LIFE CHANGES

LIFE CHANGES

Laura E. Greenway

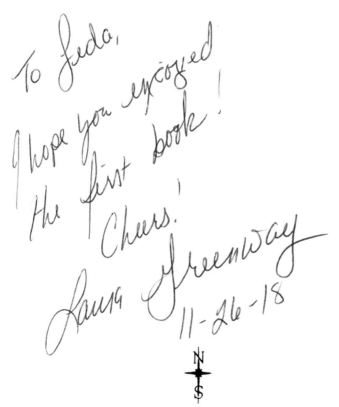

To Jada,
I hope you enjoyed
the first book!
Cheers!
Laura Greenway
11-26-18

NORTH STAR PRESS OF ST. CLOUD, INC.

ISBN: 978-0-87839-572-9

First edition, September 1, 2011

Printed in the United States of America.

Published by North Star Press of St. Cloud, Inc.
PO Box 451
St. Cloud, MN 56302
www.northstarpress.com

CHAPTER 1
MEETING THE STONEHENGERS

Y ou can't do this! This is my house!" My stepdad, Ben, called from the front door. The wood nymphs surrounding me in the living room, ignoring his protests. I heard the front door open and close, but the wood nymphs paid little attention to that either.

Ben and I had almost been killed in a tornado just an hour or so ago, but we were rescued by my fiancée, Ash, and his dad, which was a surprise since Ash's dad, Elm, hated my family. I was surrounded by the king of the wood nymphs and his minions.

King Cornelius Stonehenge and Queen Delphine, his wife, came here because I was the first human and wood nymph mixed person born. The thing is, I just found out last year that I was half human and half wood nymph. I had no idea how the king and queen found out. My biological dad's family, who were all wood nymphs, kept my birth a secret from the rest of the wood nymph world. They even kept my heritage a secret from my mother, who had no idea that the man she had fallen in love with years ago had not been a human. After I found out, I told my mother, who had trouble believing it. Finally we told Ben, my stepdad, who had even more trouble believing the truth of my birth. Believe it or not, I exist, but, beyond Mom and Ben, we tried to keep my genetics a secret. Who would understand?

Visually wood nymphs look human, but they don't act human. It is hard to reject out-of-hand when your eyes see someone move at the speed of sound without creating a sonic boom or jump thirty feet in the air and land safely in a nearby tree. Humans just can't do that.

Wood nymphs are born with a lot of gifts that humans don't have. However, not all wood nymphs had the same abilities. All the ones I have met could "jet," which was their word for running faster than the speed of sound and jumping really high. But, only Olivia, my biological father's cousin could "see" events just before they happened. She didn't see everything, but what she did see usually came true. Before the Stonehengers arrived, she complained of having an ominous feeling. She never actually "saw" them packing their bags and coming here, but I have a feeling we were about to find out just exactly what the Stonehengers wanted and how they felt about a human and wood nymph mixed girl.

Some wood nymphs can read the emotions of cognitive creatures. This includes animals. That's one of the gifts I received with my wood nymph blood. I can tell the emotional state of any creature within one hundred yards of me.

1

The king was staring at me with curiosity. We were still in my living room, and everyone's attention was on me. I could sense the curiousity from the wood nympth gaurds around me, along with some revulsion.

"Why are you here?" I blurted out. I knew the answer, but I didn't like being handled like this, and I was very afraid.

"Why, because of you, of course," he responded with a smile. Was it me, or did the smile not quite reach his eyes? It didn't seem like a natural or real smile. Maybe I just felt that way because I could feel the tension radiating from Olivia and Forrest, my cousin and uncle, in waves. "You are the first of your kind," he continued. "We have never had a wood nymph breed with a human before. I cannot understand why a wood nymph would want to have a sexual relationship with a human. Speaking of that, where is your biological father? Who is the wood nymph who sired you? I should like to have a talk with him."

"He's dead," Forrest said. "He died within a week of meeting Laurel's mother. They only had one weekend together." Forrest stood outside the royal entourage. That was another thing about wood nymphs. They all had really keen hearing.

"Hmm. Interesting. How did he die?" the king asked Forrest. Forrest was my biological dad's brother and Olivia was his cousin. That made her my cousin, too. Since I found out about the wood nymphs last fall, I had become quite close with Forrest and Olivia.

"He died saving humans," Forrest replied quietly. He may have spoken quietly, but I heard a certain amount of pride in his voice.

Good for you Forrest, I thought. Humans are worth saving!

"Two things I find really interesting," said the king. "One: your brother gets killed off trying to help humans, and yet you still care about them. And secondly," the king said and turned to look at my mother, "I really find it interesting that the human became pregnant after just one weekend together with a wood nymph. It was just one weekend, right?"

"Yes," my mother said quietly, blushing slightly.

"I'm sorry, my dear," the king said kindly as he looked back at me and patted my hand. "As a species, humans just don't measure up to wood nymphs. Also, it is very important for our species to remain hidden from humans. When a human see a wood nymph, the human just thinks it is another human. We prefer it that way. The question is, what do I do about you and your human parents? I have to say that if the girl's biological father were still alive, he would face some consequences for his behavior. But, as he is already dead, well, I have to think," he said pulling his hand away.

"Why does anyone have to do anything at all?" I asked compulsively. I didn't think about what I was saying. It just came out of my mouth. "I understand the need to protect the private lives of wood nymphs and so do my parents. We would never tell anyone about them, ever," I said jerking my arms away from the guards and crossed them in front of my chest.

As I waited for the king to respond, I tried to read his emotions and got nothing. He either felt no emotion at all or had some kind of block preventing me from seeing his emotions. I began to read the other wood nymphs. The queen was curious about me, but she felt apprehensive about being in a room with humans. The guards were all on high alert. I could see the intelligence and wariness in their eyes. They were not only really big, but they were really smart. I could hear Chuck, my part-wolf pup howling outside. He must have been hunting when the Stonehengers arrived.

After a moment, the king finally gave a little sigh. "Oh, I am quite sure that your wood nymph friends have told you not to say anything. I stay up to date on the news of the world and if the actual fact that wood nymphs existed were to become known to the humans, well, then we would have had to do some damage control," he said giving me a scrutinizing look. "We are here because of you. The question is not that you actually exist. We can see that you do. The question I have is what do we do with you?"

I heard Olivia take a sharp breath. This had been her fear since the beginning. For the last eighteen years, Olivia and Forrest had known about me and kept an eye on me from a distance. Humans were not supposed to know that wood nymphs exist. Their clan kept my existence a secret from the rest of the wood nymph world.

"How did you find out about me?" I asked. I wasn't sure if I was allowed to ask questions, but I just had to know. Even though I was scared out of my skull, I figured I had nothing to lose by asking an innocuous question.

"We had a visit from some friends of yours," King Cornelius said, looking at Elm. Ash and I were planning to get married in a couple of months and then go to college. Until today, Ash's family had been against his marrying a human-wood nymph mix. After fighting with Ash's father for months about accepting me as a match for his son, the day he finally did accept me turned out to be the day that the Stonehengers arrived. Were they going to try to keep us apart now, too?

"Chester Quince," Elm whispered with a chagrined look. Chester Quince and his family had come from Europe to stay with Ash's family last fall. Both families were hoping for a love match between Ash and one of Quince's three daughters. This did not happen, since Ash and I had already bonded. When wood nymphs fall in love, they create a kind of bond much stronger than the love humans possess.

Wood nymphs never got divorced because, once bonded, their souls combine. When one of the pair of wood nymphs feels pain or discomfort, the other one does as well. Ash and I bonded last year. The life expectancy of a bonded wood nymph after his or her spouse has died is not very long.

"Yes!" the king said with a dramatic sigh. "Chester Quince came to see us last week. Of course when we found out that wood nymphs knew about this mixed girl and hadn't told us about it, well, as you can imagine, we had to come see for ourselves. The question is, why didn't anyone tell us about her? You know the rules. Humans are not allowed to know that wood nymphs exist. Just imagine the chaos! Humans would try to butt into our business, and they would try to use our abilities. Humans are selfish creatures that do nothing but pollute the world we live in. And now, we have a human-wood nymph mixed creature to deal with. The big question is what to do about her?"

"Laurel and I have bonded. We're to be married in a couple of months," Ash said to the king. Ash then squeezed between the guards to get to me and held my hand as he spoke. "Your highness, I thought Laurel was selfish when I first met her. I didn't know any humans personally. I find now that my views on humans have changed as I got to know her. Please, sir, give the humans a chance," Ash pleaded to the king.

"A wood nymph conjoined with a human? Outrageous! I cannot condone such a thing!" the king roared.

"You don't even know her! She could be good for the wood nymph population!" Forrest cried. Immediately, the biggest guard was beside him and I never even saw him move from the other side of the room. Forrest sat down in a nearby chair.

"Good for the population, you say? How can that be?" the king asked with a quizzical tone. He was working hard to regain his composure. I was grateful he was giving any thought at all to what Forrest had said instead of just disregarding him.

Olivia answered the king with a soft voice. "As you know, sir, the wood nymphs have not been breeding normally for years. Our species is slowly dying off. We used to number hundreds of thousands throughout the world, but now we number only in the thousands. We don't live for hundreds of years anymore. Very few of us live to one hundred years. We have been blaming it on the pollution that the humans created. Maybe our mixing with the humans on a selective level will keep our species alive."

"Keep our species alive? Nonsense. Mixing with humans will only dilute our species. Are humans fast? No. Do humans have special abilities? No. Why would we want to mix with humans?" King Cornelius scornly said.

"Because we're capable of great love," my mom said softly. "We're loyal and most of us are honest. No, we don't have the special abilities that wood nymphs have, but we can do other things really well. We can be great mediators, as Laurel was with the water sprites."

"Water sprites? What about water sprites?" the king asked as he uncrossed his arms and leaned forward to look at my mom. "What did this human and wood nymph girl have to do with water sprites?"

"First, my daughter has a name. It's Laurel. She's not a thing. She's a person. She's more than just a person. She's the mixture of two species and she's special." My mom smiled at me and then focused back to the king. "While humans may not be as powerful as wood nymphs in many ways, we can communicate. We have cognitive minds and practice many other aspects of humanity that wood nymphs could learn from, like the understanding of diversity. Laurel may be different. She's not entirely human and she's not just a wood nymph. As a combination, she's the best of both worlds. Being different isn't bad. It just makes her unique. Everyone who gets to know her loves her. She's a good person, as a wood nymph or as a human."

The king stared at my mother for a minute and then he said, "I don't know humans very well. I only know what I read and hear about them. I have to think about this. You are right. I should not make a hasty decision." He turned to look at Olivia. "What you say may be right, too. We do not have as many wood nymphs in the world. We are dying off younger, and we are not having as many offspring. We may need to study this situation. Tell me about the water sprites."

I felt Olivia and Forrest relax a little at that comment and I felt myself relax a little, too. Focus had shifted away from me. I smiled at the king and said, "Once you get to know us, you'll like us. Not all humans are bad. Some are quite good. Look at our schools of higher learning. Many people are trying to figure out how to reduce and remove the pollution in the world. Human doctors are trying to cure diseases, and they may find the reasons that cause the different diseases. Wood nymphs are in the human universities trying to study the same thing. Imagine if humans and wood nymphs collaborated! Just as the water sprites were concerned about the possibility of some drilling near one of their underwater villages and we negotiated a peace with them. There will be no drilling near their village. My parents and I have talked to the water sprites, and we won't divulge their secrets, either," I said in a rush.

I heard the front door open and close along with the tell-tale metallic sound of the slide on a rifle being rammed closed. That got the wood nymphs attention. I saw all heads snap towards the front door.

"This is my house," Ben said calmly. "This is a fully automatic rifle. If you don't let her go, we will see how well wood nymphs handle getting shot." Ben may have sounded calm, but he was seething. That much I could easily tell. Wary wood nymphs stood aside as he entered the house.

"Really? You think you can hurt a wood nymph?" the king laughed with derision. He may have sounded confident, but his emotions were conflicted. Was it possible that Ben could actually shoot one of the guards? If he did shoot one, what were the chances of any of us surviving the aftermath?

"Well, well, well," the king replied. "Perhaps I have underestimated the humans." I felt the king's curiosity growing. The king then looked at me and asked, "Why are you so interesting? Why would anyone be willing to die for you? Do you have any wood nymph abilities?"

I was so afraid I would say the wrong thing. While I wasn't normally tongue tied, I couldn't seem to gather a coherent thought as the king directed his question to me. "I, uh, um, I think I can summon fish. I've been told that I have an ability called 'the call,' which I can honestly say has come in handy at least twice now. Once was just a couple of hours ago when a tornado came through this area. Um, ah, I can also read emotions," I mumbled to the king. I was so nervous! This king had control over everyone in the room! While Ben was trying to protect me and my mom, I knew at any time the king could kill him, and there would probably be nothing that anyone could do about it.

"She's been touched by the essence at the Essence Bowl Ceremony," Forrest said with pride. "I took her to the winter solstice ceremony in my village near Presque Isle."

"Mixed humans are affected by the essence passing over them? I find this very interesting," the king said rubbing his chin thoughtfully. He looked from Forrest to me.

"Your highness, please, may I speak?" Olivia asked the king. She had worked her way through the royal entourage until she was almost next to me.

"Are you Olivia? As I understand it, you are the one who foresaw the birth of this child, but you didn't notify me. Is that correct?" the king stated as he gave Olivia a penetrating stare. The king was the only one to look away from Ben.

"Yes, sire. I apologize for not telling you, but I believe that this young woman may be a benefit to the wood nymphs," Olivia said as she dropped her gaze from the king's glare. She looked at the floor, but she didn't lower her voice. "We have been watching her since she was born, and she has only recently been made aware of our existence and of her genetic background."

"How so?" the king asked. I think he was purposely ignoring Ben, as if that would make his threatening posture, well, less threatening.

"She possesses certain abilities, and she is both smart and kind. She, along with others like her, may be the future of the wood nymphs. I'm not saying that all male wood nymphs should find a human mate, but if Laurel and Ash have children, the children would only be a quarter human. There's the possibility that their children may have all of the abilities that wood nymphs usually have, even with diluted blood. Wouldn't diluting our species be better than having the wood nymphs die off altogether?" Olivia looked up as she pleaded with the king.

The king sighed and looked at Ben. "Let's sit down. That is something to think about. Everyone find a seat. You, Laurel, will sit next to me." He looked over at Ben again. "You are wholly human and you find out that your stepdaughter is not. Yet, your feelings for her have not changed. I find that very interesting. I need to find out some things about you. Are you employed? What do you do?" The king radiated mistrust mixed with curiosity.

Ben sat in a chair near the entry to the dining room and held his rifle at his side with the barrel pointed towards the floor. He looked the king in the eye and said, "I just returned home after an extended deployment away from my family. I have just retired from the United States Army."

"The Army? A military man! I can see why you would feel comfortable with a weapon," the king replied thoughtfully. He was quiet and appeared deep in thought for a moment and then he looked at my mother. "Do you work outside of the home?"

"Yes. I'm a therapist in a counseling center," my mom replied as she sat in a chair next to Ben. My mom was very proud of her career, and I believed she was making a difference in the local community. Although she would never talk about specifics of her work, I knew there were times when something really good happened at work and we would go see Chris at the Silver Bird for dinner.

"What does a therapist, do?" the king asked. I could tell he was puzzled by my mother's response. How could he not know what a therapist was? Didn't wood nymphs have to deal with mental health?

"As a therapist, I help people deal with issues they're unable to handle on their own. Sometimes it might be depression. Other times it can involve substance abuse. I help people who are unhappy learn to enjoy their lives and find ways to make their lives better," my mom replied with pride. This was a really condensed description of what my mother did, but it seemed to make sense to the king.

"What is an award?" the queen asked. She glided over and sat on a chair next to my mother and leaned forward in her seat to listen intently.

"An award can be a medal, a trophy, or even just a document given to someone as a way of showing appreciation for a job well done. I was just thinking about an award certificate I received about a month ago for the positive things I've been doing for this community," my mom said. "Did you know I was thinking about that?"

"I have a limited telepathic ability. While I don't hear all thoughts and words in someone's mind, I do hear words that seem to have importance," the queen replied thoughtfully, giving my mother a measuring look. "Have you had much experience with human addictions?"

"Yes, sadly, there are addictions all over the world. Even here in our north woods of Wisconsin, there's alcoholism, drug addiction, gambling addiction, and other kinds of addictions," my mom said to the interested queen.

The emotion that the queen was radiating went far beyond what I thought she should be feeling. When my mother told the queen that she helped with addictions, the queen felt a surge of hope. Why would she feel hope? Why would any kind of human addiction problem be of interest to the wood nymph queen?

The king looked at his wife, and they shared a look for a long moment. I saw the king give an almost imperceptible nod. "I have a solution! You will all come to my palace as my guests for a month. This way I can study the mixed human girl and make a determination about what I should or should not do about her," the king proclaimed as he stood from his chair.

"Oh, hold on there. We're not going anywhere," Ben said and stood up. Immediately, another guard was by his side. The guard was taller and bigger than Ben, but Ben did not back down. "Call off your henchman," Ben said to the king while staring at the guard.

The king was becoming very interested in me. I could feel it in his emotional state. The question was, was this a good thing or a bad thing? "I see loyalty on the faces of all of the wood nymphs associated with these humans. However, I will not tolerate anyone to point a weapon at me!" The king stated from his seat as he glanced around the room and then settled his glare on Ben.

Ben lowered his gun, but his hands remined gripped in firing position. "I will not allow you to take Laurel anywhere," Ben said as he sat on a dining room chair.

"Yes, I see you could be a problem," the king pondered. He thought for a moment. The room was so quiet. I could hear the mixed emotions around me. The big guards standing next to the king were angry. I assumed that they were angry with Ben. My mother's fear combined with a certain amount of curiosity, while Ash only felt a deep concern for my well-being.

"Can we all sit down, please? You and your guards could certainly outrun us humans," my mom said quietly. She spoke softly, but everyone in the room could hear her. A few wood nymphs stood to the side of Ben as he rose abruptly.

The king scrutinized me again. "Humans that can keep a secret about water sprites or wood nymphs, imagine that! I need to learn more about this whole situation without making a hasty decision. I do not like to think about mixing humans with wood nymphs, but I find the idea of our species dying off appalling. I need to study humans and I need to study you. I think you need to come and stay at Stonehenge for a while until we figure all this out. I think your whole family needs to come to Stonehenge. Since your family seems to be the only humans who know wood nymphs exist, we will bring all of you. Pack your things for an extended stay. We will wait for you." The king sat back on the couch. "I need to study this one. What other abilities does she have? Does she really have any value?" The king seemed to ask himself while stroking his chin.

"What if we refuse to go?" Ben asked, still holding his rifle.

"Then I start killing off wood nymphs," the king simply said. "I really don't want to gain the attention of the local law enforcement by killing humans. I see that there is loyalty on both sides here. If these misguided north woods wood nymphs really believe that humans can be trusted, then we shall put that trust to the test. If the humans run, then wood nymphs die."

"Think of it as a vacation," the king said with crooked smile. "It will only be for a few weeks. You do want to make a good impression, don't you? If you don't do as I say, I will start killing wood nymphs until you agree to come."

The queen said softly to me, "I look forward to spending more time with you. I can sense the wood nympth character within you. I can tell these things and you have a good character, even if it is muddled with your humanity. Please don't be afraid. I have a good feeling that things will turn out the way they should."

Forrest jumped up again, causing the guard to his left to grab him by his should and hold him in place tightly. I could see Forrest go pale from the pain. However, he maintained his position and said, "If we agree to this, I want to go, too. Laurel has been under my protection her entire life. Ben is her stepfather and I'm her uncle. We should go together to help protect her."

Olivia calmly stood up next to Forrest and said, "I too, wish to go. As I understand it, the Stonehenge palace is very large. It could easily accommodate all of us. Valerie, Laurel's mom will need someone familiar to help her learn the wood nymph culture."

At that moment, the door bell rang. All heads turned. "May I?" my mother asked the king for approval and then answered the door.

It was Ash's mom, Willow. "I see you have important company. Is Ash here? There was a tornado and I was worried," she asked my mom as she stepped in the house. I didn't hear what my mom said, but I saw that Willow walked with my mom toward the living room.

"Oh! Your highnesses!" Willow cried when she saw the king and queen of the wood nymphs sitting in my living room. She gave the royal pair a deep curtsy.

"Who is this female who interrupts us?" The king said, sounding exasperated.

"This is my wife, Willow," Elm said softly as he went to seat his wife in a chair next to his. He put his arm around her. She looked at him with questions in her eyes, but he subtly shook his head at her.

"Fine. We will kill her first," the king said firmly. He stood up and waved one of his body guards toward Willow. The body guard was beside Willow faster than I could blink.

"What?" Willow cried. "What's going on, Elm?" she asked her husband. She clutched at his arm. Elm looked worriedly at the bodyguard as he put his arm around Willow in a protective gesture. I knew that Elm would be no match for the bodyguard and for the first time, I felt sorry for Elm and Willow. She could not have arrived at a more inopportune moment.

"If Laurel and her family do not agree to go with the royal family to Stonehenge, then the king will have the guards kill the wood nymphs in this room, one by one, until they agree to go to Stonehenge. The king wants to study Laurel," Elm said softly to his wife. Willow stared at me with terror in her eyes.

"I'll go with you," I said to the king and stood up. "Leave my family alone. They've done nothing wrong."

"I'll go with you," Ash said as he stood up next to me. "I love you. Whatever happens, I want to be with you."

"You know, when the king's no longer entertained by me, he'll probably kill me," I said softly to Ash.

"How long would we be gone for?" my mother asked in a defeated voice. "I can't be responsible for someone else dying because of my decision."

"Oh, a month or so should do it. I'll either deem you worthy of life, or I won't," the king replied. He started to the door and brushed off his robes as if our home contaminated his attire.

"Can we have more time to get our affairs in order?" Ben said with a sigh. "We need to close up the house, my wife needs to take a leave of absence from her job, and the kids start school at the university in the fall."

"I expect you to be at the Stonehenge palace two weeks from today. I will allow everyone in this room to come. In fact, I insist that everyone here, wood nymph and human alike, come to Stonehenge. I will send my private plane and arrange transportation to Stonehenge from the airport. You will meet the plane at the Rhinelander airport. Look for the sign with Laurel's name on it at the London airport. A limousine will be waiting," the king stated as he stopped and counted around the room. "There will be eight seats."

I counted in my mind. The first three were probably me, mom, and Ben. Then there was Ash, his parents, Olivia, and Forrest. That made eight. We were all going.

"Should you not be there and I have to come back, a lot of wood nymphs and possibly humans will die. I will use the guards and no one will see it coming," the king said as he started walking to the door again. "This meeting went better than I thought it would. Please think of the invitation as a vacation and not a summons. It is up to each of you on how the vacation will end."

We all walked the Stonehenge royal family, their staff, and guards to the door. We followed them outside and watched them get into their limousines.

"Two weeks! See you then!" the king called out of his window as the limousines departed down the driveway.

"Two weeks. That is not a lot of time," said Ben. "I feel so helpless. I think I could have taken one of those gaurds down with me, but the other three would've annihilated everyone else." Ben heaved a frustrated sigh.

"We should try to think of it as a European vacation. Just think! We'll see things humans never see on vacation!" My mom said, trying to put a positive spin to our situation.

"Do we know that we're the only humans who've ever been to the palace?" Ben asked, turning to Forrest and Elm. "We can only hope they decide to let us live after being with them for a month. Do you think they'll let us live? Your king was willing to sacrifice his own subjects to ensure that he got his way."

"Of course as wood nymphs, we've known of our royal family," Forrest said. "However, the truth is, we've never had anything to do with them. We stay here, and they stay there. We follow the rules and once in a while one of the royal representatives shows up to see that we are indeed following their dictates, but mostly they just leave us alone. We don't even pay taxes or anything to them." Forrest watched the dust settle on the driveway from the departing limousines.

"What's going on?" Willow cried. "What happened here today?" She grabbed Elm's arm and shook him. Having come late to the party, she truly had no idea.

"Come on. We'll fill you in on the details," Elm said, gently taking his wife's hand. She glared at him. I guess I was glad she wasn't glaring at me.

Mom smiled at Elm and Willow and said, "I need a drink. Would anyone else care for one? I have some scotch."

11

"I'll be right back," Olivia said. "I'll get some wood nymph wine." She jetted off. I never got tired of watching the wood nymphs take two running strides and then disappear. That was one wood nymph characteristic I hadn't inherited and sure would have liked to have.

Mom, Ben, Elm, and Forrest went into the house. With the limousine gone, my pup, Chuck, came out from around the house. He whined as he sat down next to me. He seemed to have sensed the danger the wood nymph royal family represented. I sat on the ground and buried my face in his fur. "What are we going to do?" I asked, my voice muffled by his fur. I could feel the tears running down my face. "What if . . . what if they decide they don't like me. Will they really kill me?"

Ash sat down on the ground next to me and gathered me into his arms. "If they kill you, they'll have to kill me, too. I don't want you to die and I don't want to die, either. We need to come up with a strategy to show them that humans aren't all bad. Let's brain storm on what we can teach the Stonehengers."

As we got up to go into the house, I wiped my eyes on my sleeve. We would get through this. We were still alive right now. If they truly wanted me dead, I'd have been dead already. As we walked up the stairs into the house, Olivia jetted up with a couple bottles of wine.

"You know," I said as we approached the house. "The last thing the queen said to me as they were leaving was that I had good character and that things would turn out as they should."

"They should leave us alone. That would make things turn out as they should," Ash sighed as we walked up the steps.

"Yes, that would be nice. We'll do our best to make that happen in the future," Olivia stated as the three of us walked into the house together.

Chapter 2
Accepting the Summons

When Olivia, Ash, and I walked into the living room, everyone else had already taken a seat. Olivia went into the kitchen to open the wine. Mom and Ben each had a glass of scotch with ice. As Ash and I sat on the couch, my mom swirled her drink and clinked the frozen cubes softly against the side of the glass. I didn't want anything to drink. I was too nervous.

"This is all about Laurel?" Ash's mom, Willow, finally asked her husband as Olivia came into the living room with a tray of wine glasses.

"Yes, my dear. It is," Elm replied reaching for a wine glass with one hand and massaging his wife's hand with his other. He kissed his wife's hand. After he gazed into her eyes for a moment he said, "This is my fault. If I had only paid attention and accepted the truth before my own eyes, instead of trying to fight it, this would never have happened." Elm stood up, walked across the room, and sat next to Ash on the couch. He looked at his son and said, "While Laurel would not have been my first choice for you, she *is* your choice, and I should have accepted that before today. I'm sorry. If I hadn't invited Quince and his family to come here, we would not be in this predicament."

Willow stood up and walked over to her husband. "Elm, you only wanted what was best for our son. Do not be so hard on yourself." Willow took Elm's hand as they went back to their chairs. "So, what happens now?" Willow asked as she sat down.

I couldn't take this calm discussion anymore. "This isn't fair! I'm half human! They have no right to threaten me or any of you!" I said loudly as I stood to face everyone. I wasn't the type of person to shout, but this was making me really mad and I was really scared, too. I could feel the panic creeping around the edges of my consciousness.

"Laurel, honey, calm down," Ash said softly as he pulled me back down to my seat. "We'll figure out what to do." I shuddered as I leaned against him. I closed my eyes. I could see my whole future disappearing. I was just beginning to live and now I was going to die. There had never been a person like me before. The king was never going to let me live.

"It's obvious. We'll have to go to Stonehenge," Forrest said with a sigh while shaking his head. "Of all the things I could have imagined happening, if or when

13

the Stonehengers found out about Laurel, I guess I never expected a royal summons, let alone the king and queen coming here themselves."

"Have you ever been to Stonehenge?" Mom asked Forrest while sipping her scotch. I sat up to look at her and noticed her hand was trembling.

"No. I never wanted to go. The Stonehengers usually leave us alone and we like it that way. As far as I know, a wood nymph only gets summoned to Stonehenge for some kind of punishment. The king's a hard disciplinarian about his rules of conduct and behavior for wood nymphs. As long as we follow the ordained rules, he leaves us alone. I've never heard of anyone being invited to Stonehenge as a guest of the king. I'm glad that my brother isn't here to be a part of this. No offense to you, Valerie. I believe that he loved you, but I don't think the king would have been reasonable with Leif. He broke one of the biggest rules by falling in love with you."

Forrest didn't say it, but I knew what he was thinking. Humans were beneath wood nymphs in every way. Humans didn't have the speed or strength of wood nymphs. My biological father had a different attitude about humans. He genuinely liked them and was working to help his clan get over their aversion and prejudice against them. I was proud he was able to fall in love with a human. My father's brother, Forrest, accepted me, and he had been kind to me since I met him last fall. He told me that he had been watching out for me and my mother since I was born. He just couldn't let us know of his existence because of the wood nymph rule about humans finding out that they were a different species.

"Yeah, I believe I heard that threat while he was talking about consequences," my mom said with a shudder.

We all sat pondering our own thoughts for a while. "Olivia, you're very quiet," Mom said, looking at Olivia.

Olivia was sitting on the love seat next to Forrest swirling the wine in her glass. She looked up at my mom with a scared look on her face and said, "I can't see anything in the future. Nothing at all. I can't see anything in our immediate or distant future. Nothing. It's like my ability has been turned off." Then Olivia turned to look at me. "Plus, I guess I agree with Laurel because this isn't fair. We kept her hidden from the king and queen for fear of his reaction to her existence. I can't say we were wrong."

"Is that a bad thing?" Mom asked. "Has this ever happened before? I'm not talking about the fact that you agree with Laurel. But, you really can't see what's happening?"

I looked closely at Olivia. This was really making her nervous. She was pale and her body was trembling.

"No. I don't remember this ever happening before. Most of the time I at least get a little something when I concentrate on the future, but now I'm drawing a complete blank," Olivia replied appearing near tears.

Forrest reached over to put his arm around her. "Olivia, a lot's happened. It could be that stress is blocking your ability."

"Could be," she replied softly. She looked down at her hands in her lap. I wondered if it was just the stress, or was it something else blocking her gift.

"At one time, I would've thought this a stupid question. But, with everything I've learned and experienced in the past year, is it possible that the Stonehengers have some kind of magic that would block your ability?" I asked Olivia.

"Not that I know of. But, there is magic in the world. Look at the way the plants bloom every spring. That's a form of magic. It's a natural magic, perhaps, but magic just the same. Although, come to think of it, I've heard talk of certain wood nymphs experimenting with magic called, *necromancers*."

"What's a necromancer?" I asked. I still didn't know lots of things about the wood nymphs.

"A necromancer is a wood nymph who practices dark magic. Some of us have a special ability making us able to change the natural course of things. You know that I can sing to wooden objects and they'll grow in certain shapes. This is a natural phenomenon for me. Not all wood nymphs can do this. It's a form of magic. However, there are other wood nymphs who practice a darker form of magic. We have never encouraged anyone in either of our clans who practices the 'dark arts' as it's called, due to negative consequences that can occur," Forrest said thoughtfully as he leaned back in his chair.

"There is the possibility that one of the king's attendants is a necromancer who can subdue or eliminate a wood nymph's abilities," Elm stated flatly.

"Would that be a bad thing?" I asked. If the wood nymphs didn't have their abilities, would that mean that they could no longer jet? Would I be prevented from reading emotions? I was able to read each person's emotion quite clearly, so if a necromancer was in the house, he or she had not affected me. "I can still read emotions," I said after no one replied to my question. "Olivia jetted to get the wine."

"Let's hope the rest of us haven't been affected. It'd be a long walk home," Forrest stated dryly.

"Very funny. But Laurel is right. I jetted to get the wine, and I was able to do that without difficulty," Olivia replied sarcastically. "Maybe I'm just nervous and that's affecting my ability."

"We'll see, won't we?" Elm replied. "As to answering your question, to lose my ability would be to lose my livelihood. I would no longer be able to find natural resources in the ground, and that would definitely be a bad thing. We live in a human world and the human world requires money."

My mother took a deep sigh and changed the subject. "Well, okay. It is obvious we have to go to Stonehenge or people are going to die. Do you all agree with me that this is an accurate statement?" She looked around the room. We all nodded.

"Okay. So, I guess we need to decide what to bring and get our affairs in order so we can leave for a month. We have to believe that we'll be returning to Wisconsin. Otherwise, what's the point of anything?" Mom said leaning back in her chair. "We're all still alive. If the king really just wanted us dead, we'd be dead already. We're far from the normal human world in this house. If the king murdered us here, no one would have heard a thing. Our driveway is a mile long."

We all sat in silence for a while, each of us lost in our own thoughts. Then, my mother looked around and said, "We need to show the king and queen that humans and wood nymphs can live together in harmony. We need to show that humans are not devils of the world. We especially need to prove that Laurel is a benefit and not a mistake. Actually, humans and wood nymphs have been living in the same communities for years. It is just that the humans never knew that the wood nymphs were different."

I thought about what Mom said. "Ash, I'm not picking on you. I love you, you know that. But once, when we first met, I overheard you call me an abomination. I know you don't feel that way anymore. I know you love me now. The point I'm trying to make is . . . what changed your mind about me? How did you change from hating me to loving me?" I asked Ash as he turned to face me.

Ash put his arm around me. I loved the way he smelled when he was close. "I got to know you. You're not the self-absorbed human I thought you'd be. You're smart and kind. The truth is, the imperfections you do have, I find endearing," Ash replied and kissed me on my nose.

"Imperfections? What imperfections?" I said playfully and punched his arm.

"You can't jet," Ash said smiling. "I have to carry you. I found out today that I can do it with no trouble. In fact, I kind of like it."

I cuddled closer to him. I wished at that moment we could just run away. I wished we could leave all this mess behind us and start fresh, new lives. At that moment, I wished wood nymphs did not exist, that Forrest, Olivia, Ash, and his family were just normal human beings.

"Yeah, okay," I said leaning back into the couch. It was true. While I was part wood nymph and exhibited certain abilities, such as the ability to read emotions, I couldn't jet. While I was disappointed I hadn't inherited that ability, I was glad Ash loved me enough and was strong enough to be able to jet while carrying me. If he hadn't been able to pick me up and jet, we would have been killed by a tornado.

Olivia perked up. "That's it! Instead of going into the Stonehenge underground palace like fearful mice, we'll go into the palace with the attitude that we have been invited to go on the vacation of a lifetime."

"You are absolutely right," Mom said with a big grin. "We may have no real choice about whether we're going to Stonehenge or not, but we do have choices about our attitudes. I like that idea! We really should treat it like a vacation. We'll all be our most charming and gracious selves. Those of us who are human will need to be tutored in wood nymph etiquette, though. We need to be on our best behavior. The king won't be able to help himself. We'll make him like us!"

"I'll help," Willow said getting into the spirit of the situation. "We can practice having royal dinner parties at our house. We have a large table with chairs and are used to catering to big wood nymph gatherings."

Forrest said thoughtfully, "I think we need to keep a limit on how many of our people we tell about where we're going and why. If the king and queen decide that they don't like us, they may decide to come back here and do damage control. We have no idea what that could entail. If our people are sincerely ignorant of where we are, I think they'd be safe from any repercussions from the Stonehengers, don't you?"

"That's a good point," Ben agreed. "We don't want to put anyone else in danger."

"There is the real possibility that we won't come back from Stonehenge, isn't there?" Willow asked with a catch in her voice.

"I guess that's true, but we can't think like that," Ben stated. "We need to set up an offensive strategy of kindness. We'll be the best, most well-mannered guests they've ever seen."

"Is anyone hungry?" Mom said and stood up. "It has been a rough day and we all need to eat something." Her idea of handling a stressful situation was to eat something.

"That's a good idea. Let me help you," Olivia said, getting up as well. "You guys can help Ben and Laurel with their wood nymph cultural lessons while we put something together for dinner."

"I can listen while we cook," Mom said as she headed for the kitchen. "This is just another reason why I love the open-air concept of this house!"

"While some of the cultural norms are different from humans, a lot of them are similar. The basics shouldn't be too hard to learn. You probably already know them," Forrest said as he stood up and appeared to put on his best lecture voice.

I sat back to listen to Forrest's lecture.

"First and foremost, our manners and behaviors are very important. You never speak to a royal person unless he or she addresses you first. If you have to interrupt them in an open room, you slowly walk toward the person you wish to address until you know you have his or her attention. At that point, you bow to show respect. If it is his or her convenience to have you state your business, he or she will address you. If after a minute or so of being in a bowed position, you find you're not addressed, you straighten up just enough to be able to back out of the room and take your leave. If you're asked to state your business, you straighten to your full height, look the person in the eye, speak in an even and normal voice, state your business, and wait for the response. If you ask a question and the question is answered—positively or negatively—you give one quick bob of your head to show that you understood the answer and turn to leave. If you have additional questions, you bob your head and then go back into the bow. This indicates you have an additional question. At that point the person may ignore you or ask what other business you have."

Forrest paused a moment, took a sip of his wine and continued. "Always speak in a normal voice, not too loud or too soft. At no time should the person addressing the royal personage use an excited or loud voice. This will almost always ensure the person speaking will be evicted from the royal person's presence or possibly a worse consequence," Forrest said with a sigh.

The lessons went on for some time. I listened to everything, trying to file it all away in case I needed it.

"Dinner is ready. Come to the table," Mom called as carried a big bowl of cold shrimp salad to the table. I was amazed. It felt like only a few minutes had passed.

"We have enough chairs for everyone. Please sit wherever you like," Mom said, heading for the chair nearest the kitchen. Olivia stood by the chair next to her.

"No, I'll sit next to Valerie," Forrest said. "We should get used to the seating arrangement now. It's male, female, male, female around the table. That's the proper way. We need to start with our table etiquette now. Since Ben and Valerie are the hosts, it's right that they sit in the end chairs as they usually do. However, once we get to the underground palace, there'll probably be place cards on the plate chargers designating where everyone will sit," Forrest said, holding the chair out for my mom.

"What's a plate charger?" I asked. Did we have to pay for our food?

"A plate charger is a larger plate, usually of gold or silver that the dinner plate would be placed upon by the server. Your knife, fork, and spoon will already be set at the table," Forrest replied. "Humans usually use placemats instead of chargers to place the dinner plates on, although I have seen chargers at some homes."

Willow stated that the fork was held in the left hand and the knife was held in the right. Then, the fork was kept in the left hand to eat. I found this awkward. I had always cut my food while holding my knife in my right hand and my fork in my left hand, but would switch the fork to my right hand to put the food in my mouth. While it felt funny to try to use my left hand to eat, I was going to practice it until I got it right. I only had two weeks to be on my best behavior.

Forrest stated that no one was to leave the table until the king and queen got up to leave. We practiced that with Mom and Ben acting as the king and queen. Once Mom and Ben stood up and walked away from the table, we all got up at the same time and stepped away as well. This waiting part was going to be difficult for me since I was used to leaving the table as soon as I was finished eating. I had never thought that our table manners were bad, but we had never eaten with any kind of royalty before.

I had never thought I would meet any kind of royalty in my life. I certainly never expected to have royalty come to my house. After we cleaned up and the dishwasher was running, Ash said to me, "Laurel, let's take a walk outside. I want to be alone with you."

"Okay," I replied. I agreed with Ash. I had to get out of there.

"Mom, I'm going for a walk with Ash!" I called as we walked out the front door.

Chuck ran up to us as soon as we came down the porch stairs. He was whining and felt the tension in the air. I ruffled the fur around his neck. "We'll be fine, boy!" I stood up and faced Ash, "Who'll take care of Chuck while we're gone?"

"I guess you should give Adam a call. He'd take care of him," Ash said as he took my hand and we started down the driveway.

"Yeah, I'm sure that he would," I responded, relieved. The porch lights faded behind us as we walked further down the driveway. I held Ash's hand as he guided us down the dark driveway, able to see better than I could. The stars provided the only light. I could only tell we were on the driveway by the gap in the trees when I looked up. I could not see the driveway in the dark. Ash could though. That was another wood nymph characteristic I hadn't inherited. We walked in silence awhile.

The night was getting cooler. Ash put his arm around me when I shivered. "Are you cold?" he asked.

"Kind of, but I'm not ready to go back to the house yet," I replied as I snuggled into the warmth of his body. I hadn't thought to put on a jacket when we left the house. It was summertime but I forget that it could get cool at night in the north woods. A lot of things sure had changed since I left Washington, D.C., last year.

I stopped and put my arms around Ash. He stared into my eyes and enclosed me in his strong arms. He felt so warm and comfortable. He smelled so good. "I could just stay this way forever," I whispered into his neck.

"I'll always be here for you. I won't let anything or anyone separate us," he replied softly near my lips.

"I love you," I said as his lips touched mine. He gently put his hands on each side of my face as we kissed. I leaned into him and increased the pressure of the kiss. I kissed him with such intensity that I felt him give me his soul in return. My legs grew weak from the sensuality of the kiss. My breath was coming in little gasps, and I could feel a heat building inside of me. I could smell the wood nymph musky arousal emanating from him and the kiss deepened into an even more sensual kiss. About the time I felt my legs weren't going to hold me up any longer, Ash pulled his lips away from mine.

"If we keep this up, I'm going to pick you up, jet to my house, and make love to you right now," he said with conviction.

"Okay," I responded with a sigh, placing my face on his chest. I was eighteen years old and I really didn't want to die a virgin. I was ready for sex with this man.

"Oh, I want to! But, I don't want our first time to be tonight. My parents could come home at any minute. I couldn't handle our first time being interrupted by my parents. We've had enough stress for one day. Don't ever think I don't want to! I think about you day and night. Let it be enough for tonight that I want you desperately," he said as he held me tight.

With a deep sigh, I replied, "Okay." I knew he wanted me. Wood nymph males had a gland that excreted a hormone that was extremely pleasant to the senses when he was excited.

"We may not have a long life. I want to experience you completely before we go to England," I said a little breathlessly as I felt my legs getting stronger. I knew nothing was going to happen tonight. I was disappointed, but also excited about the prospect of Ash and I being alone together in a bed.

"Maybe we can find a place to be alone together before we leave," Ash whispered as his voice trailed away. I shivered again. While I was getting a little cold, I shivered with excitement. Ash said, "I better get you back to the house before you get too cold."

I shivered again with the anticipation of experiencing and seeing all of Ash. He looked like a sculpted god with clothes on. I had imagined many times what he would look like with clothes off. I had seen him without a shirt before, but never without pants or a swimsuit. I wondered if we really would have a chance to be able to fully express our love to each other before we left for England.

He took me by the hand, and we walked back to the house. Maybe with Olivia's "sight" not working, we could manage to find a place to be alone and undisturbed. The last time Ash and I had come close to actually making love, Olivia had interrupted us.

When we got to the porch, we saw that Ash's parents, Forrest, and Olivia were leaving. "Ash! Laurel! I'm glad you came back in time to say goodbye," Olivia called to us as she walked down the stairs of our front porch. She gave me a hug and as she walked past Ash. She took a discreet sniff and whispered, "Be careful you two! Don't do anything you may regret later."

"She smells me," Ash laughed and whispered in my ear. "I thought that the scent would dissipate before we got back to the house. I guess I thought wrong."

I giggled and whispered back, "Don't stand near anyone else." I squeezed Ash's hand before I went up to Forrest to keep him away from Ash. Ash's sensual scent was dissipating in the night air, but there was enough of it left that if anyone got close enough, they could probably smell it. Ash angled himself to ensure he was downwind of everyone else.

"Good-bye, Olivia. Good-bye, Uncle Forrest!" I said as I gave Forrest a hug. "When are we getting together again? I'm sure there are other details we need to work out before we leave."

"I'm using tomorrow to go to work and get a leave of absence from my job," Mom said from the porch.

"I'm going to talk to the utility companies and the post office about mail, tomorrow. I'll have the mail held for a month," Ben said as he stood next to my mom.

"I'll get someone from our clan to watch our properties while we're gone," Elm stated to Ben as he walked with Willow to the driveway. "I'm not sure what I'll tell them about our departure, but you don't have to worry about your place while we're gone."

"That would be great. Thanks!" Ben said with a smile. I was amazed at how many changes had taken place in just one day. Ben and Elm were now allies, where before they were at a minimum, estranged neighbors, if not enemies.

"I'll call Adam and have him come and get Chuck," I said as I reached down to scratch Chuck's head. I was really going to miss my pup while I was gone.

I watched Forrest and Olivia jet. I wondered if I'd ever get the ability to take two steps and disappear like they could.

I pulled Ash aside before he left with his parents. "I really am terrified about going to Stonehenge. I shouldn't want you to go with me, but I'm really glad syou are. I feel like I'm being selfish to want you with me, but I don't know if I could handle this without you." I wrapped my arms around him and buried my face in his neck.

"I told you, dear girl, I'll never leave you. For good or bad, our futures are linked," he replied as he gently pulled away from me. He gave me a quick kiss that was filled with meaning and then gave me one last look before he jetted home with his parents.

As I walked silently into the house with my parents, I thought about what my life was going to be like in the palace. Would we learn enough etiquette to show the king and queen we were civilized? Could we really get them to like us? We were creating history here. No humans had ever been inside the Stonehenge underground palace. At least, that's what we'd been told.

The three of us went into the living room and sat down. Ben started a fire in the fireplace and then sat on the loveseat. Mom got herself another glass of scotch on ice and one for Ben. I sat on the couch.

We silently watched the fire until it dwindled down to glowing coals. I guess we all had our own thoughts to deal with. I sat thinking about Ash and our future. And I wanted a future with him. We had to survive England. We just had to! I wanted little wood nymph babies. I wanted the blended life that I could see with humans and wood nymphs for my relatives. Ash's dad had just accepted me!

As I watched the fire burn to ash, I realized how tired I was. This had been a stressful day. Ben and I were almost killed in a tornado, Ash's dad had finally accepted me as his future daughter-in-law, and I'd met the king and queen of the wood nymphs. With a big yawn, I got up to go to bed. Mom and Ben followed shortly after.

CHAPTER 3
LIVE FOR TODAY

It had been a week since the king and queen had been to my house. In that time, I arranged for Adam to watch over Chuck, started packing for the trip, and Mom took a leave of absence from her work due to emergency family business. I guess this could be considered an emergency because, if we don't go to England, people's lives are at stake.

I got dressed and cleaned up. I heard the doorbell as I was walking down the stairs. I went to open the door to find a special delivery man with a package and an electronic clipboard.

"Is this the Redmond residence?" he asked glancing up from the clipboard.

"Yes," I replied with my back against the door and Chuck to my left sniffing the stranger.

The man seemed uncomfortable when he glanced down at Chuck. Looking back at me with nervous eyes he said, "Do Laurel, Ben, and Valerie Redmond live here?"

"Yes, I'm Laurel," I replied as I nudged Chuck away from his leg.

"Great. Please sign here," he said handing me the clipboard. I took the stylus and wrote my name next to the "x." The delivery man handed me the large envelope and left quickly.

I turned to walk into the house. As I shut the door behind me, I heard my mom call from the kitchen.

"Who was that?" she asked, wiping her hands on a towel as she came out toward me.

"Some delivery guy. He dropped this off," I said as I handed her the package.

We went into the dining room and sat at the table. "The return address is from England," she stated looking at the package.

I leaned closer to see for myself. "Shipped from Salisbury. I wonder if that is near Stonehenge," I said as we both looked at the package.

"I think it is our instructions," Mom said nervously.

Just then, Ben came in the house. "I was hoping the king and queen would forget about us and not follow through with sending us the information he thought we should have. I saw the delivery guy, so I am assuming that's what he left."

"We haven't opened it yet, but you're probably right. Look at the return address. There's no name," mom said as she handed Ben the package.

With a deep sigh, Ben opened the package. Inside were the instructions for when we were to board the plane that departed from the Rhinelander airport.

"Is there a return date on the tickets?" Mom asked.

"No. No return information," Ben said softly. "I went through the package twice. There are instructions for who we're to meet and where, but no return info."

"That can't be good, huh?" I asked. "If the king intended for us to return to Wisconsin, he would have included the return information, right?"

"Maybe he doesn't have an exact date for us to leave," Mom replied.

"Yeah, or he has no intention for us to return," I said softly.

"Now, we can't think like that. We have no idea what kind of agenda he's prepared for us," Mom said with a brave smile.

"Regardless. We're jumping to conclusions. We should call Forrest and see if he and the others have received their flight information too," Mom said.

When the doorbell rang, we all jumped. I got up. Ash was standing there.

"Did the delivery guy come by yet?" he asked as he walked in and kissed me on the cheek.

"Yeah, we each got one-way flights to England along with detailed intructions," Ben replied.

"Same with us. My mom is worried about the no return ticket. She thinks we're traveling to our deaths," Ash said with a sigh and a shake of his head.

"Come on, I made breakfast. Let's eat," Mom said trying to lighten the mood.

"I'm not very hungry," I said. How could anyone eat at a time like this? I knew my mom dealt with stress by eating, but I didn't.

"Eat anyway. You'll think clearer with something in your stomach," Mom said as she put a bowl of fruit on the table. "I have waffles with real maple syrup, too."

"Okay. I'll eat because you say so, not because I'm hungry," I said as I walked slowly toward the table.

I only ate a few pieces of fruit and some of my waffle, but everything tasted like cardboard. Nothing had any flavor. As I looked around the table, everyone poked at their plates soberly. You would think we were eating our last meal.

As Mom and I finished loading the dishwasher, the doorbell rang again. It was Forrest and Olivia.

"Hi! Where is everyone?" Olivia called as she entered the house.

"In here. We just finished breakfast. Did you get your package yet?" Ben asked as he got up from the table to shake Forrest's hand.

"Yeah, that's why we came over. Did you get return flights in your package?" Forrest asked Ben.

"No. Neither did Ash or his family. What could it mean? Does it mean the obvious? That they are planning to kill us off?" Ben asked Forrest.

"I don't know. I have no experience with anything like this," Forrest said as he followed Ben into the living room.

The doorbell rang again. This time it was Ash's parents. Willow was in tears. "What are we to do?" she wailed.

"First of all, we don't panic," Forrest said sternly. "We may be jumping to conclusions. There's probably a good reason why there's no return information. Besides, it's not like we're flying on a commercial airline. The king will send a private plane to pick us up. Hopefully he'll make arrangements for the same plane to bring us home."

I backed into the kitchen, pulling Ash with me. I whispered, "I can't take any more of this right now. Let's take a walk."

"Okay," Ash said, and we headed for the door.

"Ash and I are going out for a while," I called.

I wondered what an England summer would feel like. I wondered if we would be able to go outside once we were settled in the underground palace. I hoped we were allowed to, since summer was my favorite season, especially in the north woods of Wisconsin.

"Let's go to your house," I said as we climbed into my Jeep Wrangler.

"Why there?" Ash asked.

"I want to be alone with you. Your parents will be at my house for at least another hour discussing the flights and instructions. Olivia does not have her visions, and we can be entirely alone," I said as I started to drive down the driveway. I looked at Ash, and he gave me a big grin. I think he knew what I wanted. I hope he wanted it as much as I did.

It only took me a couple of minutes to drive the distance between our houses. As I had predicted, it was empty.

"Do you know, I've never seen your room?" I said as we walked into his house.

"Let me show you," he said as he took my hand and led me up the stairs to his room.

Ash's room was very large and painted forest green. The furniture was a dark wood that looked stained, but not varnished. He had a large chest of drawers and a roll top desk. There was a queen sized bed in the middle of the room with the headboard against the wall.

"Show me more," I said as I reached for the bottom of his shirt and started to lift it up.

"What do you want to see?" he asked with a big grin and helped me with his shirt.

25

"I want to see you. All of you. Now!" I said as I pulled off the last sleeve and dropped his shirt to the floor.

Without his shirt on, he looked like my very own personal god. I could see why Greek mythology considered wood nymphs demi-gods. Ash had very little chest hair and no fat.

"Fair is fair," Ash teased as he pulled my shirt over my head.

I unstrapped my bra and dropped it on the floor. For the first time in my life, a man other than a doctor, was looking at my body.

"You're truly beautiful," Ash said as he put his arms around me and kissed my neck.

Having my naked breasts pressed up against his bare chest was intoxicating. As I kissed him, the outside world drifted away. I'd waited all of my life for this.

We fumbled with belts, buttons, and zippers, but finally, we were standing in just our underwear. My underwear was a white bikini panty. Ash's underwear consisted of a color-changing fabric wood nymphs preferred for clothes. His underwear changed to match the color of his bedspread because we were standing next to it. It looked like part of his body had disappeared.

"The underwear has to go," I said reaching for his waistband.

"I'll do it," he said with a smile and quickly stripped them off. He stared passionately into my eyes as he gently ran his index finger on the inner layer of my waistband—this delicate motion caused my lower abdomen to ripple with nerves. I gasped quietly as his hands slowly worked the waistband down over my pelvis and then dropped the last piece of clothing around my ankles.

For a moment, we just stared at each other. His skin was a perfect golden tan and when he wrapped his arms around me, his natural musky scent enveloped my senses. He lightly kissed my shoulder blades and gradually worked his way to my lips. With our lips moist, I felt his tongue beginning to massage mine. I sucked on his tongue and then leaned away from his body.

With his naked body before me, I looked at his sensual eyes and then directed my focus on his erection—I had never seen one before. As I tentatively touched his hardened member with my hand, he moaned and pulled me against him.

We kissed wildly and somehow made it to his bed without breaking that kiss. With my back on the bedspread and Ash on top of me, I ran my hands along his muscular back, down to his buttocks. I wanted to touch every inch of his body. His erection pressed against my stomach, slowly working it's way lower to an area that had never had this experience before, but I was ready.

As we kissed, Ash broke away for a moment and whispered, "You're so beautiful, Laurel." He continued to kiss me, slowly working his way to my nipples.

Moaning, he came back to my lips. Then he licked two of his fingers and used them to enter the most intimate part of me. The passion I felt from his touch drove me wild. With every motion I wanted him more.

Without taking his eyes off mine, he leaned over me, his body pressed against mine. "I want to watch your face. I want to experience what you experience," he said as he gently separated my lower lips with his hand. He slowly pushed into me. At first I felt a sharp pain, but it vanished as quickly as it happened. The sensations I was experiencing made me feel like a whole new person. I felt absolutely whole and free. As we rocked with the rhythm of love, I knew I'd found my destiny. If I didn't have Ash in my life, I'd never be whole again.

I have no idea how much time passed before I felt reality reform around us. Ash held me tightly in his arms. Our sweat seeped into the blanket we lay upon, and our heavy breathing began to subside.

"How do you feel?" Ash whispered in my ear.

"Like I've been in heaven. I've never felt this good in my life," I said as I snuggled closer to his body.

"Me too," he said. We spooned on his bed until our sweat began to dry and itched at our backs.

"I think I need to clean up," I said sitting up. I was a little dizzy. Did sex do that to people? Did people usually feel dizzy after making mad, passionate love?

"I'll start the shower," Ash said as he rolled off of the bed. His bedroom contained a full bathroom. After he adjusted the temperature of the shower, he came back into the bedroom and held out his hand. I stumbled after him because I still felt amazingly numb from our love making. He pulled me into the shower with him and washed my entire body with his washcloth.

When we stepped out of the shower, he dried me off with a huge towel. He blow-dried my hair and we leisurely got dressed. I glanced over at his dresser and saw a clock there.

"Oh, no! We have been up here for hours! Your parents could be home at any moment!" I said worriedly.

"Okay. We'll get dressed and go. I love you," he said to me and kissed the end of my nose. He seemed so relaxed. I felt reality crashing into my fantasy.

I did not want to leave, but I couldn't stay in his room forever, though I had found such happiness here. Would we be able to do this again? What if I got pregnant? Neither of us used any kind of birth control.

I knew at that moment, that I had to live. We had to live. We had to live long enough to bring a baby into this world. For some reason, I knew that whatever baby we had, it would be special. At that moment, I kind of hoped I was pregnant.

We left in my car and went into town. We picked up some bait and decided to go back to my place and fish off of the dock.

"No fish calling," Ash warned. "The water sprites would not approve of that."

I had a skill that would make fish bite a lure or bait. All I had to do was demand a fish to bite my hook and it would. Then, I found out about water sprites and that this was poaching in their domain. It was okay to fish, but not okay to use a special ability to catch them.

When we arrived at my house, I went to the shed for the fishing gear. Olivia saw us go onto the pier and came out to join us.

"We missed you today," she said with a smile as she walked onto the pier. Then, her eyes grew wide and she looked hard at the two of us. "You didn't! How could you!"

I knew that she knew what we had done. I didn't know how she knew, but somehow she did. "What are you talking about?" I asked her.

Olivia sat down heavily on the bench and hung her head. "I had a vision once that this would happen and something intense was going to happen because of it. You weren't married at the time. I was hoping if you could wait until you were married that whatever was going to happen would be nullified because you were married and were sanctioned by the gods."

"What do you mean by something intense?" I asked, losing all pretense of not knowing what she was talking about. "Is that good or bad?"

"I don't know," she replied looking at me. "I love you so much. I don't want anything bad to happen to you, ever!"

We sat on the bench on the side of the pier quietly for a minute and then Olivia said, "Forrest will know what you have done today as well. You have a kind of glow about you. Usually wood nymphs get that kind of glow after they get pregnant. Maybe it's your mixed blood that's giving you this glow. This was your first time, right?"

"Olivia, you know we're bonded. You know we plan to get married later this summer, before school starts. But, with this trip to Stonehenge hanging over our heads, we might not be alive in a month to have a wedding and consummate our love," I said as I leaned into Ash and kissed the side of his face.

I turned back to face Olivia. "I have no regrets for what happened today. I'm really glad it happened. I love Ash."

"I love you too," Ash whispered in my ear.

"Let's fish awhile and see if your glow dissipates a bit before we go in the house. You don't need to advertise to the wood nymph world that you both lost your virginity today," Olivia said with a wry smile as she reached for a fishing rod and the tackle box.

28

"Olivia, you fish? I have never seen you fish." I said with a smile.

"Oh, yeah. I can do lots of things," she said as she delicately and expertly cast her lure far across the water of the river.

As Olivia was reeling in her second cast, her rod was almost ripped out of her hands by the forceful yank on her line.

"You've got something!" I shouted. "Good job, Olivia!" I watched as she expertly worked the line. She gave out some line and then gently reel it back in. After about ten minutes, the fish tired, and she was able to maneuver it towards the pier.

"Do you have that . . . large net . . . handy?" she asked in an exhausted voice.

"Yeah, I got it," Ash said as he crouched on the end of the pier, ready to scoop up the fish.

I was leaning over Ash's back to see what kind of monster fish Olivia had caught. As she reeled in her line, it was hard to see deep into the water due to the tannin from the trees up river—their leaves brewed like tea in the water.

About a foot down from the surface of the water, I saw what looked like two large fish heads coming to the surface. As Ash used the large net to scoop the fish up, it wasn't just one fish. It was two! Olivia's lure had a treble hook at each end, and two large northern pikes had struck the lure at the same time, hooking the two fish.

"Should we catch and release, or eat them?" Olivia asked as she sat on one of the benches, rubbing her arms.

Ash was holding the net up for us to admire the fish, when Forrest came out of the house. "Two fish at once? You're cheating yourself out of half of the fun. Now you can't enjoy the fight with the second one, since you already caught it with the first one," Forrest said laughing as he came onto the pier. "I was watching through the porch window. It is always interesting to watch Olivia fish."

"You didn't use a special skill to call the fish, did you?" I asked. "The water sprites really don't like it when we use special abilities in their domain."

"Nope. I'm just lucky," Olivia said and laughed.

"They look like they could be good for dinner tonight. I'll clean them up," Forrest said as he took the net from Ash and started walking toward the house. After he had taken a few steps, he turned back and gave me a quizzical look. "There's something different about you today. I can't quite put my finger on what it is, but you look different. Are you okay?"

I made my cast so I wouldn't have to look at him and he'd see the red burn up into my face. "Yes, Uncle Forrest. It's been a rough week, and today, for the first time since the Stonehengers were here, I finally feel relaxed. Maybe that's what you see. No stress in my face," I said. Having flipped the bale on the reel, I threw him a big smile over my shoulder.

He looked from me to Ash and then back to me. "Yeah, you both look pretty happy, all right. Hmmm. Well, let me get these fish cleaned for dinner. I'll see you all in the house." Then, he turned back to the house.

"He noticed something," I said after he went into the house.

"Yeah, he did," said Olivia as she broke down her rod to put it away. "Now your glow has settled into a more subdued and happy look. One that says you've been enjoying the day." Olivia met my eyes over her shoulder as she began walking up to the house. "I suppose since your mom is already cooking, maybe we should give up fishing and go into the house?"

"Yeah, okay. We'll be right in," I said while gathering up our gear.

After Olivia had gone into the house and was out of hearing range, Ash whispered to me, "I have no regrets about today. I really love you and want us to be together forever. I promise you, that we'll come back to Wisconsin when this is all over. We'll come back and then we'll get married."

We held each other for a long moment on the pier. How could he make a promise like that? I knew he meant well, but if the Stonehengers wanted us dead, what could he do about it? I smiled at him and said, "I promise that I'll be with you forever, too."

Dinner went smoothly and no one questioned us about the way we looked or glowed or whatever. They were focused on the coming trip. Forrest was the only one who stared at me and Ash while we ate, still trying to figure us out. When it came time for everyone to leave, Forrest came up to me and gave me a great hug. As he hugged me, his eyes grew larger and he held me at arm's length to look at my eyes. I knew he'd figured out what Ash and I had been doing earlier, but I was happy he didn't say anything to either one of our parents.

"I love you, Uncle Forrest," I said softly.

"I love you more than you'll ever know," he replied and gave me a bigger hug.

When he released me, he looked at Ash and whispered so only the two of them would hear, "If it wasn't for the fact that I know you love her, I'd be really angry with you right now."

Ash and his parents left together shortly after Forrest and Olivia.

As I was lying in my bed that night, I closed my eyes and I could smell Ash as if he were in the room with me. If the cologne companies could figure out a way to create that scent, they'd make a fortune.

CHAPTER 4
LAST DAY IN WISCONSIN

When I woke up, I stayed in bed staring at my ceiling until I realized we had one day left. In one day I would be taking a private plane out of Rhinelander heading for England and then, possibly, to my death. I fluctuated between the thought that I should treat this trip as the vacation of a lifetime to feeling like I was heading for the gallows. At this moment, it felt like the gallows.

If we had never moved to Wisconsin, I might never have found out that I was half wood nymph. Uncle Forrest was always so careful to manage, somehow, to arrange a wood nymph to be my doctor or dentist as I was growing up so that no health care provider ever got hold of my DNA. Sometimes I wondered how Forrest had managed that. And why didn't the wood nymph doctor or dentist rat me out? I think I know the answer to that. It was because I had no idea that wood nymphs existed. As long as humans and I were ignorant about them, I was allowed to live in peace.

I dragged myself out of bed and went into the bathroom. I hadn't slept well. Hell, I hadn't slept well since the night I had sex with Ash. If I wasn't thinking about the impending trip, I thought about sex. If I did get pregnant, what did it matter? We were getting married in a month anyway. I'd still go to college. A lot of colleges had daycare centers for their students. I was sure that the University of Madison had a few daycares nearby if the college itself didn't have one.

I brushed my teeth and washed my face. I looked at myself in the mirror. I looked like I hadn't been sleeping well. I certainly didn't have a glow anymore. If anything, I looked pallid.

I went downstairs. Mom and Ben were at the dining room table. It was silent when I entered the room. Mom saw me and forced a smile and said, "Good morning, honey." She really looked at me and asked, "How are you sleeping? You don't look like you slept at all."

I shook my head. "I can't help it. I'm so scared," I said as I sat down by her. I looked at my mom and wondered how she was keeping her composure. We were leaving soon! I wasn't ready! Plus, the time had gone by so fast that Ash and I had not been able to have time alone together again. Someone was always requesting help from us for this or for that. It seemed like we were always busy doing something and it wasn't the something that I wanted to be doing.

"I know, honey. I know this is frightening. Go get yourself some breakfast. We need to eat up the food that we have in the house," my mom said as she got up to refill her coffee cup.

"Yeah, okay," I said as I got up to get my bowl of cereal. I had no appetite, but I knew I had to eat.

Chuck must have picked up on my mood, because he was looking at me and whining. I looked at Ben and asked, "Has he been outside yet today?"

"Yes, I just brought him in about ten minutes ago," Ben replied staring out the window at the river. He turned to look at me and asked, "What time is Adam picking him up?"

"Around noon, I think. Do you think Chuck knows we're leaving him?" I said as I walked around the big pup to get back to the table. I patted his head as I passed by. He thumped his huge tail on the floor.

I looked at the clock. It was 9:00 a.m. I had time for one last walk with Chuck. I finished my breakfast and put my dishes in the dishwasher.

"I'm going for a walk with Chuck," I said as I headed for the door. "I'll be back before noon."

As I walked outside, I looked up at the blue sky and saw just a few wispy clouds. It was about eighty degrees already. It was going to be warm today. I didn't know if the weather was mocking my mood by being so nice, or if some higher power was telling me that things were going to be okay.

I was just starting up the path when Ash was suddenly walking beside me. I hadn't known he was there until he reached for my hand. I jumped. "Hey! I didn't mean to startle you," he said as he leaned over to kiss my cheek.

"Come on. I want to show you something," Ash said as he took my hand again and started walking briskly through the woods. He led me down a path that was most likely a deer trail, since it had many exposed roots I constantly tripped over. "Should I carry you?" he said sarcastically, never losing his balance.

"No, I can walk just fine, thank you," I said as I tripped over another root.

"Yeah, I can see that," he replied with a laugh as he turned back to look at me. He was walking backwards on this trail and he never tripped once. It was as though his knee caps rotated on a hinge and he had radar to scout the trail.

We entered a small clearing in the middle of the woods. In the middle of the glade was a patch of very thick moss. It looked to be as thick as a mattress.

"I thought I'd bring you here to take your mind off of tomorrow," Ash said as he reached for me. He pulled me over to the thick moss and sat down. It was amazingly dry and soft.

"How did you know about this place?" I asked. It was a magical spot with the sun filtering through the surrounding trees with only one small area of sunshine directly above us.

"I found it years ago as I was hiking. The sun only shines directly on this spot for a short time each day during the summer months. The rest of the year this spot is sheltered by shade, which is why the moss loves it," he replied as he pulled me down to lay next to him.

"Are we on my land or yours?" I asked as I looked around.

"Mine. Now quit talking and kiss me," he said as he pulled me closer to him.

I pulled back and asked, "Is there any way anyone will find us here?"

"Not if you don't use the call, and Olivia doesn't have her visions back, which, as of this morning, she didn't," he said as he covered my mouth with his.

I slowly undressed him. I watched his face as I took off his clothes. His green eyes got brighter as he became more aroused. He stretched out on our mossy mattress. He reached for me, but I said, "No, I want to undress for you." I slowly took my clothes off while still watching his face. He didn't move a muscle, except for the one between his legs, which appeared to have a mind of its own. I smiled as I stretched out beside him. He took me in his arms and when he entered me, I noticed there was no pain this time, only pleasure.

When I realized the sun was no longer shining on our patch of moss, I wondered what time it was and asked Ash. He looked at his watch. "11:30. We better head back."

"Chuck!" I yelled as we started to walk back. He came bounding through the woods a moment after I called for him.

Just as we got to my house, Adam pulled up in front of the house in a brand new Ford pickup truck.

"Nice truck," I said as he jumped out of the cab. "Is it yours?" We both looked at the truck. It was blue and said four by four on the side.

"Yeah, do you like it? I got a job doing construction for the summer, and I took out a loan from Uncle George," he replied proudly as he looked at the truck and then to me. He turned to face Ash.

"Construction must pay well," Ash said as he shook Adam's hand.

"Yeah, it does, depending on what you do and who you work for," Adam said with a grin. Then the grin left his face when he looked back at me. "This is it. I won't see you for a month."

I was saved from having to answer him when Mom and Ben came out of the house. "Hi, Adam! Nice to see you!" Mom called from the top of the porch stairs.

"Yeah, and thanks for taking Chuck," Ben said as they walked down the stairs.

"It's only for a month, so how bad could he be?" Adam said as he reached down to scratch Chuck behind the ears. Chuck liked Adam. The pup wagged his tail with his tongue lolling out of his mouth.

We did not tell Adam that we might not be coming back. We just said that we were going to England for a month. I just couldn't tell Adam the truth. We had gotten pretty close in the last year, and I didn't want to scare him. There was no way that I was going to tell him that I might be going to Stonehenge with the possibility of being murdered by the wood nymph king.

"Don't look so sad, Laurel! Chuck and I will do just fine. If he has issues, I'll have Mingan talk to him. I promise! We'll be fine!" Adam said as he gave me a hug.

I hugged him back and forced a smile on my face. "I know you will," I replied. My happy mood with Ash was beginning to dissolve, and I didn't want it to! I knew Chuck would be well cared for. With a more sincere smile on my face I said, "I promise to call you as soon as we land in Rhinelander when we get back. I'll call you on my cell phone."

"Do you have time for some lunch?" Mom asked. "We have plenty of fish for lunch today! Amadahy dropped off a mess of pan fish this morning."

The water sprites had heard our conversations about leaving and were concerned for us. While we didn't exactly socialize, they did keep tabs on us and how we were doing. Amadahy—the wise man for the local community of water sprites—also promised to keep an eye on our property.

"Sure! I love your pan-fried fish," Adam replied as we walked into the house together. We had salad and fish for lunch. Adam wasn't too big on salad, but he ate a lot of the fish. I ate way more than I thought I would. I didn't realize how hungry I was until I started eating the fish. It seemed I couldn't get enough. It was a tie as to who ate more, me or Adam.

"I'm glad to see you have your appetite back, Laurel," Mom said to me as we cleaned up the dishes and loaded the dishwasher.

"Yeah, me too," I replied. I wondered if the sex in the glade had made me hungry. I went into the bathroom after my mom and I finished cleaning up and looked at myself in the mirror. While I wasn't glowing exactly, I definitely had more color in my cheeks compared to when I got up this morning.

When I came out of the bathroom, Adam was heading for the door. "Sorry to eat and run, but I have to work this afternoon. I'll take Chuck with me. Don't worry, he won't be left alone."

I bent over and gave Chuck a big hug. "I'll miss you, big guy," I said softly in his thick neck. He turned toward me and gave me a big sloppy lick across my face. I stood up and walked Adam to the door. When he realized he was going with Adam, his ears went down. While he left obediently enough, I could tell he wasn't happy with the situation. He kept looking back at me as Adam got him to jump into the cab of the truck. The last thing I saw of my big puppy was a sad face looking at me with ears hanging down dejectedly.

About an hour after lunch, Ash's parents arrived with Forrest and Olivia. We spent the afternoon discussing last-minute concerns and a final assessment of what to bring and what not to bring.

CHAPTER 5
SUMMER SOLSTICE

"Oh, Laurel, do you still have the color-shifting clothes I brought you?" Forrest asked me as he stood up. "Today is the summer solstice. We have to leave for the ceremony soon."

I had forgotten all about that. No one had mentioned it in the last few days. Was it really the summer solstice already? I was so not ready. After today the days were going to get shorter, and I was going to spend the next month in England. I was sure that summer there would not be nearly as nice as the summer in my part of Wisconsin. There was no place like the Northwoods in the summer. Of course, I liked the Northwoods any time of year.

I heard Ben say to Mom, "This is a wood nymph-only ceremony, isn't it? This is the one Laurel went to last December, the day Forrest gave her the new car?"

"Yes, dear. This is an important event for the wood nymphs. I'd forgotten all about the solstice and the ceremony. I guess because it's not a big deal for humans, we don't think much about it. It's part of Laurel's heritage from her father's side and she enjoys it," Mom replied.

"Can Ash come with us?" I asked as I stood up. Had we talked about it and I hadn't been paying attention?

"I can't see why not. He's a wood nymph. That's up to him and his parents. You go get your color-shifting clothes on," Forrest said.

I ran upstairs and dug through my dresser to find the clothes. They were a little hard to find. Because they were almost invisible, I found them by noticing the space they took up. I had to feel under the dresser for the shoes. I couldn't see them. Within a couple of minutes, I was back downstairs.

"Why didn't you mention that tonight was the ceremony?" I asked Ash when I got back into the living room.

"I forgot. With everything going on, I just forgot all about it. I'm sorry," Ash replied. "I talked to my parents while you were upstairs, and they want to come to the Solstice Ceremony with the Copper Clan, too. We have to jet home to change and then jet to Presque Isle."

In minutes, everyone had left, except for me, Forrest, and Olivia, and of course, my mom and Ben. "I'll jet with Laurel to the ceremony, and Ash can jet her back home," Forrest told Mom and Ben.

I felt like I'd just sat on the couch by Mom and Ben when the door bell rang. "Mom, maybe you should answer the door. I don't think I should be seen by any kind of salesman or UPS driver," I said, looking down at my clothes that had matched the couch. I went into the kitchen.

"That's probably a good idea, although I'm not expecting anything," Mom said as she got up to answer the door.

Ash, his parents, and Hawthorn stood there. "Is Olivia here?" Hawthorn asked looking around.

"Not yet, but she should be soon," Mom replied. "Please come in and sit down while we wait."

Everyone except Ash went into the living room. Ash saw me in the kitchen and came to me. "I really am sorry I forgot to mention this. I don't do anything for the preparation of the event. I just show up when I'm supposed to."

"It's okay. I would have liked to have had something positive to look forward to in the last few days. It's been so gloomy around here. Then with Chuck leaving, well, it would've been nice to have the anticipation is all," I replied. "I forgive you."

Forrest and Olivia arrived as Ash and I walked into the living room. "I have to try to only look at faces. It hurts my eyes to look at the color-changing clothes," Mom said with a smile.

"Do you ever get used to it?" Ben asked with a slight frown. "Disembodied heads is giving me a headache."

"We've always had these clothes. I don't remember a time when we didn't. So, I guess I never had to get used to them," Olivia replied. "We have to go, or we'll be late." Then she noticed Hawthorn.

"Hawthorne! What a wonderful surprise! Are you going with us?" Olivia asked with a huge smile.

"I miss seeing you. I know you've been busy, and I know you're going on this trip tomorrow. I don't know why you can't tell me about it or why I can't go, but when Elm and Willow came to their house to change for the ceremony and said they're going with you, well, I wanted to go, too," He said giving Olivia a big hug. "I hope some day you can tell me what this trip to Europe is all about."

"I will, I promise. I'm so glad you're here. I've missed you, too!" Olivia stated emphatically.

"I'll carry Laurel to the ceremony. Are you sure you can carry her home? She won't have a car in Presque Isle. Would you like to borrow my car to take her home?" Forrest asked Ash.

"No, I can jet. Dad will be with me if for some reason I can't carry her the whole way. I think we'll be fine," Ash replied. "But, I'm not sure if I could handle jetting both ways with her, so thanks."

We walked to the door and this time I didn't have to have a coat on. I didn't remember being cold at the first Essence Ceremony I attended in December. We walked to the foot of the stairs, and Forrest picked me up. I was just waving good-bye to my mom and Ben when the world disappeared.

The next thing I saw was that we were next to the Copper Clan community building. When Forrest put me down, I skipped over to Ash. "I'm so excited that you're here with me! This is the best thing ever!"

We walked around the building and saw the fairies flitting in a small cloud while everyone was finding seats. Just like the first time, I heard the music. This time, it was punctuated with bird song. It sounded like the birds in the trees were chirping in time to the music. I saw the dancers and the old man wood nymph carrying the bowl.

The lightning flashed out of the bowl and touched a couple of wood nymphs. I noticed that some of the bolts of light were thicker and brighter than others. I didn't understand the reason and thought about asking but didn't want to interrupt the ceremony. The lightning was randomly arching out of the bowl and touching various wood nymphs in the clearing. I watched as Forrest, Olivia, Hawthorn, Ash, and his parents got touched by the light and leaned their heads back and closed their eyes in rapture. I was beginning to think that the lightning was going to pass me by. I saw Forrest look at me quizzically and I was just beginning to shrug when I noticed the bowl glow brighter. A huge blast of light came out of the bowl and slammed into me. I started to fall backwards, but someone caught me. I thought I felt my mind explode. This was not in a bad way, though. All the fear I had been feeling for the last two weeks rushed right out of my head. Calmness overtook me. I felt at peace with the world and in my soul. I felt warm in my stomach. I wanted to feel this way forever. It was like coming through layers of sleep, when I realized the ceremony was over. Only Forrest, Olivia, Hawthorn, Ash, his parents, and I were left in the clearing.

"Are you okay?" Ash asked worriedly. "I've never seen such a large bolt of light come out of an essence bowl before."

"Me, either. That was pretty intense," Olivia said as she laid a hand on my forehead like she was feeling for a fever.

"Only the really important wood nymphs get a large dose of essence. I've never seen a dose that large, either. I wonder why the bowl gave you such a large dose?" Elm asked looking at me closely. I was feeling scrutinized.

"I don't know, but I feel great! Let's party!" I said and got up to head to the community building where the music was already starting. I didn't want to lose this wonderful feeling. I felt energized and alive. I wasn't going to wonder about it. I was going to embrace it!

I was getting a lot of looks from the wood nymphs in the room. A lot of them must have noticed the size of my essence flash of light. One of the cousins, I couldn't remember her name, asked if I wanted to learn one of the wood nymph dances. I had never been a good dancer, but I felt so good right now, that I thought it might be fun to try.

The steps were complicated, but they had a natural rhythm to them, and I picked them up easily. I tried to get Ash to dance, but he said he was having more fun just watching me. Maybe I was just a natural dancer and hadn't realized it before. Maybe I had never had a good teacher before. I felt as if I could dance all night long. When the party ended, I didn't feel like I was ready to go home. I was having such a great time.

"Honey, all good things have to come to an end. We leave tomorrow. You should be well rested before the trip," Forrest said.

"Thanks for not forgetting about the Essence Ceremony. I had a great time," I said giving Forrest and Olivia each a hug.

"We're glad you had a good time," Olivia said, putting her arm around Hawthorn.

"Come here, dancer girl," Ash said to me. He picked me up and just as I was trying to wave good-bye, Ash jetted with me in his arms. It wasn't as smooth a ride as it had been with Forrest and it seemed to take a little bit longer to get to my house, but we did jet the entire way. Ash was exhausted.

"Oh, Ash, carrying me is too much for you!" I exclaimed when he put me down and I noticed his heavy breathing.

Between gasps, he said, "I just need to do this more often and build up my endurance. I'll be fine, don't worry. I'll see you in the morning."

"Good night, Ash. I love you!" I whispered softly in his ear as he pulled away to leave.

He kissed my nose and whispered back to me, "I love you, too. I always will."

He turned toward the driveway, took two steps and was gone.

I went into the house. It was late and I still had some packing to do. I could hear Mom and Ben talking upstairs. They had to be doing some last minute packing, too. Their voices sounded normal. I sighed and climbed the stairs. It was really late before I went to bed.

CHAPTER SIX
THE FLIGHT

I was surprised that I slept at all, but I knew I had when I was jarred awake by the alarm clock. I'd set it last night just in case I actually did fall asleep, never believing that I actually would. It was a good thing I had set it after all. I got out of bed, got dressed, and washed up. I changed the sheets on my bed. I wanted clean sheets when I got back in a month. If I got back. I took one last look around my room and grabbed my purse and two suitcases. If I was going to be a prisoner for a month, I wanted to be sure I had enough clothes. The summer wardrobe I had bought this spring would do me no good in my closet here in Tomahawk.

Just as I got to the top of the stairs, I heard Mom call, "Laurel, hurry up! I made pancakes for breakfast."

"I'm coming," I mumbled. I dragged my suitcases downstairs and put them next to the others by the door. I noticed Mom also had two suitcases. Ben only had one.

Mom had on her apron, and it was all flour dusted. She looked like such a domestic goddess. She was bringing a platter of pancakes to the table. "Now eat! I have no idea if anyone intended coming here for breakfast before the limosine get here, so I made plenty. I also don't know if they're going to feed us on the plane. I packed some protein bars in my purse, just in case they don't."

"That's a good idea," Ben said as he forked a few pancakes onto his plate. I saw that the syrup and butter were already on the table. I saw Mom had set out a glass of milk for me on the table too, so I just sat down. Just as I was reaching for the pancake platter, the door bell rang.

"I'll get it," I said as I jumped up from the table. I opened the door to Ash and his family.

"We're just having pancakes. Please come in and have some," I said as I opened the door wide enough for them to bring in their luggage and stack it next to ours.

"None for me, thanks anyway," Willow stated as she set down her suitcases. She had two cases as well. "I'll take some water or juice."

"Me either, but I wouldn't mind some coffee if you have some," Elm replied after he had set down his luggage.

"We have plenty of everything. Come have a seat. I'll get it for you," Mom said as she went into the kitchen.

Ash and I were by the door. He was the last to set down his single piece of luggage. I noticed all of Ash's family had extremely expensive luggage.

"Are you okay? Did you sleep well?" Ash asked me as we walked toward the dining room.

"Surprisingly, yes, I am, and, yes, I did," I replied taking his hand as we walked. I didn't want to leave. I didn't want to go to Stonehenge ever but, there was nothing we could do about it. We had to go or someone would die. That wasn't much of a choice for me but, everything we could do prior to leaving had been, well, taken care of. Now I just wanted this over with. The waiting was killing me and the limo was coming in less than an hour.

"You didn't jet here with luggage, did you?" I asked as we sat at the table.

"No, of course not. One of the cousins will pick up our car later," Ash replied as he sipped orange juice Mom had placed in front of him. The door bell rang again.

"That must be Olivia and Forrest. They're the last to arrive," Mom said as she walked to the door. It was. "Come in and sit down. I have juice, fresh coffee, and pancakes. Please help yourselves."

After breakfast, we cleaned the dishes and went into the living room.

"Willow, who did you say was coming over to empty our refrigerator?" My mom asked as we sat in the living room to wait for the limousine.

"One of the cousins. You met her at the play last year, but I doubt you remember her. Her name is Myrtle. She actually likes cleaning," Willow replied with a chuckle.

We all sat in silence as I noted everyone deep in their own thoughts. I just held Ash's hand and he held mine tightly. His head turned and I knew he could hear the limo. It was time.

It only took a few minutes to load our luggage into the limousine. I thought with all of the people and all of our cases, we wouldn't fit. But our limo looked more like a bus than a limo. We had room for all of us, our stuff, and room to spare. It took less than a half hour to get to the airport in Rhinelander.

Our limousine took us around the main terminal and onto the tarmac. Waiting for us was a brand new jet. Customs was handled swiftly and we were introduced to our three-person flight crew. "I'm your captain. My name's Captain Blythe and this is the co-pilot and navigator, Captain Anderson. Our attendant for this flight is Ms. Holmes. I'd like to welcome you aboard the Bombardier Challenger 300. We'll make one stop in Canada for refueling, and then our next stop will be the airport in Southampton, England. Our flight departs this afternoon at 1:00 p.m. and we should get into Southampton about 10:00 p.m. tonight. If you have any needs, Ms. Holmes will be happy to assist you. Does anyone have any special dietary needs other than it has to be organic?" When no one responded, he continued. "We have a full-service bar and dining facility with a choice of meals and snacks for your comfort and convenience. Everything's been taken care of, including tipping. You are to just enjoy the flight."

We walked up the steps into the plane. Ash and I went in first. As we got to the top of the steps, I turned and heard Ben whisper to Mom, "Did he just say Captain Bligh? That doesn't sound good."

Forrest was right behind Ben. He chuckled and whispered to Ben, "No, he said Blythe, with a T and an H in there. We're not going to have a mutiny on the jet."

"Well, that's comforting," Ben replied with a dramatic sigh and a shake of his head.

Mom was in front of Ben and elbowed him. "This isn't the time to make jokes! What if he heard you? Do you want to piss off the captain before we even leave the ground?" she hissed at him.

"Relax, dear. I'm just trying to have some fun. I'm sure the captain's heard worse than that in his life. If that little bit of teasing would piss him off, I'm pretty sure I wouldn't want to fly with him. I think he'd be too much of a hot head," Ben said as he put his arm around my mom as they entered the cabin.

The seats were arranged almost like living room recliners. There were eight seats altogether. Each was a leather recliner and could be spun in a circle and locked facing in any direction. We could all set our chairs facing forward, or four chairs could face the others. This was the position they were in when we entered the seating area. Ash and I took two seats in the middle. Mom and Ben took the two seats closest to the cockpit. Forrest and Olivia took their seats next to Ash and me, and that left the two seats in the back of the cabin for Ash's mom and dad.

I leaned my head back after everyone had been seated to talk to Forrest. "Uncle Forrest, I bet you never counted on this when you found out about me." He knew I was referring to all of the years that he had been keeping an eye on my mother and me.

Forrest leaned back so that he could talk softly and I would still hear him. "I didn't know what to expect. I guess I kind of always suspected something like this would happen. It was only a matter of time. I guess I'm just grateful I could be with you when the summons came."

"Me too," Olivia interjected. I guess she couldn't help but overhear as she was sitting right next to Forrest. "No matter what happens, I'm glad we're together."

After she said that, we all sat in silence. We observed the flight crew prepare our plane for the first leg of the flight to Canada. After the pilots went into the cockpit, our flight attendant told us to buckle our seat belts. I was surprised that she didn't make us sit facing forward and to have our seats in an upright position for takeoff. In no time at all, we were speeding down the runway and into the air.

After we were at cruising altitude, the pilot announced that the attendant would be serving drinks and snacks. We could also unbuckle our seat belts if we so desired.

Ms. Holmes made several beverage suggestions and when she said that she had a particular wine, a lot of wood nymph eyebrows went up. "How did they get that type of wine?" I heard Olivia whisper to Forrest. "That's nymph-made wine."

"Don't you make your own wine?" I whispered to Olivia's back. "You bring wine to our house regularly, but I don't remember seeing a label on any bottle. I guess I never thought to ask where you got the wine from."

She turned to face me and replied softly, "Our clan does make some wine, but not a lot. There are some wood nymph vineyards in France, Germany, Spain, California, and Washington. There are a few nymph vineyards, but not many in Wisconsin. This is from a very exclusive and expensive vineyard in France. Even wood nymphs can be quite capitalistic in their endeavors. They sell the wine at a very high price to humans. They give it to the wood nymphs that request it at a much more reduced rate."

"That's pretty unfair," I whispered back. "Humans help them by buying their products and then they rip off the humans."

Olivia sighed as she leaned back in the chair and turned her head to face me. She said, "I know, dear. Don't forget, most wood nymphs don't like humans. We've had eighteen years to get used to having a human in the family. Forrest's watched you grow and has given reports about you throughout your life. By direct observation, we know that not all humans are selfish and egotistical. Even though I didn't know you, I felt an attachment to you."

I sat back in my seat and thought about my future. I thought about the wine being served to Ash's parents. The crew on this plane was human. Where did they get the wine? I was curious. I asked the flight attendant, Ms. Holmes, as she came up to Forrest and Olivia. "Where did you get this wine?"

"I'm sorry, my dear, you're too young to have any," she said as she poured for Forrest and Olivia.

"I know. I'm just curious where you got that type of wine," I asked feeling slightly ruffled at her condescending attitude.

"The client who hired us for this trip asked for this type of wine by name. He was very specific about all of the beverages and food served on this flight," she replied giving me her professional smile.

"Who hired you for this flight?" I asked. I knew that she wouldn't tell me that it was the king.

"The CEO of the Stonehengement Corporation. It's a fairly big corporation in England. I would've thought you would have known that, since you're a guest on this flight," she replied giving me a quizzical look.

42

"Of course she knew that. She just forgot," Forrest said to Ms. Holmes. He had an interesting tone in his voice as he said it. It sounded almost hypnotic.

Ms. Holmes blinked a couple of times and looked around. She noticed she had the bottle of wine in her hands, shook her head and said, "Can I get you anything else?"

"No, not now. Thank you," Forrest said softly but firmly.

"Uh, sure, I'll check back with you," she answered as she walked up to my parents and offered them some wine.

After she was out of hearing range, Forrest leaned back in his chair and whispered to me, "Be careful what you say and ask. We don't want this to look like anything more than a vacation retreat paid for by friends."

"What did you do to her? Your words seemed to vibrate through me. If I didn't know any better, I would've thought you were hypnotizing her," I said leaning back to hear him more clearly.

"It's a form of mesmerizing. Kind of a glammer, if you will. Every now and then, we need to rearrange a human's thinking. Sometimes they get too close to the truth and then we have to do something about it. Like this. She's not hurt. She just forgot what we were talking about, or that we were even talking. She won't remember what you said," Forrest responded. "I find it interesting that it didn't affect you. It was possible, because of your human blood, that you'd have been confused as well," he said as he leaned back and kissed my cheek. "I'm glad you weren't affected."

I thought about it. Then I smiled. "I'm glad you never tried to use a glammer on me."

"Me too, since now we know it won't work," he replied and laughed.

"What's so funny?" Mom asked, sipping the wine. "This is really good wine!"

"Oh, we were just discussing the different things that make Laurel special," Forrest said as he lifted his wine glass in a toast to my mom. "I'm so glad you are part of the family."

"That's an interesting thing to say, especially considering what's going on at the moment," Mom said as she looked pointedly toward the flight attendant's back.

I was sure my mom was talking about why we were on the flight in the first place. As we sat there, the flight attendant brought out cheese, crackers, and a fruit tray. It seemed in no time at all we were stopping in Canada to refuel for the long flight across the Atlantic Ocean.

When the plane ascended back into the air, I rested my head on Ash's shoulder, and we both fell fast asleep.

I woke up with the plane bouncing up and down. Just as I awoke, the pilot came on the intercom and suggested that we put our seat belts on because we were experiencing some heavy turbulence. I had a hard time getting to my own seat, as we bounced around so roughly. When I finally made it. The next thing I noticed was that I felt weightless. The plane was losing altitude at an unreasonable speed. We weren't free falling exactly, but close. The flight attendant staggered to the cockpit. I assumed she was going to go see what was going on. She came back with a wild look in her eyes but stated calmly, "The pilots are out cold. Can anyone fly this plane?" she asked our group.

"I think I can," Ben replied as he got up.

"You? I didn't know you could fly a plane!" Mom said.

"I learned lots of things in the Army," Ben replied as he staggered to the cockpit. Shortly after he closed the door behind him, the plane leveled out. Soon I could tell we were gaining altitude again.

A couple of minutes later, the pilot and co-pilot came out of the cockpit with handkerchiefs pressed against bleeding heads. "Unbelievable. The odds of that happening are so slim," the pilot said as he wrapped some ice in a towel to put on his head. "To have stuff fall out of an overhead compartment due to the turbulence and knock both of us out just would not have been a concern before this. I've never heard of anything like this happening before. The auto pilot was reset . . . but Mr. Redmond is keeping an eye on things for us while we get some ice for our heads."

The pilot put the ice pack on his head and went back into the cockpit. The co-pilot looked like he had taken a harder hit. He was very pale. He sat in the flight attentent's chair for a few minutes before going back into the cockpit. When he finally stood up, his face had a lot more color. Ben remained in the cockpit until the co-pilot felt well enough to operate the plane.

The rest of the flight was uneventful, and we landed safe and sound at the airport. Ms. Holmes handed out Customs forms and we filled them out. The flight crew apologized to us as we left the plane.

"I don't know what we would have done without you, Mr. Redmond." The pilot stated as he shook Ben's hand.

"Me, either!" Forrest said.

"I was happy to help," Ben replied. He smiled at the pilot as he walked off of the plane with my mom.

Customs took no time at all and within minutes a black stretch limousine sat outside of the terminal waiting for us.

CHAPTER 7
THE STONEHENGERS' PALACE

The limo driver was a wood nymph. He had non-descript brown eyes which matched his hair. He introduced himself as Whitey Pine and didn't say much more. He loaded our luggage into a trailer attached to the back of the limo and then we departed for the palace.

I noticed Whitey's skin and I could now tell the difference between humans and wood nymphs. The wood nymphs had a slightly different cast to their skin. Some had darker complexions and some were lighter but, they all had a slight glow.

I whispered to Ash, "Does my skin glow, too? I can't tell. I can only see the glow on a wood nymph."

"You glow from the inside," he replied as he kissed my forehead.

I pushed him back. "No, seriously. I want to know. Do I have that glowing cast to my skin like you do? I can't see it on me."

"Yes, you do, but it isn't as discernible as it is with a full wood nymph," Forrest answered for Ash.

"I don't see a glow," my mom said from her seat in the limo. "You all look like humans to me."

"I don't either," Ben stated sitting next to Mom. "Can all wood nymphs determine a wood nymph by this glow?" he asked looking around the car as if all of the wood nymphs would suddenly look different. "Is that how you can tell a wood nymph from a human?"

"Not all of us see an actual glow. It is more like an instinctual thing. We can tell by looking at someone and immediately know if the person is a human or something else. A lot of times we can tell by the scent. Only a few wood nymphs can see the aura. All living things have an aura. It's just that not everyone can see them," Olivia said to Ben, but looking at me curiously.

As she said that, I noticed that the limo driver was watching me through the rear view mirror. I intently looked back at him and he took his eyes off of me. He seriously gave me the creeps.

We didn't drive for very long when I noticed the mountains. I saw the Stonehenge ruins in the distance when the driver stopped the car. I thought we would stop by the ruins. We stopped next to a mountain. When we got out of the car, I noticed that we were at the end of a dirt road. I didn't notice when we had gotten off of the highway from the airport. Everything about this place was creeping me out. I didn't like the driver or the way he looked at me. It wasn't like he did anything in particular that was offensive, it was just the feeling I got being near him.

I didn't like it that he drove on the wrong side of the road. I knew in England that it was normal to drive on the other side of the road, but it still made me uncomfortable. I wondered if that was what was making me feel creepy. I wondered if I had taken a normal trip to England with my parents as tourists if I would have felt this creeped out. I doubted it. Sometimes I really hated the whole human- wood nymph thing.

"This is the entrance to the palace," the driver said to us as we got out of the limo. "You all need to carry your own luggage now." Well, so much for being treated like honored guests by the staff.

We all grabbed our individual pieces of luggage with Elm and Ben taking their wives' extra bags. Ash also took my second bag. I looked up and noticed that while we had picked up all of our belongings, there was nowhere to go! All I saw was a wall of a mountain in front of us. Were we supposed to hike all of the way to the ruins? I knew that tourists went to the Stonehenge ruins all of the time. Why were we being dropped off next to a mountain? I stood there and looked around.

A few boulders stood next to the mountain. I assumed that they'd fallen off and I wondered if there was the chance that any could drop on us. I was just about to ask where we were going when Whitey put his hand on one of the boulders and the huge rock recessed into the mountain as if it were on hinges. The opening had to be at least twenty feet in diameter. There was now a huge hole in the mountain and all I could see was black. "I'm not going in there," Ben said flatly.

The driver gave Ben a disgusted look and went inside the black hole of the cavern. Just inside the entryway, he put his hand on the inside wall. Immediately the entire cave was illuminated on all sides. As I looked closer, I noticed it wasn't just the whole wall that lit up. There were lots of veins of what appeared to be white light inside what otherwise looked like carved granite on the inside of the mountain. In this case, the lighter color streaks inside the granite had lit up. I wondered what caused that. I noticed as I entered the cave that there were enough veins of light in the rock to brightly light the entire cave as far as we could see. After we had all entered the cave, the boulder slammed back into place. I did not hear it move until it finished closing. We were now in the cave. I felt kind of trapped and panicky. The only thing that kept me from freaking out was that Whitey was still with us. The driver started walking into the cave and told us to follow him. I noticed that the floor of the cave was smooth and easy to walk on. He walked us about one-hundred yards over to what appeared to be railroad tracks, only of a smaller gauge from what I had known. They reminded me of the train tracks for the small zoo train children rode. A little ways down the tracks was a train car. Whitey seemed to be taking us to it. The thing was fully enclosed and reminded me of a bus or a trolley. Whitey told us to climb in and we would be on our way.

"Come on, Ben, we have to board he train," I heard my mom say to Ben. "I don't want to do it either, but it appears this is part of our journey." Mom put her bag down and put her arms around Ben.

With a deep sigh, Ben looked at me sadly and said, "I know you love Ash, and I really like Olivia and Forrest, but right this moment, I wish we never built the house in Tomahawk."

I sighed and said, "Let's go. They're waiting for us."

Ben gave me a long look, sighed, and picked up the luggage. I picked up my mom's other suitcase since Ash had already handed ours up to Forrest on the train. Forrest put the luggage on the pile in a cargo space on the train and once we were all seated and the door closed. The bus/train thing started moving. While it started out slowly, within seconds we were flying down the track. This was no kiddy train. We were going so fast, I couldn't see the walls anymore, just a blur of white light from the veins in the rock.

After a while, I felt the train gradually reduce its speed. We stopped in a large valley inside of the mountain, but, even though we were inside the mountain, the landscape was a beautiful, living green with many trees and grasses spread as far as three football fields.

On our right as we exited the train, was the wall of the mountain. I noticed. If I looked in one direction, I saw a green valley that was beautiful and alive. If I looked toward the mountain, I saw darkness and felt despair.

The doors displayed carvings with some kind of runes. Whitey touched a panel on the right side of the door and the veins of color shined brightly.

As we approached the giant illuminated doors, they slowly began to open up to great walls with gigantic tapestries displaying scenes of wood nymphs dancing and feasting. The figures on the tapestries wore ancient Greek chitons or Roman robes. When the doors closed, the breeze from the massive doors caused the tapestries to flow in such a way that it looked like the wood nymphs were dancing on the fabric. At the end of the room there was a wide staircase that gradually became more narrow with each upward step.

The stairway continued for six floors. There were hallways branching off from the stairway in six places. The hallways branched off to both sides of the

47

staircase. Each landing had a hallway balcony that reached halfway around the room. Each successive floor was set back farther then the landing or hallway beneath it.

At first I didn't notice the petite wood nymph girl standing before me, until she cleared her throat. I noticed that wood nymphs stood before all of us and each of them wore the same type of clothing. The new nymphs wore patterned tunics and trousers similiar to the color-changing fabric Olivia enjoyed wearing. I looked back at the girl in front of me, and she smiled shyly. She said her name was Moss Grass and that she was my personal servant while I was a guest at the palace.

The rest of the servants that accompanied Moss introduced themselves to the individual they would be serving. Just as Moss picked up my luggage, the king of the wood nymphs called out to us from the bottom of the massive staircase. Moss put my luggage back down and went into a deep bow.

"Welcome, my friends! I hope you have had a comfortable journey over to England," he said with a flourish. "Welcome to Stonehenge palace. As you have probably figured out, most of the palace is inside the mountain. Some of it is goes beneath the Stonehenge ruins." He spoke with a booming voice in order for us to hear him clearly as he approached the group.

After several moments, I noticed the nymphs in my group beginning to bow in respect for the king. I looked at Mom and Ben, and we followed their actions.

"Please rise! Welcome!" he said as he walked up to us.

I noticed his clothing no longer resembled the eighteenth-century style anymore. He looked like he had just stepped off the cover of *GQ* magazine. There was no royal cape and he still wore his crown.

He walked up to us and shook our hands. "I am so glad that you are here. This is a momentous occasion. This is the first time that we have had humans within the palace."

He looked at each of us as if we were science projects. I heard the words, but I didn't get the feeling. I did not believe that he was really glad to have humans in his palace. He was just glad that we were there and that he could do damage control in keeping us from telling other humans about the wood nymphs and this place.

"I hope you will find everything comfortable. If you need anything at all, your assigned servant will take care of it for you. All you need to do is ask. You are welcome to wander anywhere in the palace you like, except for a few areas that will have a guard by the door and the sixth floor. Those are the royal quarters. I have put you all on the third floor. Those are the suites reserved for our honored guests," he said as he smiled. He acted as if he was doing us a huge favor. Maybe he was, but it didn't feel like it at this particular moment.

"Please allow my staff to show you to your rooms to freshen up. The servants will wait while you get ready for dinner and will show you to the reception and dining rooms. I will see you all in say, one hour?" He then slightly bowed to us and turned away. He did not look back. I wondered where the queen was.

As the king headed for the stairs, I turned to look at Moss who was watching me. "I didn't know wood nymphs were servants to anyone," I said as I watched her pick up my luggage.

I looked back to where the king should be on the stairs, but he was nowhere to be seen. I wondered if he had jetted up the stairs. Come to think of it, I didn't see him walk down the stairs either. He was just there. I guessed either he came from a side door or jetted down the stairs when he came to greet us. I looked back at Moss and saw her patiently waiting for me.

"I will answer all of your questions to the best of my ability. But first, will you follow me please?" she asked as she started toward the stairs.

I looked around and saw that all of the servants had their respective person's luggage and were all starting toward the stairs.

"Just a minute!" I said to Moss. I turned back to Ash. "I need to know what room you're in." Then I faced everyone else and spoke louder. "Actually, I want to know everyone's rooms. Once we get our room assignments, can we meet on the balcony hallway? It shouldn't be too hard to find everyone since we are all on the third floor."

"That is a good idea. I'll meet you in the hall as soon as I get my stuff put in my room," Ash replied giving me a kiss on the cheek. Then he pulled me close and whispered to me, "I wish we could share one room."

"Me, too!" I whispered as I smiled back at him.

Mom, Ben, Forrest, and Olivia agreed knowing where everyone was, was a good idea. Elm and Willow looked at each other first, and then they agreed as well.

Moss was a tiny thing, but she handled both pieces of my luggage with apparent ease. I followed her up the stairs. We went first, with everyone else behind us.

"It is an honor to be able to work in the royal palace," she said as I walked beside her on the stairs. "Those of us not born with gifts are given positions as servants in the palace."

"No gifts? What about that hyper-speed running thing? I thought all wood nymphs were born with that one." I asked in surprise. I thought all wood nymphs had multiple skills.

"Yes. That is one of the gifts that some of us are born without. That is why we have the train you rode in on from the outside world. Jetting is not a universal skill, and some of the old and infirm nymphs can't jet anymore. If we need to go to the outside world, we can take the train," she replied. She didn't seem bothered by the idea of being a servant. I actually thought I heard pride in her voice.

"I am not sure what all I can or cannot tell you. I have never personally dealt with humans before. In fact, other than being in the valley just outside the palace, I spend almost no time outdoors," Moss explained as we reached the third floor.

I was sidetracked as we turned onto the long balcony that led off from the stairway. Set back from the railing so far that I didn't see them from the foyer were doors into the rock walls of the mountain. The walls and ceiling were smooth granite with the glowing veins of light. Each door also had the glowing veins of light adding to the brightness of the main hall.

My room was the second door from the stairway. However, it had to be one-hundred feet away from my parents' door. This place was massive. It seemed built for giants. Even the doorway to my room had to be nine feet tall.

Moss opened my door by placing her hand on a rectangular panel on the wall just outside my door. When she put her hand on the panel, it glowed for a moment and the door opened. After it was open, she took my hand. Reflexively, I jerked my hand away. She smiled at me and asked me to please place my hand on the flat panel. I asked her why, and she said the door would remember my handprint. I agreed and when I rested my palm on the panel, it glowed again for a moment and then went dark. "This door has now been activated to your hand. Only my hand or yours will allow this door to open," she said as she carried my luggage into my room. She waited for me just inside the door.

I hesitated. "I want to try it," I said. "I'll shut the door. If I don't come in right away, come back out, okay?" I said as I was closing the door. I saw her nod.

I closed the door and took a deep breath. I put my hand on the panel, and the door immediately opened. Okay. I agreed that she and I could open the door, but who else could open the door? I was sure that the king and queen had some kind of master handprint or something that would open the door. I only had that amount of privacy the king or queen deemed me worthy of. I was certain of that.

I went into the room. Calling it just a room was wrong. It was a suite of rooms. Upon entering, I saw what appeared to be a living space. I saw chairs and tables built into the walls. There were shelves with books on other parts of the wall. In the middle of the room was a sunken area with circular couches with padded seats carved into the rock of the mountain. In the center of the room was a circular table that also appeared to be carved from the mountain itself.

The walls still glowed in here, but not as brightly. I touched the wall and it was warm to the touch. Not hot, but warm. I found that interesting. I would have thought that the inside of a mountain would be damp and cold. The spot where my hand touched glowed brighter than the rest of the room.

Moss smiled at me as she walked into a room off of the living room area and said, "The walls both give us light and control the temperature of the room. If you are too hot, you put your hand on the wall and think about cooler temperatures. If you are too cold, you put your hand on the wall and think about warmer temperatures. Oh, but, since you're part human, it may not work for you. You should try it, and if it does work. If not I'll do it for you. But, the entry door did respond to you, so the temp control should. Why not give it a try?"

I put my hand on the wall and thought about winter in Wisconsin. Where my hand touched the wall I could see that the outline of my hand had a brighter glow compared to the rest of the wall. When I thought about colder temperatures, the light flared brightly around my hand and the room immediately became colder.

"Oh! Don't think such cold thoughts!" Moss squeaked as she put her hand on the wall and closed her eyes to concentrate on a more comfortable temperature. Immediately the room was comfortable again. Moss pulled her hand away from the wall and looked at me and smiled. "I guess it does work for you, but maybe until you feel more comfortable with it, I should do it for you?"

"That might be a good idea. I'll make sure you are here if I decide to practice," I replied as I followed her into what would be my bedroom. The bed was a huge canopy bed. It was at least a king-sized bed. It had a lot of white lace and ruffles. This was definitely a feminine room. However, on the far side of the room found a window looking at forest and a lake. I thought we were in the middle of a mountain. How could there be windows? I walked over to it before I realized it was an illusion. The light and colors in the wall were set in such a way as to appear to be a summer day in a forest by a lake. The leaves on the trees even fluttered as if in a wind. It was so real looking and in a strange way, very comforting.

"That is amazing!" I said as I backed away. I would have sworn that I was looking through a window at a forest view.

"We're wood nymphs," Moss said. "We need the comfort of the woods, even if it is just an illusion. It helps the mind adjust to living in a mountain." She started hanging my clothes in a huge walk-in closet. "Many centuries ago, as humans populated the world, we had to hide ourselves away from them. Most of them meant no harm—in fact—humans idolized us, called us gods. But, there was no privacy from them. As more and more of them were born, we had to hide ourselves away. So, we have this mountain. Smaller clans populated different areas of the world. For centuries, we appeared to humans at certain times of the year to give blessings to their crops or their health. Years ago, we could help the humans with famine or diseases. However, now it's our species that needs help for our health. More and more of our children are born without natural gifts, and those are the children lucky to being born at all. Our life expectancy is shorter than it used to be and many of our conjoined couples are having no children at all. Is that why you are here? I heard that you were coming when I got you as an assignment. You're the first human-wood nymph child born. Is that why the king brought you here? I have always been afraid of humans, but you seem nice," This last part she said with a look of embarrassment. "I'm sorry. I tend to talk too much."

I walked over to her and put my hand on her arm. She jumped as she looked up at me, frightened. "It's okay," I said. "The more I learn about the nymph culture, the better chance there is that I'll learn how to help. Wood nymphs have helped humans in the past, so maybe I can help the wood nymphs? Maybe that's why we are here?"

She looked at me with such hope when I said that. I blushed. Was it possible that I might be able to do some good? If I was able to help the wood nymphs, it would show that I had value, and we would be allowed to live. I smiled at her. But, what could I do to help? I had no idea. But, I was alive so far, and that was a start.

"That would be really great," she said with a smile. "I don't know much about humans, but I think you have something good about you. I like being around you. I'd like to think that maybe you are the hope for our future."

She was still smiling as she turned and finished hanging all of my clothes. As she was putting things away, she said, "What would you like to wear for dinner tonight? Ooh, this is a nice dress. How about this one?" she asked as she held out the dress I had bought a week ago in Wausau. Olivia had said we should have some long dresses for dinner, and this one was a light-blue satin gown. Olivia went with me and Mom to do the shopping. Olivia stated that price was no object to her, and she wouldn't take no for an answer no matter how expensive the shoes and dresses were for either of us. Olivia could be quite forceful when she wanted to be. She made sure that my mom and I had plenty of evening wear to go along with what we already had to wear during the day.

"Sure," I said. I found the matching sandals that went with it. While I was looking for the shoes, Moss went through a doorway on the other side of the bedroom and I heard water running. She came out a moment later.

"I'm running a bath for you. Will you need assistance?" she asked as I walked into the bathroom. The bathroom alone was the size of a small house. There was a standing shower, a Jacuzzi-style tub with mirrors from floor to ceiling around it, and an elaborate sink with makeup lighting surrounding it. Just the fixtures in this bathroom would have fed a small country. I wondered how the wood nymphs were able to get the light fixtures and wiring through the marble walls.

I was gawking around the room when I noticed that Moss was waiting for a response. "Um, no. I don't think so. I'm used to bathing myself. When do I have to be ready to go downstairs?" I asked Moss.

"I'll be back in a half hour to do your hair. Is that enough time for you? We have almost an hour to get you downstairs to the reception hall," she replied, heading for the door.

I just remembered that Ash and everyone else were probably waiting for me in the hallway outside the suite. "Oh!" I said as I ran out of the room. "I'll be right back! Please don't let the tub overflow!"

When I got out into the main hallway balcony area, I saw that everyone was outside their rooms, leaning over the railing and looking down into the great hall. When everyone saw that I was out of my suite, we met in front of Ash's door, which was two doors down from mine. I figured out that Mom and Ben were the first door, then me, then Olivia, then Ash, then Forrest, and finally Elm and Willow's suite. Conveniently, there were six suites on each side of the stairway. I wondered if anyone would be staying on the other side of the stairway while we were here.

"Is everyone's suite as grand as mine?" I asked everyone. "You should see my rooms! The bathroom alone is as big as a house!"

"Yes, our rooms are fabulous. I've never seen such opulence," Mom replied, smiling. "I think it's a good sign that the king kept us together and gave us such a nice place to stay."

"How are your rooms?" I asked Ash. "Do you have a gigantic bed, too?" I whispered, hoping only he would hear.

He squeezed my hand and nodded. There was a definite gleam in his eye when he smiled. I wondered if he was thinking what I was thinking and that maybe, just maybe, we might have some time alone to try out his bed or mine, or both!

Olivia raised her eyebrow at us. She was the only one paying attention to us. Everyone was fixated on the glowing veins of light in the marble looking rock walls.

"Isn't that something!" Ben exclaimed. "I've never seen anything like it! And the temperature control in the room! Just touch the wall and think of a temperature and that creates the comfort level of the room. Amazing!"

"Did you try to change the temp in the room?" I asked Ben.

"Yeah, I made it too hot. I was thinking at first of how the inside of a mountain should be damp and cold, and thought it should be warm and thought about a hot sandy beach in the tropics. It instantly got really hot in there! Spruce Pine, our assigned person, had to change it back," Ben replied with a self-deprecating smile.

"Servants. They are servants," Elm stated. "They are proud of their station and what they do. While that may seem strange to you, it is a proud vocation for them. They may be offended at being called an assigned person," Elm stated with a sigh. I wondered if Elm was getting all haughty because us mere humans had no way of understanding all of the wood nymph culture.

"Oh, I would never mean to offend!" Mom said softly as she went to stand next to Ben. "We're only trying to give their position dignity."

"That's true," Ben agreed as he squeezed Mom's hand. "We would never want to intentionally hurt anyone's feelings."

Elm sighed again. "I understand. Some of our culture is different from what you're used to. That doesn't make it better or worse, but it is different and you are here. We'll try to guide you, but things are not always what they seem." Elm looked down at his watch. "We better get cleaned up now. We don't want to be late to meet the king."

Silently, we went back to our rooms to change for dinner. I had spent too much time with my family and was worried when I got back to my bathroom that my bath water would be cold. "I'm sorry," I said to Moss. "This is just so different from anything any of us have experienced! I had to check on my family. Did my water get cold?"

"No, I was able to keep it warm. The tub works like the walls. You think of the proper temperature of the water and place your hand on the tub here, and the water temperature is raised or lowered depending on your desires," Moss explained, showing me where to place my hand for the adjustment. "I'll be back in fifteen minutes. Is that enough time?" she asked as she headed for the door.

"Yes. Plenty. Thank you!" I called to her retreating back as she left the room.

She gave me what appeared to be a sad smile as she left the room. Why would she be sad? Was she sad that she had to wait on me? She seemed happy enough to do it. Did she know something I didn't? I thought about that as I undressed and stepped into the tub. Moss had put some kind of bath oil in the water and while I had never smelled anything exactly like it before, it kind of reminded me of a feminine version of Ash's aroused scent. Interesting.

CHAPTER 8
THE ROYAL FAMILY

I got into the tub and stretched out. It was the size of a hotel hot tub, the kind found by an indoor pool that can comfortably fit eight people. I looked around the tub and found the switch that turned on the jets in the tub. I sat back and luxuriated in the feel of the warm, bubbly, scented water. It seemed that I had barely relaxed when I realized it was time to get out and get dressed. I turned off the jets and drained the water. I was just getting dressed when Moss came into my room.

"Knock, knock," she called from the bedroom doorway. "I'm here to do your hair."

"Great. Can you zip up the back of this dress, please?" I asked as I turned towards her.

"Oh, of course! I'm here to help you with anything you want!" she gushed as she rushed over to help me.

I felt stupid. I never needed help like this. "I can usually get dressed just fine by myself, but this dress seems a bit tighter than it did a week or so ago. It fit just fine when I bought it. I guess I must have eaten too much on the flight over," I complained as Moss zipped me up.

"The dress looks perfect," Moss said as she appraised me. I twirled in front of the mirror to see how I looked. I really did look good. The dress didn't look too tight once it was zipped up. The skirt flared around beautifully. It was a sky blue satin dress with one shoulder sleeve and one bare shoulder. I had on aquamarine earrings and an aquamarine pendant necklace. My high-heeled sandals were dyed to match the dress. With my light-brown hair—I had to admit—this light-blue color looked good on me. I couldn't wait to see Ash's face when he saw me.

"Now let's do your hair," Moss said as she reached into a cabinet near the dressing table to pull out my brush and combs. She gestured for me to sit on the stool by the vanity table. I sat and watched her pull out a package of hair pins from a cabinet. The hair pins matched my hair color perfectly.

Moss pulled my hair up into a French twist and expertly applied the makeup that she had brought out with the hair pins. Did wood nymphs wear cosmetics? I didn't remember ever seeing Olivia with makeup on. How did Moss know how to apply the eye shadow? She wasn't wearing any makeup that I could see. I was about to ask her, when she said, "It is time for us to go now," as she sprayed my hair. I got up and looked at myself in the full-length mirror. I was so pleased by my appearance in the mirror, I forgot to ask her where the cosmetics came from or how she knew how to apply them. There was no label on the containers. She gave me one last approving look before we headed for the stairs. I grabbed my white shawl just in case it was cool where we were going.

"Do you want to take the stairs, or would you prefer to take the lift?" she asked me as we exited my suite into the hallway. I looked around for my mom and Ben, or Ash but didn't see anyone in the hall. They must already be where we were going. I wondered why my mother hadn't knocked on my door.

"You have an elevator, I mean, a lift in this place? Sure, with these heels, I'd much rather take the lift," I replied. We went to the end of the balcony corridor on the end away from the stairway. There, sure enough, was an elevator door with a hand panel similar to the one next by the door to my room. The whole elevator system was placed into the wall of the mountain as if the mountain had grown around the elevator. It looked like the elevator and its casement had been there since the mountain was built, which was of course, impossible. I wondered if someone here could talk to stone or rock the way Uncle Forrest could talk to wood and make it do what he wanted it to do. I decided in the near future I was going to ask Moss about that.

We entered the lift and Moss placed her hand on the inside panel and said, "Main floor." The doors closed and then immediately opened. I had not felt the elevator compartment move. I just saw the doors close and then open again. It reminded me of the time Ash jumped out of a tree with me so long ago. It happened so fast.

When we exited the elevator, I saw Mom and Ben just coming down the stairs. I went over to greet them. "Where did you come from?" Mom asked me as I walked up to them.

"I took the elevator down with Moss," I replied. "See, it is right there." I pointed to a little alcove off of the main room where they could see the door to the elevator.

"Nice!" Ben laughed and then looked at my mom. "That may come in handy if your feet hurt by the end of the night." She was wearing really high heels with her long gown.

"True. These are new shoes." She laughed as she pointed her toe.

"I wore comfortable shoes with my tuxedo," Ben said and showed us his feet. He had on his old dress Army shoes.

Now that we were all together, I wondered where we were supposed to go. Moss must have guessed what I was about to ask because she walked up to me and said, "Please follow me. We do not want to be late."

We followed her. My parents' servant had left when Moss and I joined my parents. Moss was leading us in a direction that I hadn't noticed before. This was off of the main entryway. She turned to look at me. "This is the way to the reception and dining rooms."

The hallway was covered in wall to wall carpeting. I thought my heels would get stuck in the loops of the carpet, but they didn't and it was quite comfortable to walk on. The carpeting was forest green, the color of pine needles in the filtered sunlight on a forest floor. The lighting on the walls appeared diffused. They were the color of what the sky would look like as you looked at it through the branches and leaves of a forest just before dusk.

I was just about to comment on it when Moss opened a set of sliding doors that led to another large room. This room had the same lighted veins in the walls, but while they were more subdued, there were a lot more of them. I saw that one wall had the illusion of a huge picture window overlooking a forest in bright daylight. There were small tables with chairs set up throughout the room. There was also a huge fireplace along another wall with a blazing fire in it. The room was large, like a ballroom with the center cleared for either dancing or standing and talking. As I entered the room, I would have expected the room to be stiflingly hot due to the roaring fire. But, it wasn't. I had the impression that no matter how close I got to that fire I would not get too hot, that the fireplace was for ambience and not heat, or maybe it was for both but was controlled like the heat in my room.

Ash, his parents, Forrest and Olivia, were already there. Their servants were handing them beverages. Ash had what appeared to be a glass of wine! We walked over to them. "Is that real wine?" I asked as I walked up to him.

"Nice to see you too. You look beautiful," he said to me as he reached over and kissed me. "Is that a new dress?"

"Um, yeah. Olivia took us shopping, remember? This is one of the dresses she bought for me. Mom's dress and shoes are new, too," I said as I watched my mom and Ben walk over to us.

"You are both very beautiful," Forrest said as he walked up and put an arm around each of us. "Olivia has impeccable taste."

Olivia put an arm around Ash and one around Ben. "You guys dress up pretty nice yourselves," she said with a smile.

"So, is that wine?" I asked Ash again. I hadn't realized how thirsty I was. While as a rule I didn't drink alcohol—if he was willing to drink it—I was too.

"Yes. Want to try it?" he asked as he handed me the glass. I could see the disapproving look on my mother's face. Mom had dealt with childhood alcoholics while she had worked as a school counselor in Virginia before we moved to Wisconsin. She was strict about no drinking before the legal drinking age.

I took a sip. At first it tasted really good. But, by the time the wine made its way to my stomach, it seemed to have turned sour. I felt that if I took another sip, I might throw up and that would definitely be a bad thing here. "It's okay, but I think I'd like some juice or water, please," I said to Moss as she hovered nearby waiting to hear what I wanted to drink.

"Is there beer?" Ben asked his servant, Spruce. Spruce had already been in the room when we arrived.

"Oh, yes. We have beer here. It is from an original German recipe. The German humans got the beer purity laws from their local wood nymphs. It is unfiltered. I'll get it right away. What can I get for you, ma'am?" Spruce asked my mom.

"I would like the same as well pleas," my mom replied. Then she walked over to me and whispered, "I'm glad you're not drinking. I don't know what the rules are here, but I still don't like the idea of underage drinking. You don't turn twenty-one for a couple of years yet."

I looked at her and said, "You know mom, at first it tasted nice, like grape juice, but better. Then it hit my stomach, ooh. Not good. Maybe I have some kind of jet lag or something. The last thing I need to do is to throw up here."

Mom looked at me and then around the room and sighed as she said, "I'm sure we are all tired. It has been a long flight without a lot of rest. I hope that this night does not last real long."

We looked around the room. I wondered what was going to happen next. There were at least a couple of dozen people in the room. All of them were wood nymphs except for me and my parents. I was glad Olivia talked us into buying new clothes. Everyone wore expensive dressed or a tuxedoes. I guess I half expected that the wood nymphs would wear the color changing clothes like the outfit Olivia had worn to the Essence Ceremony. I was surprised to see obviously human type clothes.

Some of the people were sitting at the small tables talking. Some playing a kind of board game with stones that I had never seen before. Most of them would discretely look toward us. None of them looked very friendly, at least not in the expressions I saw on their faces when they looked our way.

The servants brought our drinks and we stood there for a moment and sipped on them while looking around. Moss had brought me some kind of nectar. It was sweet and thick. It was very soothing to my stomach. "This is perfect. Thank you," I said as I smiled at Moss.

After serving us our drinks, I watched as Moss joined the rest of the servants who stood along the wall. They stood far enough away to allow privacy in conversation and close enough to be available in case we might need something. We were just commenting on how far down we should bow down for the king and queen when they arrived. Mom and I decided that we would copy Olivia and Forrest. Just then, we heard a servant announce the arrival of the king and queen from the other side of the room. I was taking a sip from my glass when the main sliding doors opened and the king and queen entered with some of their attendants.

All of the wood nymphs bowed low as the king and queen entered. Mom, Ben, and I bowed along with Ash, his parents, Olivia, and Forrest. I felt all of this bowing was a bit much but, it wasn't my home or culture, so I had no right to criticize. After a moment, the king asked everyone to rise up and continue on with what they were doing. I had held my drink in my hand as I bowed, and I was glad that I hadn't spilled it. I was just wondering why the women didn't curtsy as I watched the queen walk over to us.

Forrest and Olivia gave a quick bow and with a suppressed sigh, I did the same. I noticed that Ben and my mom also gave a quick bow. The queen smiled and asked us, "Are your rooms acceptable? We do study human behavior and tried to ensure that you would be comfortable. Bath tubs are so much more civilized than bathing in a forest lake, don't you think?" she said with a smile. I wondered if at one time the wood nymphs really did bathe in the lakes, but didn't humans bathe in lakes years ago, too?

"I love the bath tub! I really like the temperature control," I replied. I was thinking how beautiful the queen was.

She laughed and said, "Well, that is one thing the wood nymphs have finally been able to do. We're learning how to link human technology with wood nymph gifts. One of our nymphs can sing to the wall to get it to accept orders, like changing the temperature or light of the room. This is something we have always been able to do, to talk to the naturally occurring things, like wood and stone. But combining technology with nature—that is new to us. We have learned that once the wall is taught to accept these orders, it will do so as long as the wall lasts. But, having the lift, or elevator as you Americans call it, is new for us. It has been quite handy for our older subjects." Then after a moment of thought, she said, "I'm glad the bath tub temperature control works well for you." She then looked over at my mother and held out her hand.

My mother wasn't sure what to do and looked to Olivia for guidance, but Olivia just nodded her head. My mother took her hand and nodded while giving a slight curtsy like something that would have been done in the Victorian era.

"We will soon be going into dinner. I would very much appreciate it if you would accept my request that you sit next to me at dinner," The queen said still holding onto my mom's hand.

Mom looked in surprise to Olivia. Olivia, looking confused, shrugged. I remembered our lessons in etiquette we expected in the king and queen's palace. Seating was always male, female, male, female, around the table. The queen seemed to understand the unspoken discussion between mom and Olivia and still smiling said, "Yes, I am changing the seating arrangement, but I have so much I want to talk to you about! I will see you at dinner." With that last comment, she glided away to greet the king who was talking to some young male that appeared to be about my age that had just entered through a side door.

He was well dressed in an expensive tuxedo. He reminded me of a young actor. He looked like a younger version of the king. I wondered if they were related. I couldn't help but pay attention to the queen as she walked up to him. "Darling, you really should enter formally and be announced to our guests. It just isn't right that you enter a side door like a servant."

"Guests? Humans? Why should I worry about what they think? Everyone else knows who I am. I am only here now because you ordered me to be here," he said as he turned and looked me right in the eye. His voice carried quite clearly across the room.

I thought, here we go again. Another wood nymph who hates humans. Big surprise there! On appearance, wood nymphs were a beautiful species. However, this one reminded me a lot of that horrible European wood nymph girl, Stella Quince. He was beautiful on the outside, but ugly on the inside.

"My dear, we are not sure what we are going to do about the whole human-wood nymph issue at this time. I would like you to be patient. Your father knows what he is doing, and to be honest, I kind of like the mixed girl," the queen said softly to her son.

I wondered if my hearing was getting stronger, as I heard the conversation clearly. I looked over at my mom and Ben, but they were talking to Forrest and Olivia and hadn't noticed the newcomer to the room. I looked at Ash and he gave me a worried look without saying anything. He obviously heard that exchange, too.

I tried to ignore the king, queen, and the new guy. I turned my back to the royal family and Ash put his arm around me. "This is an interesting place, isn't it?" I said as I tried to change the subject from the conversation we had just been eavesdropping on. We talked about how nice the rooms were and how big they were.

But, I couldn't help glancing back over my shoulder to see what the royal family was doing. They seemed to be having a quiet disagreement. They had lowered their voices to the point that I couldn't hear what they said anymore. Maybe that was a good thing.

Mom and Ben were the only full humans in the room. I was the only mixed human-wood nymph child anywhere, so my being the only one in this room didn't surprise me. I wondered again what was going to happen to us. It was all I could think about. I looked up at Ash and felt him stiffen. I looked where he was looking and saw the queen walking back towards us with the angry looking young man.

"Please allow me to introduce you to our son, Prince Andrew," The queen said. Mom, Ben, and I bowed when we saw Olivia and Forrest bow down. When we had straightened back up, the prince was giving me a sneer. He never even glanced at my parents when they said hello to him. He barely gave a nod to Ash, his parents, Olivia or Forrest.

He stared at me. I held out my hand in greeting. I wasn't sure of the complete etiquette thing, but I thought it would be a nice thing to do. He looked down at my hand and then back at my face. He didn't touch my hand. "You shouldn't exist," he stated flatly.

"Yeah, I've heard that before," I replied as I dropped my hand and looked up at Ash. Ash was looking at the prince. I looked back at the prince. "However, I do. Deal with it," I muttered at him.

I knew I was being rude in front of the royal family, but I couldn't help it. There was no reason he couldn't say hello or even try to be friendly. I felt the animosity come off him like steam from a kettle. Sometimes being an emotion reader gave me way too clear an insight into someone else's feelings and emotions. I heard Olivia gasp and realized that I wasn't doing us any favors by being rude to the royal prince. Just because he was rude and inconsiderate didn't make it right for me to be just as awful back at him. I sighed and straightened up and held out my hand again.

He raised an eyebrow as he looked at me. I felt as if I was being inspected, like some interesting science experiment. Then, an interesting thing happened. The emotions coming off him shifted as quickly as the thunderclouds in a tropical storm. It was like he wanted to hate me, but found me interesting at the same time. He was confused by his own shifting emotions. He stared at me for a moment and then laughed. "You are feisty, I will give you that. Maybe I need to study this mixed creature," he said as he looked over at the queen. The queen's face was like stone.

He looked back at me. "I have studied humans, and what I have learned about them, I don't like. But, you now, you might be interesting after all. I have heard that some of our kind believe that you, or ones like you, may be the hope to our future," he said as he reached down and took my hand and kissed the back of it. It felt like he held my hand longer than he should have. I actually had to pull my hand out of his grip. His emotions had shifted definitely into interest, but it was not the kind of interest I wanted from him. This felt sexual, and I was getting creeped out.

The queen still had the flat look on her face. I don't think she approved of her son's reaction to me. I looked at Ash and he looked disturbed. My mom and Ben looked confused. Forrest and Olivia tried not to have any expression at all, but I felt shock coming off of them. What reason did they have to be shocked? I had never met any kind of royalty, either human or wood nymph. I had no idea what to expect. Forrest and Olivia were not emotion readers like I was. Was there a different way in which they could tell his interest in me? Or, was his behavior just obvious?

"Come, dear, we need to go over by your father," the queen said sharply. Why was she unhappy? Her displeasure oozed from every pore of her body. Was she mad at me? She took a deep breath and seemed to compose herself. She looked over at my mother and repeated in a kind voice, "Please sit by me at dinner."

My mother replied with a slight bow, "Yes, your highness." She stood up and we stood in silence as we watched them walk away.

"What was that all about?" I asked Olivia when they had reached the other side of the room.

"I don't know. I've heard rumors that both the royal children have issues. I don't know for sure what kind, but certainly some kind of behavioral issues. Andrew has a younger sister, Elizabeth, who's having some . . . difficulties. I don't see her here," Olivia replied looking around.

"I think the problem is that the royal children have been given everything that they've ever wanted their whole lives. Nothing has any real value. Neither of them had ever had to wait for anything. If they can think of it or want it, the king and queen give it to them. As you well know, the things we work for have the most value in our lives. At least, this is what I think," Olivia said thoughtfully.

"I agree," Mom replied as we stared at the royal family. "We value what we work hard for. A lot of times, things that come too easy just don't seem as important or as valuable."

A gong sound. Next thing, we were all herded through another set of double doors into a huge dining hall with a long table down the middle of the room. The lighting was different in this room. It looked like trees were growing out of each of the rock walls and the branches spread out just below the ceiling in the middle of the room. Each branch had what looked like thousands of tiny light bulbs or candles. It felt like we'd entered a forest glade in the middle of the mountain with bright fairies in the trees.

I let Moss guide me to where I was to sit. The king and queen stood at opposite ends of the table. Next to the queen on her left side was my mother. Then Ben stood next to my mother and then it was my place. To my left was an older male wood nymph. He was definitely older than Ben or Forrest, but not as old as some of the wood nymphs of the Copper clan I had met. There was a female wood nymph I hadn't met and then Ash. I didn't see Forrest, Olivia, or Ash's parents across the table from us, so I assumed they were on the same side of the table we were, just farther down the table. I thought it best not to crane my neck to see. We waiteding for the king and queen to sit before we could sit. I remembered that from our training at my house.

I saw the looks and felt the emotions coming off of the different wood nymphs seated around us. It felt like a cacophony to my new emotion reading sense. I felt a lot of curiosity but also a lot of hatred. Many of the people—even though they are wood nymphs—looked like people to me, and they really hated us. Or was it just me? All of this went through my head in the first few seconds after getting behind my chair. I turned my head to face the king. He said something in a language I did not know and then he sat. Moss pulled out my chair for me.

After we were seated, I was so busy watching the king I did not pay much attention to the man at my side. I picked up on his interest by my emotion sense. He was really curious about me. I wanted to focus on him and tune in to what he was feeling, but I had to pay attention to the protocol at the table. I didn't want to show bad manners. Once we were served our soup and I saw how everyone else was eating it, I was able to pay more attention to the male wood nymph next to me. He was also an emotion reader! His emotion changed as soon as I tuned in to him.

He must have felt my attention as he said, "Yes, I too, can read emotions. I am what you would call the physician to the royal family." He smiled at me.

"How did you know I could read emotions?" I asked, forgetting all about the soup in front of me. I put my spoon down.

"I heard from the queen upon their return from your country that you were an emotion reader. Just now, I could tell when you focused on me." He then slowly sipped soup from a spoon. He turned to face me again. I was still staring at him.

"I am Dr. Box Elder. During your visit here, if it wouldn't be too much trouble, I would like to examine you. I have never met a human-wood nymph born person before," he said kindly.

Even though he was treating me with respect, I got the feeling he was only asking me as a courtesy. If I denied him, he could force me to submit to an examination. It wasn't like I had never been examined by a doctor before. In fact, all of the doctors I'd had in my life had been wood nymphs that Uncle Forrest had arranged for me without my or my mother's knowledge while I was growing up. He had been trying to protect me and the wood nymph race, afraid that a human doctor's blood tests would show that my blood was not normal human blood.

I thought about it for a minute. That was why I was here—to satisfy the king's curiosity about me. Why should I be surprised that a physician wanted to check me out? After being poked and prodded, as well as interrogated, the king was going to determine whether I had the right to live or not. I decided I needed to get this over with as soon as possible. If I did this with a good attitude, it might make it easier.

I smiled at him, forced myself to respond positively. I wondered if I could force my own emotions. Even though I was really appalled at the idea of being this guy's science project, if I could pretend I was interested, would that help our cause? Would that help keep us alive? Anyway, isn't that what people did during a lie detector test? Didn't they fake their emotions? I wasn't sure, but some people were able to beat the system. Maybe I could. Was this guy a living lie detector? For that matter, was I one, also? Would I be able to I tell if people were faking their emotions? "When would you like to get together?" I asked.

He seemed surprised by my response. I couldn't tell if he knew I was faking interest. The smile looked sincere, but who knew? His emotions were shifting around, but kept coming back to curiosity.

"I will have someone bring you to my suite tomorrow when you arise," he said and then turned to Ash. I felt like I was dismissed.

I looked down at my bowl and noticed that I had hardly eaten any of my soup, even though it was really delicious. I wasn't sure what kind it was. It was green, but did not taste like pea or broccoli soup. There was a slight bitter edge to it, but instead of detracting from the flavor, it made the soup better. Just as I was about to really enjoy the soup, Moss took the bowl away and replaced it with a salad. I looked around and noticed that all the wait staff was replacing the soup with the salads. There were greens I couldn't identify with some kind of fruit on top. I took a small bite and found the mix of vegetable leaves and fruit delicious. I made sure I ate all of the salad before Moss could take it away. We had four more courses that were all delicious. The main course was a small type of chicken. I thought it might be a game hen but wasn't sure. To my taste, it was cooked perfectly. It just didn't taste like the game hens my mom made.

After dinner, the king and queen stood from their seats and took their leave. The rest of the guests at the table stood and followed them as well. All of the women went in one direction and the men another. I looked for Olivia. I saw her standing up near the end of the table near the king. There was another male wood nymph on her other side. He seemed to be fawning all over her. She didn't look interested. In fact, she looked relieved when she saw me waving at her. We walked together as we followed the queen. The queen was in a deep conversation with my mother. I wondered what they could be talking about so intently.

We entered another large room that reminded me of an old fashioned Victorian sitting room. Overstuffed couches and high-back chairs created relaxed seating. In one wall was a fireplace with an overstuffed couch in front of it. I also saw gaming tables with cards and other board games. Olivia and I took one of the two-seat tables so that we could talk with a semblance of privacy. We looked over at my mom. She was still with the queen and they were sitting together on a love seat. All of the queens attendants stood nearby, but not within hearing range. Some were openly frowning. I got the impression that the attendants did not like the attention my mother was getting. Was it because she was human or that she was getting so much attention from the queen?

I tried to reach my mother with my emotion reading sense, but with all the wood nymphs between us, I couldn't tell how she was feeling. I could see her face from where I was sitting, and she looked like she was paying close attention to what the queen was saying. She looked intense, but not in any kind of discomfort.

"Why are we in here and the guys in another room?" I asked Olivia after we sat down.

Olivia looked around the room and said, "Males have their own business to attend to, I suppose. I have never been here before, so I'm not sure."

Olivia and I talked about the dinner. We had not been sitting for very long, maybe a half hour or so, when the queen got up and said that she was going to retire for the evening. We were invited to continue to talk or play games as long as we liked. When she said that, we all stood up and bowed. She left with her attendants, and in no time it was just me, my mom, Olivia, and Willow in the room, with our servants standing along the far wall.

"I think our first dinner went well," Willow said as we watched them leave.

"Mom, what did the queen talk to you about?" I asked when just the four of us were left in the room with our servants.

"Oh, she wants me to talk to her daughter, Elizabeth," my mom replied distractedly.

I wasn't expected to here that. Questions about being human, about me, sure. "What about Elizabeth. Why wasn't she at dinner?" I asked leaning my head in such a way as to make my mom look at me instead of away. She didn't seem to want to look at me. This was her way of avoiding a discussion. She'd change the subject and not look at the person asking her a question she didn't want to answer.

Mom sighed, realizing I wasn't going to stop until I got an answer. She looked at me and said, "Elizabeth is sick. The queen wants me to talk to her."

"I sat next to a doctor at dinner. He wants to run tests on me, starting tomorrow. Why isn't he dealing with Elizabeth if she's sick?"

Mom looked pointedly at me. "It's not that kind of sick, and I don't want to talk about it."

I got it then. Elizabeth had some kind of mental health issues. Wow! A wood nymph royal princess with psychological problems! Who would have guessed that?

Mom realized that I had connected the dots and nodded. The queen was hoping that my mom, as a mental health counselor, could help Elizabeth. I wondered what the problem was, but I knew better than to ask. Mom wouldn't tell me anything. She probably felt she'd already told me more than I should know. I wondered if human privacy laws applied to wood nymphs.

I saw my mom try to suppress a yawn, and I realized that I was really tired, too. "Okay. I'll drop the issue. Well, we made it through our first day here."

"That we did. One day at a time," Olivia said with a sigh.

I didn't see when Ash, Forrest, Ben, and Ash's dad entered the room. Ash came up behind me and put his arms around me and said, "We'll continue to make it, and we'll make it home. I promise you."

I hugged him and hoped he was right. We all took the elevator, or lift, as it was called here in England back to our floor.

When we all got off of the elevator, I said to Moss, "I can get undressed by myself. Why don't you head off to your bed?"

She seemed unsure about that, but I insisted. I wanted time alone with Ash.

The rest of my group also sent their servants off to bed, too. We were not the type of people used to having people do stuff for us. We were used to being independent. After all of our sevants left, we said good bye to Ash's parents, Forrest, and Olivia as we walked past their doors and they went into their rooms. Ash walked with me to my door. Ben and my mom each gave me a hug before heading to their suite. "We made it through the first day. Let's get some sleep so we're ready for whatever tomorrow brings," Ben said trying to hide his yawn.

"Don't stay up too long," Mom called softly as she and Ben went into their suite.

"I'll see you in the morning," Ash said as he hugged me outside my door. We were alone in the hallway. There were no other sounds other than our breathing.

I whispered in his ear. "I wish you could stay with me! Who would know?" I held him tight.

"I don't know. But, I don't want to get us into trouble on our first night here. What if we fall asleep and our servants show up and I'm in your bed? That'd be embarrassing. Plus, I don't think either of our parents would approve of that. I don't want you to think I don't want you. I think of you all of the time. There's never a minute that goes by when I'm not thinking about you and wanting to hold you. You know that, right?" He pleaded with me as he whispered in my ear and wrapped his arms tightly around me.

"Yeah, I get it. But, I don't have to like it," I said as I kissed his neck.

He pulled away from me. "You need some sleep. You look tired," he said as he walked backwards down the hall to his room.

I watched as he opened his door and I blew him a kiss as I went into my room. I slowly undressed and hung my dress up. I was tired. I didn't ever remember being this tired. I went to bed and I fell asleep wondering what kind of tests that Dr. Elder was going to put me through in the morning.

CHAPTER 9
PREJUDICE AND BIAS

When I opened my eyes, I saw that Moss was already in my room waiting for me to wake up. She had a breakfast tray in her hand. When she saw me look at her, she put the breakfast tray on my lap. Whatever was under the lid smelled really delicious and when she removed the domed covers, I saw what looked like some kind of oatmeal and fruit. She tapped on the marble walls and the veins lit up.

"Miss Laurel, I was sent to get you up. Dr. Elder is expecting you in about a half hour," Moss said as she went to my wardrobe to get me out something to wear. "Would you like to wear this today?"

"Yeah, the blue suit is fine," I replied. It was another one of those expensive outfits Olivia had bought me in Wausau before we left Wisconsin.

I stretched as I reached for my spoon. This had to have been the most comfortable bed I had ever slept in. It was like sleeping on a thick feather-stuffed comforter. I stretched as I took a couple of bites of the fruit. It looked really good, but I must have been nervous about seeing the doctor. I had a hard time swallowing. Maybe I was still full from last night.

"I'm not very hungry right now. If I get hungry later, can I get something to eat?" I asked Moss as I pushed the tray away from me to get up.

"Of course! Just tell Aron that you want something to eat and he will get word to me," Moss replied.

"Who is Aron? Won't you be with me, today?" I asked as I got out of bed and headed for the bathroom.

"No," I heard Moss say from the bedroom. "Aron is waiting outside your suite. He will be your bodyguard while you are here."

Bodyguard? Why would I need a bodyguard? Then I thought it might be the other way around. Aron was my jailer. The king probably thought he couldn't let the little human-mixed girl escape. I sighed as I washed up.

"Would you like help dressing or your hair?" Moss asked as I started to dress.

"No, I got it, thanks," I replied as I pulled on the blue pants. I was not used to strangers in my room while I got dressed. Moss didn't act weird or anything. She acted like she saw people getting dressed all of the time. This was just a new experience for me.

"Then I will see you later. Just let Aron know what you need and he will make sure that I get it for you," Moss said as she walked out of the bedroom. I heard the door to my suite open and close. A couple of minutes later, I had my hair in a band that matched my suit and was ready to go.

When I walked out of the door, I saw a huge, very dark-skinned man waiting just outside. I thought I had seen him before.

"Are all of you humans this slow?" he asked. But, before I could answer, he said, "Follow me, and keep up." He turned in the direction of the stairs.

I looked around as we walked toward the stairs. I had forgotten to grab my watch and I had no idea what time it was. It would have been nice to have had at least a skylight to see the sunshine.

"What time is it?" I asked Aron.

"It is time to get you to Dr. Elder. That is what time it is. What does it matter what time it is? Do you have a date or something? It wouldn't matter if you did. You will do what you are told," he said with a mean tone to his voice. I could tell he really hated this guard duty. I wondered what his normal job was.

"Why do you hate me?" I asked. I could feel the contempt coming from him as we walked.

He stopped and looked at me. "You don't belong in this world. I can't understand how a wood nymph would even want to be with a human. Humans are stupid and slow. They cause all the problems in this world. You're an embarrassment to the wood nymphs. It is a good thing your father's dead," he said with a sneer.

How could he say such a thing? I had never met my biological father, but everything I'd heard about him made him sound like a really good man. "How dare you? My father was a good man!" I yelled at him. "I never knew my father, but from what I've been told, he was a good man, well, er wood nymph. You have no right to say anything about things you know nothing about."

"What is going on here?" I heard a voice behind me. It was the prince, Andrew.

"I have to take this human to Dr. Elder, and she is being difficult," Aron said with a disgusted sigh as he bowed to the prince.

"Well, I heard you and you do not have to be mean to our, ah, guest, Aron," Prince Andrew said softly as he touched my cheek. I jerked my head away. I glared at him.

"Oh, the human does have spirit! How interesting!" the prince chuckled. "I have never spent any, ah, time with a female human. My sister likes humans. But, she's an idiot. I avoid them. Maybe I should take a special interest in this half breed."

69

My stomach turned as he looked at me with what appeared to be undisguised lust. The prince was good looking, but only on the outside. Everything I'd seen of this guy had been self-serving. I wanted to keep him at a distance. I wondered what Ash was doing at this moment.

He seemed to notice when I stopped paying attention to him and scowled at me. I noticed that. I decided it was time to get out of there. "Well, while it's great just standing here listening to you talk, I have an appointment to keep. Aron, lead on," I said as I glanced over at him and then looked at my guard.

Aron raised an eyebrow at me but didn't move. I got the feeling that no one talked to him like that. Aron looked at the prince. I didn't look directly at him, but I could see him out of the corner of my eye. He laughed and said to me, "Do I scare you little girl?" He looked over at Aron. "Take her to the doctor's laboratory. I appear to bore our guest. She won't be bored when she gets to the doctor's laboratory. Then she will learn what bad is!" The prince turned away and laughed all of the way down the stairs.

I watched him walk down the stairs. I turned to face my guard. "Which way, Aron?" I asked impatiently. The doctor wasn't scary at dinner last night, but I was afraid to meet the doctor in his lab. Aron didn't need to know that. I think he would find it entertaining.

"At the top of the stairs. Let's go," he replied. He turned and started walking up the stairs. By the time we got to the top floor, I was almost out of breath. I had a hard time keeping up, which Aron thought was funny. He stood at the top watching me force my legs up the last couple of steps. "You are a feeble and insignificant creature. What good are you?" He laughed as he led the way to the doctor's office.

Aron knocked on the door. A female wood nymph who looked about my age and was dressed like a nurse answered the door. She looked me at me slowly from my head to my feet. I felt like I was being judged and not in a good way. Before she said a word, I heard a male voice call out, "Is that our young lady visitor?"

"It must be. It is a female human," she stated with no attempt at concealing her contempt. Great. Another wood nymph who'd convicted me as being unworthy without a trial.

I could not help but feel a little bit of fear of what the doctor had in store for me. He had been nice last night, but could that have been an illusion to make me comfortable? I wondered if I was going into the office of a Dr. Mengele, the angel of death from World War II Nazi Germany. I had studied World War II history in high school and Mengele had been horrendous in his treatment of Jews. He performed horrific experiments on them.

"Please bring her in to my office," I heard the voice say.

The nurse rolled her eyes at me and said to Aron, "How horrible for you to have to do escort duty for this creature." She then walked into the hall to get closer to Aron. "If you have some free time later, maybe you could spend some time with me. I would make it worth your while to escort me." I could smell her female wood arousal musk scent and it made me nauseous.

"Can you at least wait for me to go in to the doctor before you do that? Ewww," I said with a grimace.

She snapped her head back and glared at me. I think she had forgotten that I was there. I could tell that she was really interested in my bodyguard. Aron showed no emotion at all. If he was interested in her, he sure didn't show it.

"I'll see you later?" she asked Aron as she led me into the office. I looked back at Aron, but he didn't say a word. He just maintained his bored attitude.

I followed Nurse Ratchet into the office. She reminded me of the horrible nurse in the movie, *One Flew over the Cuckoo's Nest*.

Dr. Elder wore a white lab coat and sat at a desk when we entered. It looked like a regular human doctor's office. I was surprised and it must have shown on my face. "Good morning, Laurel. You look surprised! What were you expecting? Something medieval? Don't you worry about a thing. I promise that this will be just like any other interview you have had with any other doctor. By the way, I understand all the doctors you've seen in your life have been wood nymph doctors? The truth is you wouldn't even know how a human doctor would act around you since you have never been treated by one.

"Have a seat," he said, waving me to a chair across from him. "I want to ask you some questions," He took up pen and paper. He looked up at Aron and said, "Come back in a couple of hours." Aron nodded and left. He did not look at me or the wretched nurse. I wondered if he was hoping the doctor would torture me.

"Miss Thornbush, please continue with your filing. When you're finished, you are free for the day, unless Miss Laurel would like you to stay?" he asked looking at me.

I thought about his question. At least Dr. Elder acted like he liked me. This Thornbush bitch clearly hated me, so I was relieved to have her out of the office. I could only hope Dr. Elder wouldn't do anything that would make me uncomfortable. I had to stifle a laugh. So, her name was Thornbush, a fitting name for such a nasty person.

"No, Dr. Elder, I think I'd be more comfortable if she wasn't here," I said as I sat in the chair. I wasn't worried about the questions he was going to ask me. I was worried about what was going to happen *after* the questions. I grabbed the arms of the chair as I sat down.

"Okay, Laurel. I'm glad that you are here today. Don't be afraid," he said with a smile.

I watched Nurse Ratchet Thornbush walk out of the office. A moment later, I heard the door to the hall open and close. I was now alone with the doctor.

As an emotion reader, he had to know I was terrified. I didn't try to hide it. I just looked at him. I was so frightened, I couldn't respond. I looked around.

"Laurel, relax," the doctor said kindly. "I had my medical training at a human university.

When he said that, I turned to look at him. "Really?" I asked. For some reason, that made me feel less fearful.

"Does that surprise you?" he asked as he leaned back in his chair and cocked his head as he looked at me.

"Yes, I guess it does. You aren't the first human-trained wood nymph doctor, I've ever met, but I mean, you're right. My uncle always had me see a wood nymph doctor and neither I nor my mother ever knew it. But, I guess I just didn't expect to see all of this human stuff in here," I said with a self-deprecating sigh. "I don't know how Uncle Forrest managed to always ensured that I had a wood nymph for a doctor, though. I never thought my doctors were anything but human. This room looks like a typical doctor's office. But then again, so did the other offices and clinics I've been to. What surprises me is why you don't have wood nymph décor in your office. You live in a wood nymph palace and are surrounded by wood nymphs.

"My cousin Olivia has color-changing clothes and her whole house is decorated like the inside of a forest. I also thought that the wood nymphs would have their own universities," I said. I knew I was rambling. I wanted to relax, but I was still uncomfortable.

"I like the human decorations better," the doctor said, glancing around the room. "But, to answer your question, I think that the human universities are better than the wood nymph higher schools of learning. We get so preoccupied with our natural abilities, that we lose sight of the science and learning aspect. As far as my office goes, I got used to humans and their ways while I was away at the university. This looks right to me. Now that I've answered your questions, You don't mind answering some for me?" He asked as he leaned back in his chair.

I was surprised at his frankness and honesty. He didn't seem like a bad guy. "Sure, fire away," I replied with a smile.

The doctor smiled back at me. It was a natural smile, the kind that a person reserved for those moments when they'd met someone they wanted as a friend. I got the impression that he wasn't just doing his job. He wanted to like me. I could feel it. But, was this another level of subterfuge? Again, the thought crossed my mind as it had at dinner. Could this guy fake his emotions?

He started with basic questions like where did I grow up? What were my friends like? Did I get along well with others? Did I like new experiences? Was I shy? The next couple of hours flew by. As time went by, I found I relaxed with Dr. Elder. He was easy to get along with and didn't ask anything uncomfortable.

"After lunch, you don't mind if I do an examination, do you? I need to know how the human body is different when blended with a wood nymph. I will take some blood tests and check your heart and basically give you a physical. Is that all right?" he asked as he got up from his chair.

"Sure. I guess that would be all right. Nothing will hurt, right?" I asked as I got up from my chair. He hadn't been scary so far, but that could change.

"The only pain you may feel would be the stick of the needle in your arm. Everything else will be just like any other physical you have ever had," he replied as he walked me to the door. Aron was just coming up the hallway when the doctor opened it. "Please have her back in one hour," the doctor said to Aron without looking at me or saying goodbye. He went back into his office and closed the door. I looked after him. He didn't appear nearly as friendly once Aron showed up.

Aron turned away from me as soon as the doctor went back inside his office. "Where are we going for lunch?" I asked Aron's back. He was already speeding down the stairs. I had to rush to catch up with him.

"There is a cafeteria on the first floor. You are to go there. Moss is waiting for you there," he replied without slowing his steps.

Going down the stairs was at least easier than going up. Still, I almost had to run to keep pace with Aron.

The room we entered must have been an employee cafeteria. It reminded me of a school lunch room. All of the wood nymphs in this room had on some kind of palace uniform. For the first time, I noticed that Aron was wearing a black uniform. I asked him what kind of uniform it was.

He puffed out his chest and said proudly, "I am part of the king's guard. I should not have to be escorting a human around. You are a waste of my time."

"Hey, I didn't ask for you either. I didn't ask for any guard. I only asked what your uniform represented," I replied as I got into line. Aron didn't reply. Moss joined me in line. I greeted her and when I looked back for Aron. He was gone. Once I was with Moss, I guess he felt he didn't need to guard me anymore.

"Where did Aron, go?" I asked Moss. "Not that I miss him. He's not very nice," I said as I looked at refrigerated case in the lunch line.

"He will be back after lunch," Moss replied grabbing a tray. "I wonder why he told me to meet you here in the servant's lunch room? I would have expected you to go to the formal dining room for lunch with your family and friends. I would bring you there now, but it is a long walk, and you didn't eat much breakfast. I should have insisted that he bring you there and not here," Moss said.

"Oh, it's no big deal. The food looks good. If it is good enough for the staff, it is good enough for me. Besides, I would rather eat here than do a lot of walking to go somewhere else. It smells good in here," I said as I looked at the lunch choices. There was a variety of sandwiches and fresh fruit. It was plain food, with nothing that looked fancy, but looked like it would taste good.

"You really don't mind?" Moss asked with a surprised look on her face. She turned to pick out lunch items for herself. "There are more choices and much fancier selections for the guests and the royal staff in the dining room. Why aren't you offended that Aron brought you here? From everything I have heard about humans, they always want the best of everything. They get insulted easily and are offended if they are not offered the best of the best. I thought humans were greedy and selfish. At least, that is what I have been told."

She must have realized what she had said because she looked back at me with horror and said loudly, "I didn't mean that. I truly do not want to offend you!"

I looked around. Everyone in the lunch room had stopped what they were doing to stare at us. I realized I had a chance here to eliminate a human stereotype.

I smiled at Moss and said, "There are selfish people and there are people who are not selfish. Some humans, a lot of them, are really kind and generous. Some humans are greedy. I can't speak for all of the human population, but I would like to think that I'm easy going and not selfish. I really don't mind being here. This food looks really good!"

Moss still stared at me without moving.

"And, after running to keep up with Aron, I appreciate not having to do so much walking," I said as I picked up a sandwich on whole wheat bread. It looked like some kind of tuna salad. I also picked out a salad with endive lettuce, tomatoes, and cucumbers. There was iced tea, too. "Pick out your food and we'll find a place to sit."

Moss made her selections and, since there was no check out line, I started looking for a place to sit. I picked out a table along the wall and as I placed my tray down, Moss started to walk away from me. "Where are you going?" I asked.

"Oh, I could never sit with a guest of the king and queen. It would not be proper," Moss said.

I didn't want to eat alone. While I barely knew Moss, it was better than eating by myself. "No, would you please sit with me?" I asked as I sat down.

"You are a guest! You shouldn't be sitting with the servants!" Moss replied, sounded appalled at the very idea. However, she just stood there with her tray. Her emotions were conflicted. I think she wanted to stay with me, but protocol required her to not sit with me. She was confused.

"Hey, I'm in the servant dining room, right? Who's going to care who I sit with, unless you don't want to sit with me? I don't want to sit alone." Then I realized that maybe Moss didn't want to sit with me. She had to take care of me. That was her job. Maybe she didn't want to have to deal with me in her personal time. "Oh, Moss, I shouldn't try to force you to stay with me. You can eat wherever you want," I said with a sigh and looked at my tray.

She stood there for another minute. "Ah, no. I mean—sure. I would be happy to sit with you. I have never eaten a meal with anyone I've served, though." She offered a tentative smile as she looked around and sat down.

I saw some curious looks directed our way. No one said anything though. As we ate, I asked Moss about herself. Moss told me about her childhood in the palace. Her mother worked in the kitchen as a pastry chef. As a child, Moss would hang out in the kitchen and get samples of the treats made specifically for the guests.

An older woman who looked just like Moss came and stood by our table.

Moss smiled tentatively at the woman and said to me, "Laurel, this is my mother, Gloretta. Mom, this is Laurel."

"This is the human girl?" Gloretta asked quietly. I felt concern coming off of her in waves. She looked at Moss. "You are not supposed to bring the king's guests here. You are not supposed to eat with the people that you serve."

"Moss didn't bring me here. My guard, Aron, did. I asked Moss to eat with me so I wouldn't have to eat alone. Moss is the only one I know here," I said softly. I know I sounded a little pathetic, but I couldn't help it. I wondered where my parents were. I wondered where Ash was. I was tired of walking. I wondered if I should have insisted that Aron take me to the guest dining room. I didn't know about such things, though!

Gloretta must have seen how vulnerable I felt. She softened towards me. She gave me a small smile. "Well, there's no harm being done now, is there? This is just another way that Moss is taking care of you. It does seem strange that Aron brought you here, though. I wonder why he did that? I'll be right back," Moss's mom said and walked toward the kitchen.

"You are not in trouble, are you?" I asked as I ate the salad. I really didn't want Moss to get in trouble because I was feeling a little sorry for myself.

"I don't think so. It's not like the king or queen will come in here and catch us eating together. Besides, you asked me to eat with you," Moss replied with a smile and then took a bite of her sandwich.

The food was good and I was really hungry. I didn't notice Gloretta returning to our table until she put what looked like a slice of strawberry pie in front of me. It looked like the strawberry filling was one huge strawberry that had been cut to fill the pie crust. "Is this strawberry?" I asked.

"Yes, we grow them the exact size of a pie plate. One strawberry will fill two pies. The glaze fills in around the bottom and it's topped with just one strawberry in the middle. The king prefers this kind of pie, so I make it for him whenever we have fresh strawberries," Gloretta said as she pulled up a chair to sit with us.

"It looks delicious!" I smiled at Gloretta and took a forkful of the pie. It tasted as good as it looked.

I was quite full when I noticed Aron standing next to me. I did not see him come up to the table. "It is time to go. Moss will clean up after you. It is her job after all. Follow me," he said as he turned away, expecting me to just follow after.

Knowing now that he had treated me badly by taking me to the servants' lunchroom, I had to assert myself. I was not a door mat. I would not accept mean treatment. I had a really good time with Moss and her mother. But, I didn't like that Aron could act like I was less than nothing. I didn't get to have lunch with my parents or Ash. I worried about them.

The high handed way Aron treated me had to be stopped. Whether he liked me or not, I was still a guest of the king. The king could decide to kill me in a month, but I was still a guest right now. I shouldn't be treated with such disdain. I ignored Aron and stayed with Moss and her mother. I watched out of the corner of my eye as he turned around and gave me an exasperated look and stormed back to the table. "I said you were to follow me!" He thundered at me.

"Yeah, I heard you. I am a guest. You may have forgotten that with your prejudicial and bigoted attitude about humans. But the fact remains that I am a guest of the king. You will treat me with respect. You will *ask* me to accompany you. You will not order me around again, or I just won't go," I said as I sat back in my chair with my arms crossed. "You will get to explain to the doctor and the king why I chose not to go."

"Get up!" he snarled and reached for me.

Moss gasped. I slapped his hand away. "Stop that! I'll tell the king if you ever try to touch me again! You will not grab me and you will not order me around. I forbid it," I stated as regally as I could.

Moss and her mother were staring at me with their mouths open. I don't suppose that they ever saw anyone order one of the king's guards around. Well, I was not used to being treated as something less than well, human. As a human, I was a creature with a mind. I may not have all of the abilities of a wood nymph, but I still had the right to be treated with respect whether Aron thought so or not. At least I thought so, and that was what mattered to me.

He stared at me with loathing. I could feel the anger coming from him. I could almost see the steam rising from him, he was so hot. Then I felt him get himself under control. He must have wondered what the doctor would say if he brought me back to the laboratory bruised. He took a deep breath and said, "Would you please return with me to the doctor's office?"

"Yes," I said and turned to Moss. "Thank you for having lunch with me. I appreciated the company. And, Gloretta, thank you for the wonderful pie."

They stood up when I did. "You are so welcome. You can come here anytime you like," Gloretta said as she headed back to the kitchen.

"I enjoyed lunch with you, too. Maybe we can do it again," Moss said as she picked up our trays to return them to the kitchen.

"I will see you later," I said as I backed away from the table. I wanted to help Moss with the clean up, but I knew she wouldn't appreciate my gesture. It was her job to take care of me. If I took care of myself, then she would have no job.

As we left the cafeteria, I walked down the hall to the elevator. "We will take the lift back to the top floor. Please take me to the nearest lift," I said.

Aron gave me a long look before he nodded and we found the nearest elevator that would take us to the doctor's floor. After we got off of the elevator, I followed Aron back to the doctor's office.

CHAPTER 10
Learning More About Me

I felt respect coming from Aron as we walked to the doctor's office. He didn't talk to me, but I could feel his emotions. I had a full belly and I was tired when I got back to the doctor's office. The confrontation with Aron and the worry about dealing with the doctor's examination was exhausting me.

The door was open and we walked in. "Ah, there you are! Right on time! Please put this on in the back room and come back out," Dr. Elder said as he handed me a hospital gown.

"Okay," I said as I took the gown and went into the dressing room. I noticed the dressing room looked like something out of Olivia's house. It was decorated in shades of greens and browns and looked like a forest glen.

"How come the dressing room looks like part of a wood nymph house but the rest of your office does not?" I asked as I held the hospital gown tight against my body. Aron was gone when I came out of the dressing room and I was relieved. He did not need to see me in a hospital gown.

"Well, I try to accommodate my patients. The forest look of the dressing room relaxes my patients before I have to examine them. I'm sure you can imagine that all of the humanness in the rest of these rooms could make a wood nymph uncomfortable," Dr. Elder explained as he led me to an examination room.

I hadn't thought of that! The wood nymphs were using more human technology, such as the elevators, but I wondered if doing this was causing them to lose some of their own culture. There was a difference between science and natural ability. *Magic and technology can be considered one and the same*, I thought. But on the other hand, wood nymph natural abilities could not be duplicated. Or could they? Would humans come up with a way of being able to jet? Could science come up with a way to cause trees to grow in certain shapes? Of course they could! Look at the bonsai trees in Japan! Were wood nymphs losing their culture due to human encroachment in more ways than one?

I thought about this as I sat on the edge of the table. I looked around in the examination room and there was nothing of the wood nymph culture in the room. There was not even one picture of a woods or river or even a tree in the room. The only thing hanging in frames on the walls were the different certificates and licenses Dr. Elder had received from human institutions!

"Dr. Elder, you've been around humans for most of your life. Do you really like them?" I asked as he had me lie back on the table and put my feet up in the stirrups.

"I do." He smiled. "And I always hoped that one of our species would mix with one of your kind and create a mixed child. I always wondered what such a child would look like," he responded as he put normal looking tools on a tray next to the table I was laying on.

"One of my kind?" I asked. "I thought I was the only one?" I sat up.

"I mean human. I always wanted to see what would happen if a human and a wood nymph had a child together. I meant you, as in a human," he replied.

"You know, you're right. It's hard not to think of you as just human. Yet, here I am, about to take blood and tissue samples to see the differences in your blended cell structure. I guess I'm assuming that the dominant cell structure will be human. That's kind of a biased attitude isn't it? I'm making a judgment without having any evidence to back it up," he said as he picked up the speculum. "I assume you know what this is for?" He asked.

"Yeah," I said with a sigh. "Just make sure it isn't cold, okay?" I closed my eyes.

"Sure, I can do that. So far, everything on the human body is the same as on a wood nymph's body. I'll be quick," he said as he proceeded to take his cell samples and check for abnormalities in my internal organs.

After a couple of minutes he told me I could get dressed right after he took some blood. Other than a bit of embarrassment of being touched by a man I didn't know, this was a normal gynecological examination. There was no pain involved.

"You'll feel a little prick. I'm pretty good at this, and in my experience, the skin of both humans and wood nymphs are quite similar. This won't take long," he said as he pulled out a needle on a small tube that he inserted into my arm. He withdrew seven little vials of blood.

"That really didn't hurt, but that is a lot of blood," I said as he taped some gauze on my arm after he pulled the needle out.

"Not as much as it would have been had you donated blood," the doctor replied. "You can get dressed now."

He didn't have to tell me that, twice! I got off of the table and went into the dressing room. A short time later, I came out and found him doing lab tests on my blood. When he saw that I was out of the dressing room, he gestured for me to take a seat by his desk. After I sat down, he sat across from me.

"Can you shift colors? I forgot to ask you that, earlier," he said as he sat down.

"Shift colors?" I asked. "I don't know what you mean."

"Are you saying that none of your wood nymph friends have changed colors in front of you?" he asked surprised.

"You mean to blend in with something? Yeah, Uncle Forrest blended into a car seat once, and Olivia blended in with our couch at home. Is that what you're talking about?" I asked.

"Yes, that's exactly what I'm talking about. Can you do it?" He leaned toward me.

"I tried once. It didn't work," I replied. "I don't think it works for me."

"Can you try it for me? Just lean back in the chair and close your eyes. Pretend you're part of the chair. Feel the texture of the chair against your hands. Be the chair," He spoke with a hypnotic tone.

I looked at the arm of the chair and I leaned my head back and really felt the arms of the chair. It was a smooth brown leather, the kind often in an attorney's office. I opened my mind to the chair. I could almost see the molecules holding the chair together in my mind's eye.

"Slowly open your eyes and look at your hands," the doctor said softly.

I leaned forward and slowly opened my eyes and looked at my right hand. It wasn't there! I had no right hand! I started panicking, and my hand popped into view. My hand had blended into the arm of the chair. I had another ability! "I did it! My hand disappeared! I didn't look at the other hand. Was it gone, too?" I asked excitedly.

"Neither of your hands was actually gone. You just blended in with the chair. If you had on the special wood nymph fabric, it's possible that you would have completely blended in with the furniture," he replied with a smile. "You're a wonder, Laurel! You do have wood nymph characteristics."

"I want you to practice blending in with things. Most baby wood nymphs start color shifting on their own. Because you were not born as a pure wood nymph, you may need to train your abilities to get them to work for you," he said as he got up and walked to a cabinet and pulled out a package to hand to me. "Here is a pants and shirt set that I think will fit you. This is a color shifting outfit. Don't tell anyone I gave you this. I'm not sure how the king would feel about me giving you things to enhance your natural gifts. After we find out all that you can do, we will give the report to the king, okay?"

I felt the excitement and tension in him as he gave me the clothes. He was excited for me. I had one more ability and the doctor was happy about it! If I could show that I had enough abilities of a wood nymph, would the king allow me to live? "Sure, I'll practice in private. I get it," I responded. This was way too cool! I wondered if I could tell Ash or Olivia?

"We are done for today, I think. I'll see you in a couple of days, okay?" Dr. Elder asked as he got to his feet. I got up with him and we walked to the door.

We were standing alone inside his office by the door. "You're special, and I will help you prove it. I don't want anyone to know that I'm on your side and that I like humans. I want the king to like you, but I don't want him to think that I'm giving you special treatment. But, between you and me, 'll give you all the help I can," he said with a smile as he reached for the handle on the door. "Remember, no one is to know I like you."

"Maybe you can help me with one thing, though. Aron, my guard, hates me. He does everything he can to make me miserable. Maybe you can get him to treat me better?" I asked. I didn't mention the cafeteria, because I honestly liked it there. It was the reason that he brought me there that bothered me.

The doctor looked at me for a moment and said, "I'll see what I can do." He opened the door, and we saw Aron standing just outside. "You can get her out of here now. You treat her with respect. We don't have to like her, but she is a guest of the king and will be treated as such. Treat her as you would any other guest of the king."

Aron bowed to the doctor and said, "I will. As long as I don't have to like it." When he stood up, he said to me, "Come. I will take you back to your rooms. Would you like to take the lift?"

"Yes, please," I said as politely as I could.

With a surprised look, Aron nodded and led the way. I smiled at his back. I would get Aron to like me. The doctor liked me. I would get the king to like me, too. Humans and wood nymphs could live together in harmony! That was my new goal in life.

When I got to my rooms, I saw Ash sitting by himself on the floor outside of my door. When he saw me, he stood up and jetted to me. "Are you okay?" he asked me. "You've been gone all day! I was worried about you!" He looked me over to make sure that nothing was wrong with me. Then he picked me up to hug me.

I heard Aron make a disgusted sound. "Moss will be in your suite. Please let her know you have returned." After his parting remark, he stalked off toward the stairway and went down the stairs.

"I really missed you, today! All I did was worry all day!" Ash exclaimed as he put me down and looked me over again. "Are you okay?" he asked again.

I put my hand on my door panel and the door opened. "I'm fine! I'm more than fine, really!" I said excitedly as we entered my suite.

Moss came up to me and said, "Miss Laurel, you have an hour and a half before dinner. Would you like to start getting ready now?"

"No, Moss, not yet. Can you come back in an hour? I can take my own bath, but you can help me with my hair, if you like," I replied as I sat on the circular couch and pulled Ash down beside me.

"Yes, ma'am," Moss replied with a smile. "I will see you in an hour." She left, giving me a wink as she walked out of the door.

"What was that all about? She seems pretty friendly toward you," Ash replied with a curious tone in his voice.

"We had lunch together in the employee cafeteria. I think we're becoming friends," I replied leaning into Ash on the couch.

"When I woke up, I came to your rooms, but Moss said you had already left to see the doctor. I wondered where you were at lunch time. Your mom was not in the formal dining room, either. I saw Ben, Forrest, Olivia, and my parents at lunch. I thought you might have been with your mother somewhere," Ash replied.

"Do you have a guard?" I asked Ash. I saw a pitcher of ice water and glasses on the table and poured us each a glass of water.

"No, but I see that you do. When I talked to them at lunch, Ben, Forrest, and Olivia said that they'd been exploring the palace. I didn't see a guard with them, either. Mom and dad are keeping to themselves in their suite. I went searching the palace, too, but stopped when I walked by the library. I wanted to read some of the wood nymph histories," Ash said as he took the glass I handed him.

"The doctor was really nice to me. He gave me a package," I said as I put the package that had been under my arm on the couch.

"What is it?" Ash asked as he reached for it.

I stopped his hand. "It's a color shifting outfit. I was able to change my hands to match the chair in the doctor's office. But, he said to keep it a secret for now, although I'm not quite sure why. Maybe he wants to present a full report to the king and wants this to be a surprise," I replied as I pulled the outfit out of the bag. It immediately matched my clothes and the couch and the clothes in my hand seemed to disappear.

"Let me see!" Ash said excitedly.

I worried if I would be able to do it again. I thought about what the doctor had told me to do. He said to imagine what I wanted to blend into. I put my hand on the back of the couch as I faced Ash and closed my eyes. I felt the fabric. I pictured the color in my mind.

"That's way too cool!" Ash shouted. I opened my eyes and my hand was gone. Well, not really gone, but I couldn't see it because it had changed to match the couch.

"Shhhh!" I said, "I don't want anyone to hear you! This is supposed to be a secret. You can help me practice, and maybe I can get my whole body to change with the color shifting clothes. In the meanwhile, the doctor asked me not to tell anyone. I don't think he wants Moss to know."

My hand was back to its normal color. Ash gave me a big hug. "This is exciting news!" he told me and kissed me. "What else happened at the doctor's office?"

I told him about Nurse Ratchet. I told him about my experiences with Dr. Elder. I told him about lunch with Moss and her mother. After I told him about my day, we sat quietly for a while, just leaning against each other on the couch. "What time is it?" I asked.

Ash looked at his watch and said, "I better let you get to your bath, or you won't have time for one before Moss gets back here in twenty minutes."

Ash got up and kissed me before he walked out of the door. "I wonder what other abilities you will manifest before we leave England," he chuckled as he left.

I wondered that too. I watched the door close and then took a quick bath.

CHAPTER 11
ELIZABETH

I hid my color shifting clothes under my mattress. I liked Moss, but the doctor had said to hide the clothes and my new-found ability. I didn't understand why, but the doctor must have had his reasons. He did say he wanted to write one report for the king after he had completed all his tests on me. Maybe he was afraid that servant gossip would bring this knowledge to the king before he was ready? I didn't know.

I was just zipping up the pale yellow dress I was going to wear to dinner when Moss knocked on the door and then entered. She did not wait for my response. "Great! You're finished with your bath. Here, let me help you zip up."

I stood still as she zipped up the back of my dress. I looked at my reflection in the mirror. "How about an up-do for my hair again tonight? Not a French twist, but something else?" I asked as I sat at the vanity table.

"Sure, I can make your hair look perfect," Moss said as she pulled out the box of hair pins and a curling iron. Her hands moved so fast, I had a hard time following them. Within minutes, my head was a tight mass of curls with a couple of loose tendrils hanging down. It looked like it would have taken hours at a beauty parlor. As soon as Moss was finished with my hair, she took out the cosmetics and did my make-up. "You have such a beautiful natural glow about you," Moss said as she applied the eye shadow. "You have nice skin, for a human," Moss said smiling as she applied just a touch of powder to my cheeks.

I knew she meant it to be a compliment. It seemed everyone here was seeing me as mostly human, but I was half wood nymph. To me that meant that I was not more human or more wood nymph. I was equally both. However, the nymphs here saw me mostly as human, with little to no wood nymph. I didn't comment on it, and I wasn't sure if it should bother me or not. But the truth was it did kind of bother me.

It was true that I did not know truth wood nymphs while I was growing up and I never thought one way or the other about my humanity. But, now that I did know the truth, no one could take the truth away from me. I knew I was having a hard time dealing with my new reality, and at times I was having more than a little trouble trying to figure out my identity. However, that gave no one the right to try to define my identity for me. I might be the first of my kind but, I was exactly half human and half wood nymph. I wasn't just one or the other. I should not be treated like I was one or the other. I was something new.

I didn't want Moss to know what I thought or felt. I knew she was not trying to be mean to me. No one here had ever met someone like me before, so I guessed that Moss was just reacting to the situation. I wondered how I would feel if I met a half human and half wood nymph girl. Would I look at her as mostly a wood nymph? I agreed with the jewelry Moss picked out. It was a pair of Citrine chandelier earrings and a matching necklace. The set was perfect for the dress. They were a gift from Forrest just before we left Wisconsin.

When I got out into the hall, I saw Mom and Ben waiting for me with Ash. Ash came over and kissed my cheek and said, "You look lovely. I thought the prom dress you had, or the blue one you wore last night was beautiful, but you're even more beautiful today!"

I could feel myself blush at his words and whispered, "Thanks. These clothes make me feel beautiful."

Mom heard our exchange and said, "Olivia has perfect taste. I wouldn't have chosen yellow for you or green for me. But, she was right with both. You look fabulous."

Ben smiled and said, "You both look perfect."

"Who looks perfect?" Olivia asked as she walked up to us.

"We do, thanks to you!" Mom responded to Olivia. When my mom turned to face Olivia, I saw shadows under her eyes. She looked really tired.

"Mom, are you okay?" I asked as I walked up to her so that I could walk with her to the elevator. Ash was greeting his parents as they joined us on our way to the lift.

Mom gave me a sad look that she was trying to hide. I wasn't sure if I saw it so much as felt it in her emotions. "Mom, what's wrong?" I asked.

"I'm fine," she replied, but it was a half-hearted attempt to placate me. She took a deep sigh and looked at me as we got onto the elevator. "I really am fine. I'm just dealing with some issues right now. I don't want to talk about it."

"Is it about me? Is someone giving you grief about being my mother?" I asked. I couldn't imagine anyone giving my mother a hard time about anything but, here we were no longer in the world that we were used to.

My mom smiled a happier smile and gave me a hug. "No, honey. You're just fine. There's not a thing wrong with you. You're perfect just the way you are."

She was telling me the truth. Whatever was bothering her had nothing to do with me. At least, not directly. "What did you do today?" I asked. Maybe I could figure out what was bothering her.

"I spent the day with the royal family. I met Princess Elizabeth," my mom replied. She had a smile that did not meet her eyes. Whatever was bothering her had something to do with the princess. I felt her emotions shift when she mentioned the princess. "Maybe the princess will come to dinner tonight and you'll meet her. What did you do today? How did it go with the doctor?"

My mom knew what to say to take my mind off of what she did not want to talk about. I told her all about the time with the doctor and lunch with Moss. I did not tell her about the color-shifting clothes. In no time, we were at the doors leading to the reception room. I didn't see Moss walking with us, and when we arrived in the reception area, she came up to me and handed me a glass of nectar. "I hope you don't mind that I took the liberty of getting you what you liked last night," she said with a smile.

"No, this is fine," I replied taking a sip of the peach nectar. I saw the other servants handing out beverages. I saw another wood nymph server carrying around a tray of appetizers. I took one. It was a puffed pastry with some kind of mushroom stuffing. It was really good. I didn't realize until that moment how hungry I was.

We stood around and talked about what we did. Everyone seemed inordinately interested in what happened to me with the doctor. I tried to tell everyone that the doctor was nice to me, but they seemed to have a hard time believing it. According to some of the staff, the doctor had a reputation as an unreasonable sort of person.

I looked at my mom and she was staring off into space. She seemed lost in thought. I gave her a nudge. "Are you sure you're okay?" I asked her.

She gave a sigh and looked about ready to talk when the side door was thrown open, and the door crashed against the wall. There was instant silence in the room as everyone turned to see what happened. Just as I was about to ask, I heard, "I do not want to be here!" a young woman was yelling as she was guided in through the door. She was talking to someone out in the hall. I saw a maid wringing her hands as she tried to talk to the angry young woman. I couldn't hear what the maid was saying.

At that moment, the king and queen were announced at the great doors we had come in to the room. We all bowed to the king and queen, but I couldn't help but look at the angry young woman.

She was beautiful, with long blond hair that reached almost to her waist. Her clothes were of human origin. They were obviously from an exclusive designer. This was such an exclusive designer that I couldn't even afford to say the name. She had on a London-blue dress with matching London-blue topaz earrings and necklace.

The stones were huge! I noticed that she did not bow to the king and queen, but stood with an angry expression, her arms crossed. At least she halted the scene she was making long enough for the king and queen to come into the room.

I watched as the king and queen came over to the angry woman in the blue dress. I was glad that I had worn my blue dress yesterday. While my dress was beautiful, it would have looked dowdy compared to this dress. It wasn't until after they walked up to the beautiful and angry woman that I noticed the similarity of the queen to this woman. I also noticed the prince was walking with the king and queen. I had been so busy watching the woman in the blue dress that I did not notice that the prince. I also noticed the striking resemblance of the young woman to Prince Andrew.

About the time the royal family walked up to the young woman, I noticed she was looking at anyone but them. Then, she seemed to notice our group standing about twenty feet away. "You!" she shrieked as she saw us. For someone with such a lovely exterior, the rage she carried on the inside made her frightening to look at.

I assumed that this was Princess Elizabeth. I thought she was angry at me, and I couldn't figure out what I could have possibly done to get this woman so made at me. When she got closer, I noticed she wasn't looking at me. She was looking at my mother.

"You! You interfering bitch! You damn human! You stay out of my life!" she shrieked at my mother. Mom stood her ground and did not even flinch. She almost acted as if she might have been expecting this outburst. But, how could she have known that the princess would be here and acting like this?

"Now, my love, you need to compose yourself," I heard the queen whisper to the young woman. The princess was acting like she was completely out of control.

"You can go to hell, too," Princess Elizabeth screamed at her mother. "You are wrecking my life!"

"You will stop this behavior this moment!" the king thundered at his daughter. "You have been taught better than this!" He turned away from her and yelled, "Guards! Take the princess away. She is an embarrassment. Lock her in the dungeon. That will give her something to complain about."

I stood behind my mother who stood straight and tall. She appeared completely composed. Ben stood at her side. Ben kept looking from my mom to the princess. It was obvious that he was there to protect her. I thought for sure that crazy Elizabeth was going to attack my mother.

"I won't go! You can't make me!" Elizabeth screamed at her father and fought the guards who were taking her arms to lead her away.

"Please, Cornelius, let her stay," the queen pleaded with her husband softly. "Please don't put her in the dungeon."

"She acts like an animal and she'll be caged like an animal," the king replied coldly. "And you think you can fix this?" he said to my mother with disdain and disbelief as Elizabeth was dragged out of the room.

"This was not a good time to bring her out into the public. She is not a machine to be fixed, but I think I can help her. It just may take a while," my mom said softly to the king as the doors closed behind Elizabeth. You could have heard a pin drop because the room was so quiet. Everyone was watching the scene taking place. "She will be in the dungeons until then. I will not tolerate a scene like that in my palace again," Cornelius stated disgustedly as he walked to the other side of the room with his wife and son. His wife kept trying to talk to him, but he ignored her.

"Holy cow, is that where you were today?" I blurted out to Mom. "What the hell is wrong with her? She seems crazy!"

"I don't discuss my clients. You know that, dear," she said quietly. She slipped her hand in the bend of Ben's elbow and took a sip of her drink.

"She is your client!? Since when do you treat wood nymphs? We're prisoners here! What happens if you fail?" I had to consciously keep my voice low. Whoever was my mother's client was no one's business, not even mine. I knew that, but what was she doing? There was truth in that. What would happen if she failed? What if she couldn't fix Elizabeth? Could anyone really fix someone else? Could my mom really help a wood nymph that did not want to be helped? Could a therapist help any client that does not want to be helped? Elizabeth sure did not look like she wanted to see my mom again.

I was just about to ask the questions I had in my head when we were called in to dinner. The huge table was filled with people again. I wondered if they had this many people for dinner every night. My mother was to be seated next to the queen again, but the rest of us were all going to be seated next to different people. I was going to get to sit next to Forrest and sat across from Ash.

We all stood behind our chairs until the king and queen were seated. The queen looked miserable. It was obvious that she was trying hard to look cool and composed and failing miserably. She forced a smile. But even to me, halfway down the table from her, it did not look like a natural smile. The king looked like nothing had ever happened. He looked happy and relaxed. How could he look so composed? He had just sent his daughter to a dungeon.

As I sat and waited for the different meal courses to be served I thought about Elizabeth and where she was right now. Was the dungeon some dark and smelly place like the old movies used to show? Was Elizabeth sitting on some nasty bale of straw ruining her beautiful dress and shoes? Was she crying? Was she still scream-ing? What was wrong with her? It was obvious that something was wrong with her. Normal, healthy people did not act like that in public.

"Did you know about Elizabeth?" I asked Forrest softly as our soup was served.

Forrest looked around the room to make sure no one was paying attention to what he was saying and replied softly, "I knew something was wrong, but I did not know what. I still don't know exactly what's wrong, but I found out today that the queen wanted your mom here when she found out that your mother was a ther-apist that helped people with mental health issues. I'm not sure about how the king feels about his daughter being treated for some kind of mental issue, but the queen is relying on your mother to fix her daughter."

"What happens if Mom can't fix Elizabeth?" I asked worriedly.

"I don't think we want to find out," Forrest said, picking up his spoon.

I knew if we didn't eat our soup, in a little while, someone would take the soup away to bring the salads. We had a certain amount of time to eat each course, and if we didn't finish in that time, we didn't eat it. After the scene with Elizabeth and the worried tone in Forrest's voice, I didn't think I could eat a bite. But once I tasted the soup and found it to be delicious, I ate it all.

I ate everything from every course. I could not get over how hungry I was. Did stress make people hungry? After dinner, the king made an announcement that we were to go to see a wood nymph theater production in another part of the palace.

We walked along the hallway en masse to an auditorium. It was about the same size as the Tomahawk High School auditorium. The king and queen had a box in the front of the auditorium just in front of the stage. The wood nymph ac-tors and actresses reminded me of the dancers that I saw at the Essence Ceremony at the Copper Clan in Presque Isle, Wisconsin. They had on flowing costumes that were very similar to what I had seen before. However, these looked more ethereal. They looked like an older style, or maybe the fabric was older.

The production reminded me of a ballet. The story seemed to be about a baby. It appeared that the clan was very excited about the birth of this child. There was dancing and excitement. Then something seemed to happen and the baby died. The movements portrayed the sadness exactly. I would never have imagined having a dance display sorrow. While I didn't know the exact storyline, it was obviously a tragedy. It was like watching a foreign film with no subtitles and not fully under-standing the plot, but still realizing that it has a sad ending.

I sat between Olivia and Ash. As the curtain closed, I could feel sadness all around me. "What was that about? I didn't understand. Did the baby die?" I asked Olivia.

"It's a tragedy about the race of wood nymphs. The dying baby represented the population of wood nymphs dying off. The story was about the beginning of the end of the wood nymphs," Olivia replied softly with a sad tone.

"I know things are hard, but to make a theatrical tragedy about the extinction of a species does not really feel like entertainment to me. I wonder what the king thought about this kind of entertainment," I replied.

"We all handle things and stress in our own way. Didn't you think the dancers were graceful? Didn't they give you the feeling of sadness? Why do you think that there are tragedies? Of course, you would feel the sadness from the people around you, wouldn't you? That must be hard, feeling surrounded by sadness," Mom whispered over Ash's shoulder to me.

I knew my mom was referring to my emotion-reading sense. Mom had no non-human abilities. She was just a human.

I felt myself starting to yawn and suppressed it. I saw Mom cover a yawn with her hand. "It must be late. I'm getting tired. I think I'll go to bed now," I said and had to cover my mouth as I yawned again.

"I'll walk you to your room," Ash said as we got up from our seats. All of the wood nymphs were filing out of the room. As we followed them back down the hall, I saw some of them go into a room with gaming tables. There were billiard tables and card tables. There were other table games that I did not identify.

"Come on Ben, Valerie, let's check this out. You too, Olivia. Do you feel lucky?" Forrest asked. Ben nodded. Ben, Mom, Olivia, and Forrest went into the room.

"Don't stay up too long!" Mom admonished as she passed me and kissed my cheek.

"I won't," I replied. I watched them head to a craps table. Imagine that! There was a craps table in a wood nymph palace. Who would ever have thought that?

CHAPTER 12
A MURDER THREAT

sh and I took our time getting to the elevator and walking down the hall to my room. I put my hand on the side panel and the door opened up. There was light in the room, but it was very dim. I could see everything, but not real clearly. Moss came out of the bedroom.

"Ah, good evening! I hope you enjoyed the entertainment? I just pulled the bed covers down for you," Moss said. "Would you like help with the dress?"

"No, I think I can get it. If I can't get it, Ash can," I replied. "This has been a long day for you, too. I can manage from here on, tonight. Do we have anything planned for tomorrow?" I asked, trying to cover another yawn.

Moss smiled at me and then at Ash. "If you are sure, I'll leave you now. Tomorrow you are free to do whatever you like. I believe Ash knows the way to the breakfast and lunch dining room?"

"Yeah, I know how to get there. No sweat," Ash said as he sat on the couch in the middle of the room.

"Breakfast is served in a dining room? That's cool. I can go there for breakfast. I won't need you in the morning. I'll go to breakfast with Ash," I said with a smile.

Moss seemed uncertain about how to handle the situation. She looked confused as to what to do. I wondered if she felt bad about leaving me on my own. Would she in trouble if she wasn't waiting on me hand and foot? "Is there a way I can contact you if I need you?" I asked as I walked with her to the door.

"Yes! There's a pull cord in the corner just there in the living room and one in the bedroom. Just give it a gentle pull and I'll be right here." She pointed to where the cords were coming out of the wall. "I'll come in the morning to make up your bed around nine, okay?" she asked as she walked out the door.

"Nine is fine. I may or may not be here," I replied. "I'll see you sometime tomorrow, I'm sure." I waved and then closed the door.

"I'll be all alone until nine tomorrow morning," I said as I cuddled up to Ash on the couch.

"I think it should be both of us alone," Ash said as he pulled me to him to kiss me.

I could hardly breathe a few minutes later when Ash stood up and took my hand and helped me to my feet. I wanted Ash as bad as he wanted me. I could smell his musky aroused scent and I could feel his desire. He could probably read the desire that I had on my face.

We slowly undressed each other. Ash slowly pulled the pins from my hair and set them on a shelf in the bedroom. I hung up the dress in the closet so that Ash could get a good look at my naked backside. He came up to me and turned me around, kissing my neck and then my lips.

I pulled away from him just long enough to put my hand to the wall to turn down the lighting in the room. I imagined the room to be almost completely dark and this left a soft glow on, kind of like a night light. It added just enough light to the room to make everything black and white. I could see Ash, but I could not see his face. It was more like looking at a silhouette. I reached across to him and he reached for me. Just as our fingers touched, there was a sort of static electricity between us. There was a flash of light, but no zap like I would get from a static electricity touch. I thought of the Sistine Chapel in our touch.

I felt a warmth surround me as he touched me. "I'm giving you my soul," Ash said softly. "I've already given you my heart. I live and breathe to be with you."

I pulled my hand back and looked at his naked silhouette. I could feel his soul surround me like a comfortable and warm blanket on a cold day. I felt at peace. I knew whatever happened that we would be together forever. I believed that even in the afterlife, we would be able to be together.

I reached my hand to him. I put all of the love that I have for him into projecting it to him with my touch. He reached out to me and there was another flash of light. "I give my soul to you as well. I never want to be without you in my life," I whispered as I reached for him to hold him in my arms.

"Come," he said to me as he pulled me to my bed. I went willingly. I could smell him. I could feel him. He was my oxygen.

As he laid me down on my bed, he kissed my neck, my shoulders, my arms, and he worked his way down my body. As he reached my core, I moaned out loud because of the intense pleasure.

When I thought I would explode with the intensity of the feeling, he leaned up and kissed me and then he brought us together in the most elemental way. We reached for the stars in our passion. When I felt my rocket ship explode at the end of my universe, I heard Ash cry out at the same time. After our heart beats slowed down, we stayed that way—connected—until I fell asleep.

Ash woke me up. "Laurel, honey, Moss will be here in an hour. Do you want to take a shower or bath, or something?"

"Now that I have you here, I want something all right!" I stated as I pulled him toward me. About a half hour later, we were scrambling through a shower to be out of the room before Moss got there.

"Do you think she'll know that we were fooling around in here?" I asked as I zipped up my pants and looked around the room.

"Yes, I'm sure she will, but she'll be discreet. Besides, if we do get caught out, how bad could the consequences be? We're over eighteen and getting married in a couple of months," Ash said as he checked his reflection in the mirror. He looked over at me. I was dressed. "Let's go to breakfast."

Ash's parents, Forrest, Olivia, and my parents were already in the dining hall when we arrived hand in hand. Olivia took one look at us and gave us a look. Forrest noticed her look and then he looked at us more closely and frowned. Neither one said anything.

"Good morning, dear," Mom said as she was getting up from the table. "I'm glad you got here before I left. I'll see you at lunch, okay? Do you have any appointments this morning?"

"No, I'm free to roam around, I think," I replied as I got a cup of coffee from a side table before sitting at the table. Immediately, a servant came by with a tray of sweet rolls.

Mom kissed my cheek as she walked by on her way out. I saw a servant gesture for my mom to follow her. I wondered for a moment where she could be going and then I realized that she was probably going to see Elizabeth.

"What are you going to do, Dad?" I asked as I buttered a piece of toast.

"Forrest, Elm, and I are going to check out the valley outside the palace doors. I need some fresh air and we were told we could go out there," Ben replied as he stood up from the table.

I noticed that Forrest and Elm were finished with their breakfasts, too. "What time did you get here?" I asked as a plate of some kind of whipped and baked egg and cheese concoction was set in front of me. It looked light and fluffy. It reminded me of the meringue on a lemon pie.

"We've been here since seven. We've been waiting for you," he said with a quizzical look.

"I didn't want to get into a discussion of why Ash and I were late for breakfast. How did you do at the gaming tables last night?" I asked as I tasted the baked egg thing. It was really good!

"I won! Not a lot, around one-hundred American dollars," Ben stated proudly.

"I didn't win, and neither did Elm," Forrest said as he pushed his chair into the table. "With all of the gifts we have, you would've thought we could have won at poker or roulette. I lost fifty American dollars at the black jack table. Do you want to come with us? We can wait for you."

"No, go ahead. I didn't get to explore the palace yesterday like you guys did," I replied. "Ash can show me around the library and other things."

"Okay. Stay out of trouble," Forrest said with a knowing look. I smiled at him.

Ash and I finished our breakfast by ourselves. This was a really big room for someone just to eat breakfast in. I wondered how many people filtered through here in the morning having breakfast. I wondered what time breakfast started in this place.

"Ash, let's go to my room and practice my color shifting," I said once we were finished. "Does having a full belly affect the shifting?"

"Not that I know of," Ash replied. "Let's see if you can shift more than your hands."

We took the stairs to our floor to walk off some of the big breakfast we had just eaten. Once we got into my room, I sat on the couch and cleared my mind of everything except the color and texture of the fabric of the couch. My hand disappeared. "What happens if I have the shifting fabric on? Does that make a difference?"

"It might. Try it and we'll find out," Ash replied as he changed his hand from normal and then to blend in with the couch and then normal again.

I went into my room and found that there were two sets of color-shifting clothes in the bag. One was bigger than the other. "Hey, Ash," I called from the bedroom. "Come here!"

"What is it?" he asked as he came into the room.

"Try this on," I said as I was pulling the top of the smaller set over my head. I already had the pants on. They fit perfectly. There was also another pair of color shifting shoes.

Ash pulled off his clothes and tried on the shifting clothes. They fit him perfectly, too. "Lean against the door and concentrate on the color and texture of the door," Ash said as he pulled the color-shifting shirt over his head.

I did and Ash gave a low whistle and said, "That is awesome, Laurel," I looked to the mirror on the other side of the room. I could see the door, and I knew I was standing in front of it, but I couldn't see me. However, once I took my concentration off of the color and texture of the door, my face and hands came into view. Because I had on the color-shifting clothes, I could not see my body.

"You have to continue to concentrate to keep up the change," Ash said as he came over to me. He tried on the shoes. It was as if they were made for him.

We walked around my room. When I stood in front of the couch, I practiced blending into it. I practiced by the doorway, by the dresser, by the shower. I was able to blend into everything! The glass on the shower door was the hardest thing, but with a little extra concentration, I was able to match it exactly. We spent hours practicing my color shifting.

At lunch time, we changed back into our normal human clothes and went back to the dining room. There were a few wood nymphs there, but I didn't see Ben, Forrest, Olivia, or Ash's parents. I didn't see my mom, either, but I really didn't expect to. If she was dealing with Elizabeth, she'd probably spend the day with her. Mom had one month to fix Elizabeth if we were to be able to go home. After lunch, we went back to my room. We changed back into the color-shifting clothes.

"Let's explore the palace in these clothes!" I said excitedly. "If we see someone, we can color shift into a doorway!"

"Do you think you can hold a shift long enough?" Ash asked as we headed toward the outside door. He looked down at his feet and then looked at my small feet. "Do you think the doctor thought you might have big feet, or do you think he knew we would do this together?"

I looked at his feet and then at mine. There was definitely a difference. I said, "Maybe he did, I don't know."

"I can't get over how well these clothes and shoes fit me," I heard Ash's disembodied voice.

I opened the door and peeked out into the hallway. There was no one there, so we crept out of my room and slunk along the wall, hurrying between doors, as I could not match the light in the walls. Ash did a better job of blending with light, but I had a hard time blending with something that glowed. Ash said he could see my silhouette against the light. That might have fooled humans, but it would not have fooled a wood nymph. We were having a lot of fun sneaking around the palace and avoiding people. Some of the servants would look around as if expecting someone to be where we were, and then would get a confused look on their face when they would see that they were alone. We were very quiet. I loved these wood nymph clothes! I had to hold Ash's hand when we color shifted to know he was still with me.

For the next couple of weeks, we spent a lot of our time color shifting and sneaking around the palace. Those were the times I was not with the doctor. I saw the doctor every other day. Every time I went to see the doctor, the nurse would open the door to let me in. She always glared at me like I was the biggest inconvenience. When she did speak to me, it was to say some insulting remark about humans in general. Dr. Elder on the other hand, was really nice to me. Almost every time I came to the his office, he would send the horrible nurse home for the day. He would apologize for her behavior, but not once did he tell her to treat me better. He once told me that she had never met a human before and all of the humans she had heard about were not the best type of humans. He hinted about something to do with the princess and humans, but then must have realized he was talking too much and changed the subject.

What I liked about him was that he never treated me like I was a second-class citizen. He treated me as if I had value and was interesting. Dr. Elder had me attempt other wood nymph abilities. He tried to get me to jet. Of all of the things I could do, that was the one thing I could not do. No matter what I did, I could not move faster than a normal human.

The doctor had me practice emotion reading. Sometimes we would walk around the palace and he would have me stand near someone for a while and concentrate on what he or she was feeling. Then when we would walk off and he would quiz me on what I felt. There was a pond in the valley outside of the palace. We went out there so he could watch me call fish. I actually got fish to come to my hand. That was fun. But, that made the fish feel more like pets. I didn't want to eat fish anymore, at least not the fish I had called. I wondered what the water sprites would think of this. Were they able to call to the fish this way?

Mom was always gone during the day. I believed that she was with Elizabeth, although she would never talk about it. She was looking more and more tired. We met up and go to dinner together. Every evening there would be a concert, or some other kind of entertainment. Sometimes I would watch my mom and she would be trying hard to stay awake. Whatever she was doing during the day was wearing her out.

Ben, Forrest, and Elm spent a lot of their time either in the libraries or outside in the valley looking at the plants or the ground. Elm wanted to know what treasures in natural resources the mountain held. Sometimes he would talk excitedly about finding iron ore one day, or a cache of silver on another day, or even on one day, he found a small vein of gold.

After we had been at the palace for almost three weeks, Ash and I put on our color shifting clothes and went down to a library that was deep into the palace that we had found recently. When we went into the door, we saw that there were actually two rooms, with the inside room, away from the hallway having the oldest books. I wanted to see the old books. I was amazed at the size of the rooms. I couldn't help but gape at the floor to ceiling shelves full of books. The walls had to be fifty feet high. On each wall was a ladder attached at the top by a rail, so the ladder could be moved easily along the wall to reach any of the books. About halfway up the wall, there was a ledge that could be walked on.

We made sure that we were alone in there before color shifting back to our normal selves. We had just hit the jackpot on finding the wood nymph histories along the back wall of the second room when I heard someone come into the outside room. I looked at Ash and color-shifted into matching the ladder and books I was by. Ash color shifted to match the books and the shelves. We watched to see who was entering the room. All we could do was hope that whoever it was did not come over by this part of the book shelves or to look too closely at the books. If we moved, it would look as if the books were shimmering. A wood nymph would know what that meant. Our secret would be exposed!

I saw the king come into the room with Aron, the wood nymph guard. After the first few days, I no longer had to have a guard and was allowed to go to and from the doctor's office without an escort.

When the king had made his way into the room and the door shut behind him and Aron, the king heaved a deep sigh. He sat at one of the small marble bistro tables that were scattered throughout the room. Aron stood next to him. Neither one of them moved for what seemed like an hour, but was probably only a minute or two. The king looked up at Aron and roared, "This situation cannot be tolerated I tell you!" He slammed his fist into the marble table.

The table shuddered. I had to concentrate really hard on the books to keep from shifting back to my normal self. I was terrified. If I were to change back into my human looking self, who knew what he would do to me. It wasn't that we couldn't be in the library. That was fine, I think. The king had said we could explore where we wanted. But color-shifting was a little like sneaking around. That would probably make him mad.

"I want her dead! I cannot deal with this anymore. This is beyond anything that I have ever dealt with before, and I will deal with it no longer. I want her dead, and I want you to do it. I want you to make it look like an accident. Maybe make it look like she injured herself trying to run away. I don't care how you do it, I just want her gone so I no longer have to think about her anymore. I want it done by next week," the king stated firmly.

Next week! That would be the one month mark. I was hoping to go home next week! We had done everything that the king asked of us. I got along well with the doctor. No one else who had come with me to Stonehenge had gotten into any trouble.

I got a good look at his eyes. I had never seen anyone this angry. He was standing only a few feet away from me. If I shifted my weight or sneezed, he would know I was there and I'd be a goner. I was almost completely holding my breath. I was so scared! And I was sure it was me, he was talking about. He wanted me, dead.

Oh, what was I going to do? Aron was going to kill me and make it look like an accident. I wondered what Ash was thinking. Could we escape? If we did try to escape, would Aron catch us and kill us? Would we play right into his plans if we tried to run away? I had never been so afraid in my entire life.

"Yes, your highness. It will be as you say," Aron responded. I looked at Aron and he looked sad. He tilted his head as if he listening to something. Could he hear me? "You know that there will be questions if she disappears."

I was afraid to reach out with my emotion sensing ability. The king might be able to feel me in the room if I did that. I could tell what his emotions were. They were obvious for anyone to see. But, Aron, I could not read his. I looked at his face, and he did not look happy about this assignment. Yeah, I'd understand that. There would be a big difference between killing someone trying to hurt the ones you loved and hurting an innocent person. I was not perfect, but I was certainly innocent of any wrongdoing. I did not deserve to be murdered! I knew that Aron hated me. He showed that on my first day to the doctor. Since then, he has barely spoken to me. But, did he think I deserved to be killed?

"I will worry about that, later," the king replied. "Just make it happen." The king walked out of the room. Aron looked around the room with what appeared to be a quick appraisal just before he left.

I waited about five minutes for Ash to color shift back to his normal self. I was not going to shift until he did. I was exhausted from holding onto the ladder and for holding my concentration. After Ash went back to his normal self, I shifted, got off of the ladder and ran over to him. "Did you hear that?" I whispered to Ash, all the while watching the doorway. I was afraid Aron knew we were there. I saw him look around the room. Maybe he could sense us! Maybe he was in the outer room just waiting for us to come out and to kill me."

"Yes. Oh, Laurel, I'm so sorry. We'll get out of here, I promise," he replied in a whisper as he wrapped me in his arms. "We need to find my dad, Ben, and Forrest. They'll know what to do! I hate to say this, because I know you're exhausted from concentrating on holding the shift, but I think we need to shift back to find our dads. We don't want to be seen leaving these rooms or in our shifting clothes. I think we have a few days before he'll come after you, but I don't know that for certain. Let's go back to your room and change clothes. After we leave your room in our normal clothes, we need to be seen by somebody at all times! We can't be out of sight! It'll be hard to kill us with witnesses."

We flitted in and out of doorways as we snuck back to my room to change clothes. Just as we were going up to my door, Moss was coming out with an armful of sheets. We waited until she was out of sight before we entered my room. We did not want her to see the door open. We'd left Ash's clothes on the floor when we had changed earlier and Moss had folded them and placed them on a dresser. We quickly changed clothes and as casually as we could, we walked out into the hallway to the stairs. We walked down the stairs and headed out of the palace and into the valley. I could see our dads and Forrest about a football field away from us, looking at something on the ground. Ash picked me up and jetted us over there.

"Whoa, what's the big hurry? We missed you at lunch. Decided to join us after all?" Ben asked as he stood up. Ash put me down.

"What's wrong? I can see something's wrong, what is it?" Forrest said as he came up to us. He tilted my face up to his. I couldn't help it, I started crying and shaking.

"Hey, now, something is wrong. What is it?" Ben asked. "What happened?" He came over and put his arm around me.

"Can we talk here? Is it safe?" Ash asked his dad. His dad looked around and seemed to listen carefully.

"I don't think anyone is near us. I don't detect anyone. Why the secrecy?" Elm asked.

"A couple of weeks ago, while I was with the doctor, we experimented with color shifting. With specific concentration instructions, I was able to shift my hand to match the chair. Then, he gave me some color shifting clothes. He said for me to practice, but not to tell anyone. He said he only wanted to give one report to the king, and he didn't want anyone to tell the king of any abilities that he could determine until the final report was written. He gave me a bag that had two full sets of color shifting clothes. One fit me perfectly and just for fun, I asked Ash to try on a set and those fit him perfectly too, including the shoes." I stopped to take a breath.

"That doesn't sound bad, that sounds kind of interesting," Forrest said as he walked over to me.

"No, that's not it! I like the color shifting. There's more. We practiced in my room for a while and I found I could hold the shift while concentrating. I wanted to go exploring the palace. We spent the last couple of weeks exploring the palace in our color-shifting clothes. While we were checking out the different rooms, we found the library that we hadn't seen before and went inside to explore. While we were there, the king and one of his guards came in. We color-shifted so they wouldn't see us. The king told the guard to kill me! He said I had to be dead within a week! We've been here almost a month. I was hoping to go home in a week!" I said and started to sob. I couldn't help it. I didn't want to die! I didn't want my family to die!

They all started talking at once. "Stop! I can't understand all of you!" I shouted. I was shaking so hard.

"Don't yell, Laurel. We don't want to attract attention. Tell me exactly what you heard in the library," Ben said slowly while gently holding me away from him so he could see my face.

"I was on a ladder, looking at the old books on wood nymph histories when Ash and I heard someone come into the outer room of the library. We both color shifted and held very still. The king and Aron, the guard who took me to the doctor's office when we first got here came into the room. The king was very angry. I had never seen anyone so mad! He said something about 'wanting her dead' and 'how this was beyond anything that he had ever experienced before' or something like that. Wasn't that what he said, Ash?" I asked Ash as I turned to face him.

"Yeah, it was almost exactly like that," Ash said as he reached up and softly wiped a tear from my cheek.

"Did he say Laurel's name?" Elm asked gently. We were standing in a circle now.

"No, but who else would he want to kill? Who else would be beyond anything he had ever experienced? It has to be Laurel," Ash said slowly to his dad looking back at the entrance to the palace.

Acceptance of our doom was written all over Ash's face. He was convinced we were going to die. I could see it on his face and I could feel it in his emotions. Of course we were going to die! What chance did we have against a palace full of wood nymphs? The question coming to my mind was, when were we going to die? Who was going to die? Just me? I hoped it was just me. But, I was afraid that everyone else that I knew and loved would have to die, too. There could be no witnesses left behind. How were we going to survive Stonehenge?

CHAPTER 13
FIND VALERIE!

L et's go find your mother," Ben said. "Actually, let's get everyone together and meet in Laurel's room." We all agreed to track everyone down and meet in my room in a half hour. Ash and I went to my room. When we got there, Moss was in my bathroom. "Hi, Moss," I said feigning cheerfulness.

"Hello, Laurel. Hello, Ash. Are you having a nice day?" Moss asked as she came out of the bathroom. "I just put in some fresh towels for you."

"Thanks! I appreciate it. Have you had your lunch yet?" I asked. I wanted her out of my room.

"Oh, yes. That was quite awhile ago. Did you miss lunch? Did you want me to take you to the cafeteria?" Moss asked as she headed for the door.

"No, I had lunch in the dining room. But, I appreciate the offer. Please say hi to your mom for me, okay?" I asked with a smile. I did like Moss and her mom. That part I didn't have to fake. "What time do I have to be ready for dinner, tonight?"

"I'll be back here around five. But, if you need me before that, just pull the cord," Moss said as she left the room.

"I didn't think she was ever going to leave," Ash said as he sat on the couch. We were now alone.

I sat by Ash in silence for a few minutes as we waited for the others to show up. I wondered if they'd be able to find my mother. I wondered what I had done so very wrong that made the king want me dead. Was I a threat just by living? How was I a threat to the wood nymphs? I took a deep breath and it came out as a sigh.

"Are you okay?" Ash asked as he put his arms around me. I snuggled into him. I loved the way he smelled, even when he didn't have his arousal scent glands activated. He smelled clean and pure. He smelled like the fresh crisp air of a sunny spring day. Would I ever be able to smell spring in the Northwoods again? I felt sick thinking of everything that I would never be able to experience.

We would not be able to get married. I would not be able to go to college. I would never have a baby. The king would kill Ash, too. Ash and I had bonded and given each other our souls. Even if the king had not ordered his death, he would die without me, anyway. So, even if the king did not outright kill Ash, his heart would literally break and he would probably die within months of my disappearance. His parents would be outraged and probably try to submit some kind of protest. I am sure the king knew that. He would just kill them, too. We were all expendable.

My parents would never make it to old age. Ben would never tolerate anyone hurting me or mom and the king knew it. Ben was dangerous in his own right. Would he be able to take on wood nymph guards? I was sure that he would try. The king would have to kill Ben and Mom. He couldn't leave witnesses.

Forrest and Olivia were also guilty of loving me. They had not done anything wrong, but the king didn't see it that way. They didn't tell the king about me when they knew about me before I was born. The king could have killed me before anyone else knew about me. Forrest and Olivia would probably be the next to be killed after me and my parents.

Olivia had just gotten back with her old boyfriend Hawthorn, right before we left on this trip. If Hawthorn would have been at my house when the king and queen arrived in Wisconsin, he would have had to have been here, too. I wondered what Hawthorn was thinking right now. Did Olivia or Ash's parents tell him what was going on? Would he know when we died? Or, would he just wait for Olivia until heartbreak killed him? Would he feel it when Olivia died? Did the bond work that way?

As I thought about all of the people who would suffer because I was born, I felt myself getting nauseous. I ran to the bathroom and Ash followed me.

I leaned over the toilet. "No, Ash, don't follow me. I'll be okay," I said just before throwing up. Of course he didn't go away and he gently pulled my hair from my face. When I finished, I got up to rinse off my face and my mouth. I was sweating.

"I don't know why I threw up. I guess the stress is getting to me," I said as I used a wash cloth to wipe my face.

"We are not dead, yet," Ash said gently. He hugged me from behind and our eyes met in the mirror above the sink. He had such a loving look on his face. He also looked sad.

"No, we're not," I replied as I dried off my face with a towel. I sighed again. Yeah, we weren't dead yet, but for how much longer would we be alive?

I heard someone knocking on the door as we walked back into the living room. I opened the door and let in Ash's parents.

"I thought things were going to be fine!" Willow cried after I shut the door behind them. "King Cornelius has been so nice to us!"

I gestured toward the couch. Willow and Elm sat down. "We don't know why he does what he does," Elm said as he pulled Willow into his arms. "I never should have invited that Quince family to our house last year."

"Dad, we are not dead, yet!" Ash said as he sat by his parents. I heard another knock at the door and went to open it. Forrest and Olivia were standing there.

"I see nothing about anyone trying to kill us in any visions," Olivia said worriedly. "I see us in a group in a hallway with the king and his guards, but no one is hurting us. Could I be misreading my vision?"

"We're all stressed out about this. I guess it's possible that you're not seeing the vision clearly," Forrest said to Olivia as they sat across from Ash and his parents. "Is there any chance that you didn't hear the king correctly?" Forrest asked wistfully looking at me. His face told me that he knew the answer to that.

I gave him a grim shake of my head as I went to answer the door. I thought that my parents were finally here. I opened the door and it was just Ben standing there and he said, "I can't find your mom, anywhere! I asked some of the staff if they'd seen her, but no one could tell me where she was. I didn't see the queen, either."

"Maybe she's in the dungeon. Do you think that the king's already snatched her up and taken her down there? We've looked everywhere else, except the king and queen's personal quarters," I said thoughtfully. Then a plan started coming together in my head. It could be dangerous, but if Mom was in the dungeon, I wanted to know!

"Does anyone else have color-shifting clothes and shoes with them?" I asked. Everyone looked up at my curiously.

"Why do you ask?" Forrest asked. Everyone was looking at me.

"I want to find my mom and I don't want anyone to see me looking for her. I'm going to check the dungeon. Ash, are you with me?" I said as I walked over to stand next to him.

"Yeah, I am. We can sneak into the dungeon or anywhere else," Ash said standing up.

"I have my color-shifting clothes," Olivia said softly. "I didn't know you could color shift. When did this happen? How long have you been able to do this?"

"A couple of weeks now, but I wasn't supposed to tell anyone. I promise I'll tell you all about it, later," I said feeling guilty I hadn't let Olivia in on my secret.

"I want a full report later. For now, I want to go, too." She stood up to stand by me.

"I carry mine with me wherever I go. You're not going without me," Forrest said forcefully as he stood up. "I want to be with you from now on."

"Hey, no way! I can't do this shifting thing, and I can't protect Laurel if she isn't with me!" Ben stated as he came over and put an arm around me.

"Dad, I have a bunch of wood nymphs that can color shift with me. We need to go and find Mom!" I said with a sigh. "I don't want to leave you, either, but we have to go! You need to wait in your suite for Mom in case she comes back. Forrest will protect me. He's been watching over me all of my life. He's still watching over me," I said as I gently pulled myself away from Ben. I turned to face him.

"I'm going too," Elm said as he stood up. "I don't know why I packed them, but I packed my color-shifting clothes, too. Anyway, I can sense things through rock. I could tell if there was a wood nymph or a human behind a rock wall or door. This could protect us from accidently walking into a room full of guards. Besides, when I was exploring yesterday, I found the door to the dungeon. I think I'm the only one of us who knows how to get there. I saw someone come out of the doorway yesterday with an empty food tray. When I asked who it was for, the guard said he was returning the tray from the dungeon, but did not say who was down there."

"Oh, no, Elm! You can't leave me!" Willow cried, standing up and clutching her husband's arm.

"You stay with Ben. I'm sure he wouldn't mind having you with him in his suite. He can protect you," Elm said as he pulled his arm out of his wife's hands. "I caused this mess, and I need to try to fix it. If I hadn't opened our house to that Quince family last year, we wouldn't be dealing with this now."

"We cannot change the past. But, we can try to deal with our present. We'll meet back here in five minutes," Forrest said as he headed for the door. He stopped midway to the door and looked back at Ben. "We need to know where Valerie is and if she is safe."

"Okay! I agree we need to make sure Valerie's safe," Ben said reluctantly. "I'll be in our suite. As soon as you get back, you come over there!" Then Ben looked at me. "Promise me, Laurel! I can't stand the worrying!"

"I promise, Dad, as soon as we find Mom and either bring her back, or know that she's safe where she is, we'll come back," I said as I opened the door. I watched everyone leave until it was just me and Ash. Ash and I stood in the hallway watching everyone hurry away. When Ben got to his room, he gave me a sad look and waved before going into his suite.

"Let's change," I said heading into the bathroom. Ash and I changed our clothes together. As nervous as I was about my mom, I still couldn't help but enjoy the view of him as he stepped out of his jeans. I never got tired of looking at him with or without clothes on. We'd had a lot of alone time in the last couple of weeks. I thought about the times we had made love. I thought about him and our short time together. I really hoped our future was just beginning and not about to be cut short.

I smiled at him. "We'll get through this, one way or another," I said as I pulled my color shifting top on.

He noticed me watching him. He gave me a smile and said, "Yes, I plan to grow old with you. We'll figure out a way to survive this."

We were dressed in the color-shifting clothes and waiting in the living room for the others to come back to my room. Olivia was the last to arrive. As she sat down, Elm said to me, "Let me see you shift. Walk around the room and into the bathroom. I want to see if I can sense you in there."

"I, too, want to see you shift! I'm so proud of you!" Forrest exclaimed with a smile. "I knew you'd be able to color shift. Remember that day in my car last fall? The day you saw my hand color shift to match my car seat? I told you that I thought I saw a bit of change to your skin color."

I did remember that day. That was the day after I had almost been attacked by a hodag. That was the day after I found out that Ash was a wood nymph when he grabbed me in the dark and jumped thirty feet straight up into a tree. Oh, yes, I remembered that day. As stressed out as I was back then, there was no way I could concentrate on doing a color shift for the first time. I had just found out that wood nymphs existed. I had no idea that there was even a chance I had abilities. It was a no brainer to me why I could not color shift that day. However, I had been practicing for a couple of weeks. I was able to maintain a color shift while listening to the king ordering my death. I could color shift now.

I walked to the doorway and concentrated on it. I imagined the texture of the door. I imagined the color of the wood. I disappeared.

"Oh, Laurel, that's awesome!" Olivia said with pride in her voice. "I never knew you could do that! You say you've known how to do this for a couple of weeks?"

My disembodied voice floated back to them from the doorway. "Yes. Doctor Elder was testing me to see what wood nymph abilities I may have inherited. While there are not a whole lot of things I can do, this is one of them. So, I didn't know either, until we got here," I said. "The doctor told me what to think and feel and after a couple of attempts, I was able to concentrate, and I was able to do this. I have been practicing with Ash."

"That is really neat, Laurel. It sounds like the doctor has been nice to you. I'm glad. But, we need to focus on the here and now," Forrest said and then turned to Elm. "See if you can see her through the wall."

"Go into the bathroom," Elm said. "Don't talk and try not to make a sound while walking."

I started walking toward the bathroom. "See if you can see me, too!" Ash said as he disappeared against the wall. He had been standing by his parents and across the room from me when I shifted. I saw him disappear and then I felt his hand take mine when he reached me. I jumped, not realizing that he was going to try to take my hand. I didn't lose concentration though, and we walked as softly as we could into the bathroom. We couldn't see them and we knew that they couldn't see us. Even if we hadn't shifted, we were behind a marble wall.

We stood there silently a minute before we heard Elm call out, "Yes, with concentration, I can 'feel' you behind the wall!"

I shifted back to my normal self and Ash did, too. Well, as normal as we could be with color shifting clothes on. Our clothes were invisible. We were just heads and hands walking out of my bathroom. I smiled at Elm as we walked back into the living room. "This will work. We won't open a door into a room full of guards!" I said as we joined the rest of our group.

"Are you sure you can hold a shift? It can get tiring," Forrest said worriedly. "I'd hate to have you change back to your normal self and get caught by a guard."

"I held the color shift the whole time I was terrified in the library when the king was in the room," I said as I headed for the door. "I kept the shift then. I can do it now. We need to find Mom."

"If we are all shifted, how will we know where everyone is?" I asked at the door just before opening it.

"You're right. We need to go single file," Forrest said thoughtfully. "Elm should go first. He can make sure that we don't open a door and surprise someone. Olivia should go next, just in case she gets a vision of someone or a premonition that may save us from some problem. Ash should be next in line and then Laurel. I'll take up the rear. We'll stay against the wall. Hold the hand of the person in front of you and we won't get separated. If there are nymphs around, make sure to hold the shift and, for goodness sake, keep quiet!"

We all agreed and I opened the door. There was no one in the hallway. We would look suspicious as a group walking around in color shifting clothes, so as soon as we were all out of the door, we got in our line, took each others hands and shifted.

We silently descended the stairs. We didn't want to let go hands as that was the only contact we had with each other. We couldn't see each other. When we got to the bottom of the stairs, I felt Ash pull me in a direction I had not been before. I could see where we were going, but I wasn't sure when we would change directions, so I kept a tight hold on Ash's hand. Forrest held my other hand tightly, too. As we walked along the wall, I would see a shimmer as the color shifting aspect would change from one color to another on the people in front of me. It reminded me of how a road would shimmer in the distance on a hot summer day.

It took us a few minutes to sneak along the hallways before we reached the door to the dungeon. At times we would have to pull ourselves tight up against the wall as staff would walk by. No one seemed to notice us.

When we got to the door, there was a pause before the door opened. I assumed it was Elm making sure that there was no one on the other side. When it opened, we slipped through quickly and Forrest closed the door with an almost inaudible click. We stood on a landing just before the stairs led down. I saw Elm and then Forrest shift back to their normal selves. "There is no one on the stairs. Keep an eye on me, though. If I shift, be sure to do so immediately. That would mean someone is coming."

I noticed as we walked down the stairs, that every so often, there was a depression in the wall. If I didn't know better, I would assume that the depressions were made for someone sneaking into the dungeons. This way, if someone was coming up the stairs or down the stairs, the person doing the sneaking could back into the depression and let someone go by with no knowledge that anyone else was on the stairway. I thought that was kind of creepy. What was to stop someone else from being in the stairwell? Would guards hide in the indentations in the wall?

We must have walked down a hundred stairs before we got to the bottom of the curving stone stairwell. There were three doors at the bottom of the stairway. One was directly in front of us, and there was one to each side. Elm went to the door to the left first. He put his hand on the door and concentrated. "There's no one on the other side of the door, but I don't know if it is a hallway or something else, like a prison cell. Should I try the door?"

Forrest suggested that he check all of the doors before deciding which one to open. The door in front of us had two people on the other side. There was no way of knowing who they were. No one was in the last room he checked. There was only the one room with people in it, but were they guards? What would happen if we walked in on guards? Would we get in trouble? How would we talk our way out of that?

While everyone else was watching Elm concentrate on the doors, I was looking around the little room we were in at the bottom of the stairs. It looked like a foyer. I saw a small recessed area in the back by the side of the stairs. It was in shadow and hard to see. When I looked in the hole, I saw keys in there and pulled them out.

"Look what I found!" I whispered excitedly.

"They look the right size for the doors. I didn't think about the doors being locked," Olivia said with a wry smile.

"Me, either," Forrest said with a disgusted sound.

"Which door do we try first?" I asked holding out the keys.

"Here, give me them. I'll try this one. There is no one there, so we should be fine," Elm said. "At lease we'll know what this room looks like."

He turned the handle on the first door he had checked first. Of course the door was locked. But, we found the keys that fit the lock. As quietly as he could, Elm unlocked the door. As he started to open it, Forrest suggested, "Just in case, let's color shift." We all shifted. If anyone had been on the other side, all they would have seen is the door open by itself.

We saw a narrow hall lit with artificial lights. I found that odd, since the rest of the palace had lighting from the marble veins in the walls. There were two jail cells on each side of the hallway. Each cell had a cot, sink and toilet. They looked like the jail cells I had seen on television. They all looked unoccupied. We went back out to the room at the bottom of the stairs. We shifted back to our normal selves. Well, at least we could see hands and faces. The clothes blended into the walls and the stairs, depending on where anyone was standing.

Elm again listened to the door on the right side of the stairs. "No one is there," Elm said as he tried the keys. It took a minute, but he slowly opened that door. We color shifted and Elm opened the door. We found four more cells, but while empty, one had been recently occupied. There were sheets on the cot and a dresser with a floral arrangement on it. The flowers were real and fresh. The door to this cell was open. "Do you think someone's living in this cell?" I asked as I looked into the cell. "It looks to still be occupied by someone."

Forrest color shifted back to normal. I concentrated on his face. Seeing a disembodied head was hard on my already nervous stomach. I color shifted back to normal, too, and so did everyone else.

"Do you think the princess would still be in the dungeon? I mean, I kind of thought that maybe they put my mom down here, since we could not find her anywhere else. But do you think Elizabeth is still down here since she caused that scene with her father a couple of weeks ago? I know she hasn't been attending the dinners or social events, but really? Would they keep their own daughter in a jail cell for weeks?" Olivia asked as she looked around.

"Someone's living here," Forrest said quietly. "It looks like whoever it is, has been living here for some time. See the soap? The bar is over half gone. When we got into our rooms, we all had new bars of soap. I'd think that a prisoner would have been given a whole bar of soap."

"Well, whoever it is, she is not here now," I said. "We need to open the door with people on the other side. One of those people may be my mom."

"She? What makes you think it's a woman?" Elm asked looking around.

"I can smell her. Also, look at the flowers. I don't think a male prisoner would want flowers on the dresser," I replied.

"There is a feminine scent. Laurel is right," Forrest said sniffing the air.

"Are we ready to open the last door? We don't know what we will find," Elm said with a warning tone to his voice.

"We have gotten this far. We need to know," Olivia said cautiously.

We went back to the room at the bottom of the stairs. "Are we ready?" Forrest asked. We all nodded. "Color shift. Elm, open the door. The guys will go in first, in case it's guards. If there are guards, we hurry back out of the door and stay color shifted to our rooms. We will meet in Laurel's room."

When the door opened, we noticed that the door opened to a large room with chairs. The chairs were in a circle. Was this a meeting room of some kind? Did the guards meet in here? There were also tables and books. There was a dry erase board against the far wall. In the opposite corner, I saw Mom and a young woman in a plain adress. Her hair was a mess, but it looked to be the same color as the woman I had seen a couple of weeks ago. Could this be Elizabeth?

"Who's there?" My mother asked sternly as she stood up. "No one's allowed in here!"

I color shifted to my natural self. "Mom, it's me! We have been looking for you! Are you okay?"

"Laurel? What are you doing in those clothes? Did you just appear out of thin air? When did you learn how to change your skin like the other wood nymphs?" My mother came over to me." As she got closer, she bumped into Forrest. "Who is with you?" Of course she couldn't see Forrest since he hadn't shifted back to his normal self. When my mom bumped into him, he shifted back.

"It's me, Forrest. I'm sorry, Valerie. I didn't mean for you to crash into me. We are not alone," Forrest responded. When he said that, everyone else color shifted back to their normal selves.

"What are you all doing here?" Mom asked incredulously. "You are not supposed to be here!"

"We're in danger, Mom. The king is going to kill me. I heard him say so, this morning," I said as I rushed over to hug her.

"That's nonsense! Tell me exactly what he said," Mom said as she hugged me back. After a moment, she stepped back and said, "Laurel, you're all stressed out. Try to relax and tell me what you heard."

I repeated what Ash and I had overheard in the library. When I was finished, no one said anything for a minute, and then we heard a soft voice coming from the young woman in the corner. She said with a sad sigh, "It's not you. It's me he wants to kill."

CHAPTER 14
ELIZABETH'S STORY

I walked over to the woman sitting on a chair in the corner. "What?" I asked. Could this woman sitting here actually be the beautiful but raving Elizabeth I had seen a couple of weeks ago? She was in clothes that appeared to be made out of burlap sacks. This was a princess! Even if she had issues, I thought that she should still be dressed better.

She saw the shock on my face as I looked at her. "Yes, I'm Elizabeth, and as hard as it may be to believe, I'm the king's daughter." She spoke so softly with her head down that I had to listen hard to hear her.

"You don't have to say anything," my mother said softly as she sat in the chair next to Elizabeth. Mom reached over and put her hand on Elizabeth's arm.

Elizabeth looked up at my mom. "I know. But, I guess I want to. Didn't you tell me I need to take responsibility for my actions? Well, I'm trying to do that now. People need to know about me. Maybe if I can get others to understand what happened to me, I can get forgiveness if not redemption," she said, then turned to me.

"It all started because I was bored. I started sneaking out of the palace without my bodyguards. I got tired of having everything I did scrutinized. I felt like I was constantly watched. I thought I was being watched because I wasn't good enough. Since this had been going on since I was born, it didn't occur to me that I had to be watched over because I was a royal princess.

"I didn't have as many abilities as Andrew. He was the perfect son and the first-born. He's five years older than I am. We've never been close," Elizabeth said as she wiped a tear from her eye. "This is kind of hard to admit, this next part."

With a sigh, she continued, "A couple of years ago I started to sneak out and go to the bigger human cities. Since I am a wood nymph, I could get anywhere in England in moments. There were humans everywhere, and no one knew what I was! No one knew I was a wood nymph or that I was royalty. I watched to see how other people dressed. I always snuck out at night. It wasn't like anyone really cared about me here. At least, that is what I thought.

"I started dressing like the humans. I found some black pants and black hoodies in a human store and I stole some human money from the palace finance office and bought some of them. I didn't wear my normal clothes in the human world. I would have stood out. The places that I went to, well, the people there would not have been able to afford the name brand human clothes that I usually wore here.

"Then, I found some people who looked like they were having a good time by this bar. They were dressed like I was and I wanted to blend in with them. I thought that they'd be fun to be with. After a couple of drinks, they asked if I wanted some crack. I had no idea what that was and said sure. I didn't think anything the humans could do could hurt me. After all, I was a wood nymph! I just didn't know! I tried it. It was crack cocaine. After the first experience and coughing, I wanted more! I snuck out more and more often to meet these humans. I found I didn't care about anything except getting high. Money was no object for a princess. I could have anything I wanted. No one stole from the king, so the finance office was unlocked. No one except his daughter.

"For a long time, no one knew I was sneaking out. After a while, my mother started commenting on how I didn't look like I had been sleeping well. Sleeping well? I wasn't sleeping at all! I had no idea that I could stay awake for days at a time! Then, I guess I started acting kind of crazy. If I wasn't out in the human world and getting high, I was miserable. I was constantly angry. Andrew started to get suspicious of my behavior. One night Andrew followed me and found out what I had been doing. He told my parents. They were horrified, and my father got scary. He was so angry! He forbade me from going out of the palace anymore.

"I didn't realize it at the time, but it was not only the drugs that had been harming me. My parents without intending to had damaged me, too. They thought if they gave me anything I wanted, I'd grow up fine. But, what I needed, their attention, they didn't have time for. I thought I could have what I wanted, when I wanted, and found I wanted more and more to make up for the attention that I wasn't getting. I didn't realize what I truly needed was guidance. Maybe my parents thought servants or the wood nymph nanny was giving me the attention I needed, but it's now obvious they didn't.

"Andrew and I had always done whatever we wanted. He was getting more attention from our father, which probably kept him from being bored. We just didn't have a lot of direction in anything except lessons in royal behaviors, which was boring. That was the one thing the nanny taught us. She taught us how to act in public. She did not teach me how to handle being alone and lonely.

"In human terms, we would have been called spoiled. I had no idea that being denied things was a regular occurrence for other children. I found out by talking to humans. I'm serious. If I asked for it, I got it, except for my mother or father to have a conversation with me. No questions asked, until now," Elizabeth sat back and closed her eyes. She looked like she was going to go to sleep.

"Do you want to continue?" My mother asked softly. "I don't think anyone here is going to judge you." My mother leaned over and gently held Elizabeth's hand. When my mom squeezed her hand gently, Elizabeth opened her eyes.

"This is kind of embarrassing," she said looking at my mother with a sad expression. "I know I have to take responsibility for my actions, but I had never taken any kind of responsibility for anything before. That is, before now. I just wanted to be happy, without being responsible."

"As a royal princess, when your teacher or tutor to taught you protocol and how to behave, didn't he or she have a conversation with you?" Ash asked quietly as he sat on the floor by the princess. I sat by Ash and Forrest, Elm and Olivia sat by us. We sat in a semi-circle around my mom and Elizabeth.

"Not really. Have you ever had a conversation with a teacher? The instructor instructs. The teacher isn't there to be my friend. I hated the whole learned behaviors aspect of training to be a princess. I would act cute and charming and beg my tutors to leave me alone. Everyone thought that because I could be so charming I would naturally grow into the perfect princess. It didn't work that way. I was lonely for companionship. Andrew was getting all of the attention from my parents. He was being groomed to be the next king. I felt like I was window dressing,furniture. I was treated like a bit of fluff with no real value, at least that's how I felt. I felt I had something to say, but no one wanted to hear it," Elizabeth said looking at each of us and then she looked at my mother.

"I realize now that I was being given differential treatment. I wanted the tutors and teachers to leave me alone, because I wanted my parents to have something to do with me. This backfired. Everyone left me alone. I was my own worst enemy. None of the staff at the palace could be my friend. They weren't allowed to be my friends. The staff knew their place and I could do nothing to change it. I was the princess! No one else was good enough to be my friend. I was so lonely! I had no one to confide in, until now. Valerie's helped me realize the mistakes I've made." She stopped for a moment and took a couple of deep breaths.

"I truly want to fix my life. But, everyone thinks as soon as I have some freedom, I'll sneak out to do the drugs. Can you blame me for wanting to feel good? The drugs made me feel good. I know now that it was only the chemicals working on my brain, but that was better than nothing. For the first time, I thought I was happy. The first time you saw me, I had been under strict observation for a week. I wanted the cocaine! I wanted to feel better! Being a prisoner made me feel even more isolated. Then, after the scene I made in the reception room, I've been kept down here. I was able to sneak out a couple of times when someone took me out to bathe. Andrew would find me and drag me back here. After escaping a couple of times, I haven't been anywhere alone. I haven't been allowed to be alone to take a bath or shower for the last two weeks.

"But living in the dungeon's helped me. I couldn't sneak out, so my body's had a chance to heal from the cocaine. I don't know what I would've done without Valerie. I learned a lot about addictions and consequences since she's been coming to see me. I'm sorry, Valerie. I was difficult in the beginning," Elizabeth said.

"It's okay. I'm not offended," Mom said. "It was the drugs talking. Crack cocaine can take over your life. A lot of people don't realize what harm they're doing to themselves and the people around them. You have learned a lot about yourself in the last couple of weeks," My mom replied with a smile.

"I think I understand the addictive qualities of cocaine. I think I've learned from you that I'm an addict and will need to be careful about staying away from those kinds of temptations in the future. It's true that I learned a lot about myself. I understand my loneliness. I had never heard that word before Valerie taught it to me. I've felt lonely all of my life and have never had a word I could use to describe the feeling," Elizabeth stated with a shake of her head.

"You have a friend now," Mom said with a smile. "I'm your friend. I mean, I'm not supposed to be friends with my clients, but if it's in the best interests of the client to do certain things, I'll. Besides, I won't be your counselor forever. We can be friends. Eventually, we return to the United States. You could come and visit us there."

"I know you don't know me, but I'd like to be your friend, too!" I said as I came closer to Elizabeth.

She smiled at me. I could see the beauty in her when she smiled. It was almost like an inner light came on when she smiled and said, "I would like you to be my friend, too."

I contemplated what we had heard. Everyone else must have been thinking too, because no one said anything for a while. "What do we do now?" I asked as I stood up.

"What I really need now is a shower and some clean clothes. The guards let Valerie in to see me, and others bring me food. Everyone thinks I'll run away. Because my parents fear that I'll run away or expose the wood nymph culture, I have not had a shower in almost a week.

"I tell my mother when she comes that I won't run away anymore. She thinks I'm trying to manipulate her, because I have said that before and still ran off. I don't know what I can do to convince them that I am better," The princess said with a sad smile while looking around at us. "I know I'm not perfect, but at least the cravings aren't as bad. How do I convince my parents I'm trying to change?" This last part she directed to my mother.

"It takes time. You've damaged their trust in you. When people lie, and are caught, trust disappears. It can be rebuilt, but that takes time," Mom said with a smile.

"I don't know if I have time," Elizabeth said as she looked over to me. "Not if my dad has made the decision to eliminate me."

"I thought he was talking about me!" I said. "He was quite clear that some 'she' is going to be killed and that the guard Aron was supposed to make it look like an accident."

"That's really sad," Elizabeth said softly. "Of all of the guards, I always liked him the best. He's always been so nice to me. Now, it seems he hates me. He agreed to kill me."

"We have to show that you have changed! While a couple of weeks are not a long time for a detox program, you have made great improvements. You've figured out many things about your life that could be changed to allow you to have a happy and healthy life at the palace. You're a princess, you should be able to have friends," Mom said with conviction.

"Ah, Valerie, you're always so positive. You just don't get it. Once my father makes up his mind about something, there's no turning back. I've embarrassed the king of the wood nymphs. This's an insult he won't get over," Elizabeth said sadly. "I finally understand my life and want to make appropriate changes and now it's going to end. Kind of ironic, isn't it?"

"You are not dead, yet!" I stated. "I thought he was going to kill me, but he hasn't done that yet. I'm still here!" I said as I went to stand by the princess. "We will figure a way out of this mess. We'll get your father to accept both of us."

"You're a piece of work, Laurel," Elm said. "You're right. I would've never thought I'd like you, but I do. We should be able to do something to change the king's mind about killing anybody, especially his daughter."

"We have keys to the dungeon. If we can't change his mind, we can escape!" I said. "We'll color shift and sneak out of here."

"I can't color shift, and I won't be a part of a break out. We're trying to establish trust, not make the king and queen distrust humans even more," Mom stated firmly.

"How are we going to establish any kind of trust if the king has already made up his mind to kill Elizabeth or me? I'm still not convinced that anyone would be willing to kill his daughter no matter what she may have done," I said with frustration.

"We need a game plan," Forrest said as he stood up.

"I like games," A voice from the doorway said with sarcasm. We all jumped. As we watched, Andrew, materialized in the doorway. When we came in, we forgot to shut the door! We could see his hands and face. He had on color-shifting clothes. "Now isn't this cozy."

"What are you doing here?" Mom asked angrily. "We're supposed to be allowed private sessions in here."

"You see, I have been hearing rumors about my sister. I heard that there may be a plot against her life and I wanted to know if they were true," he said to Elizabeth. "I had also heard that a human was counseling her. It's sad to believe that a human could help a wood nymph. It is even sadder to think that a wood nymph, and a royal one at that, would need counseling. This is all an embarrassing situation."

Then he looked at me, "So, you can color shift can you? I guess you're less human than I thought you were. So what are we plotting down here in the dungeon? Are we going to help my sister escape? Are you going to help her get back to those humans that were killing her with their drugs? I'll just drag her back here again. You humans are all the same. I don't know why my mother puts up with you."

"We're not plotting anything. Why don't you just go away?" I said angrily. "Not all humans are bad. My mother is helping your sister. She's doing more than you ever did for her. You're a selfish brat. Did you even know or care that your sister was lonely, that she wanted your attention? She craved your parents' attention and the only one that got any attention was you."

"Hey, don't blame me for the mistakes she made. She had a perfect life here in the palace. She could have anything she wanted, and what did she do? She threw her life away to be with you stinking humans," Andrew sneered at me.

"Stop it! Andrew, she's right! When did you ever make time for me? When did we ever do anything together? I would see the children of the staff playing together, but you would have nothing to do with me. Andrew, we've never been close, but I didn't think you hated me," Elizabeth said softly with tears in her eyes as she walked over to her brother. He looked away from me to look at her.

"I don't hate you. I don't particularly like you, but I don't hate you. When you were born, I knew I'd have to share my parents' time with you. I did everything I could to have them pay attention to me. Since I was the first born and the heir to the throne, it wasn't hard to make Father pay attention to me. You were never anything to me, except some kind of competition.

"I hated it that you were born. Now, I hate your manipulating and lies. I hate the embarrassment you've made of yourself with humans. I hate the way you've contaminated yourself with human drugs. I hate having to drag you back here. But, I don't hate you," he said looking down his nose at his sister.

Elizabeth looked down for a moment, and then she looked up at her brother. She stood up straight and said, "I think I know the stories you've heard. They're probably true. I'm not the person you believe me to be. I've been selfish, but you are too! I may have been an inconvenience before, but maybe we could be friends? Have you ever thought about what it would be like to have me for a friend?

"Valerie told me that sometimes things seem bad because of the person's belief in what things mean. You saw me as an inconvenience or competition. But, if you tried, couldn't you see me as a friend and a sister? You don't have any friends, either. No friends that are your equal, anyway. Maybe after all of these years, we could actually get to know one another. I know I'm not the same person I was a month ago. Instead of hating me or wanting me out of the way, maybe we can help each other be better leaders for our people. Can you help me?" Elizabeth asked softly. "Father wants me dead. He said so. I don't want to die. No matter how bad the things are that I've done, have they been bad enough to warrant my death?"

You could have heard a pin drop, the room got so quiet. I couldn't even hear people breathe. Could Andrew learn to like his sister after all of these years? He has spent his entire life thinking of her as an annoyance. Was there a chance for them to become friends? Andrew and Elizabeth stared at each other.

Andrew walked closer to her. He put his finger under her chin and raised her face so that he could look her in the eye. "I have never thought of having you for a friend. Yet, as I think of the idea, I wish I would have thought of this before you started sneaking out to do those drugs. You're filthy, and yet, I've never seen you look more beautiful. I can see your eyes are clear. I haven't seen your eyes clear of those horrible drugs for a long time. After all of these years, is that possible? Do you think you can stay away from those horrible substances? Can you stay away from those horrible humans? How can I trust you?

"I feel something for you. I've always considered it a kind of contempt. But, as I think about it, I really don't want you dead," Andrew said.

Elizabeth reached up to touch Andrew's face. "I need you. I never thought I would ever need anyone. I never realized how lonely I was until the fog of the addiction started clearing. When Valerie first started coming here, she had to sit outside my cell because I'd attack her. I didn't want her help. I only wanted out of here to get more cocaine. I was out of my mind. I've had a lot of time to think in the last couple of weeks.

"Within the last couple of days I realized I was acting irrationally and irresponsibly. I learned that I'm in charge of my behaviors, good and bad. Valerie taught me that. She also taught me that I'm in charge of how I think. I want to think good thoughts. I want to do good things. I'm going to stop lying. I want to be your friend. I want you to love me.

"We know that wood nymphs heal really quickly. I think that the drugs have all been eliminated, and I can work on healing both my body and my mind. Will you help me? After all of these years, do you think you could accept me as your sister and your friend?"

116

Andrew stared into his sister's eyes. No one said a word. It appeared he was trying to look into his sister's soul. Elizabeth did not move or blink.

"I believe you're sincere. I want to believe you. But, how do I know to trust you? You've lied so many times in the past couple of years. I had no idea you wanted to be my friend. I thought you only wanted to make my life miserable," Andrew said softly.

"I wasn't trying to make you miserable. I just wanted your attention. As far as building up trust, let's start with something small. The first thing to do is to help me get a shower and clean clothes. I know I've run away before when going to the shower. I promise not to do that. I need to look good before I can face anyone else. But, how will I get out of here?" Elizabeth asked her brother.

"We can sneak you out of here," I said. "You can color shift and leave your clothes here. You would be naked, but no one would see you. When we get to my room, you can shower and put on some of my clothes. We're about the same size."

"No. There'll be no more sneaking around here. We'll walk out of here, fully dressed," Mom said shaking her head. "I think it's time for you to walk out of here with your head held high. You made a mistake and you should be forgiven. We'll avoid the main areas, but we won't sneak anywhere."

I knew my mother was talking about the last time that Elizabeth was supposed to go to dinner with her family a day or so after we had arrived here. She had embarrassed me, her parents, and everyone else!

"If we do this, will you stay with me? I'll need your support. I want to go to dinner with the family tonight," Elizabeth asked Andrew tearfully. She looked so nervous. I didn't believe anyone could doubt her sincerity. Her emotions were fluctuating between hope and despair.

He looked at her and sighed, "Yes, but if you run off, I'll kill you myself."

"Thank you, brother!" Elizabeth said and wrapped her arms around his neck. "I promise not to let you down. I'll show you that I can be trusted."

"Let go of me. You stink," Andrew said as he gently pulled her arms from around his neck. He smiled as he did it. "Hug me when you smell better."

"I will, I promise!" Elizabeth said excitedly. "We can do this! We'll show our mother and father and everyone else that I can behave like a princess. I'm afraid, but with all of you to help me, I can make this happen."

"We need to do is to get Elizabeth cleaned up. Then, we'll bring her down for dinner," My mother said to everyone. Then she looked at Elizabeth. "The first time anyone else sees you, you can't be alone. You'll need to be on your best behavior, and stay by me. We don't want you anywhere by yourself."

"I don't think we should be seen in our color-shifting clothes, Mom," I said. Would he tell the king and queen that we had been in the dungeon in color shifting clothes? "No one should know that we were down here."

Andrew looked at me while I was talking. He sighed. "You're right. I won't tell anyone you were here, at least not yet, little wood nymph hybrid," he said with a wink. "You go run off to your rooms. I'll bring Elizabeth there. Maybe there's more to humans than illegal substances and pollution."

What was with the wink? "Thank you. With your help, we can get Elizabeth back into the palace," I said as I stood up to go over by Forrest.

"Speaking of getting Elizabeth cleaned and showered, I like your idea of having her go to your rooms," Andrew said to me as he reached for his sister's hand. "I'll escort your mother and Elizabeth there. It doesn't matter if I have color shifting clothes on. This is my palace. You all color shift and get out of here. I'll handle any problems that come along. I'll meet you there."

I looked up at Forrest. He nodded. We got into the same line that we used coming down the stairs. I looked at my mom and waved. She waved back. "I'll see you in a few minutes, Mom!" I said and then I saw that Elm and Olivia had shifted. I concentrated on my surroundings and shifted, too. I heard my mom's intake of breath when I disappeared. "I love you!" I said as we filed out of the door.

We saw no one in the palace as we made our way to our rooms. Ben was standing in the hallway when we got to our floor. We took the stairs so as not to accidently run into someone on the elevator. I looked around when we got to our floor and saw that there was no one in sight. I let go of Ash's and Forrest's hands and shifted so that Ben could see my face and hands.

"Laurel! Am I glad to see you! You guys have been gone a long time!" He called to me as he ran to meet me. "What happened? Did you find your mom?"

"We did, Dad. Come on into my room. We can talk there," I said as I put my hand on the panel by my door. I was glad to see that my room was empty. We had about an hour or so before Moss would come to help get me ready for dinner. I thought about how surprised she was going to be when she saw that Elizabeth was with me in my room.

"Yes, dad, we found the dungeon. We also found Mom and Elizabeth. Elizabeth believes she's the one her father wants to kill. She's has been doing some ah, not good things lately, and has really pissed off her father" I said, hoping I wasn't saying too much. "She's been in the dungeon since that night she made the scene in the ballroom a couple of weeks ago. Mom's been with her."

"Valerie?" My dad asked, and then I heard a knock at the door and went to answer it. Mom came in, followed by Elizabeth and then Andrew. It was a good thing that these suites were large. I had a lot of people in my room. Just as I turned to shut the door, Willow came in. She ran over to Elm.

"Elm! Where have you been? Ben wasn't good company. He only wanted to stand out in the hallway and wait for you all. Now I see people going into Laurel's room, but no one came for me?" Willow whined as she took her husband's hand.

"Not now, dear. We have more pressing issues." Elm looked toward Mom.

Willow's opened wide and she covered her mouth. "The princess and prince!" She squeaked and curtsied.

I didn't even think about giving Andrew a curtsy when he surprised us in the dungeon. I wondered belatedly if I should have.

"My dear, you look awful!" Willow blurted out to Elizabeth. "What happened?"

"It's a long story that can wait until later." Elizabeth gave a self-deprecating laugh. "Laurel, can you get me a nice dress for dinner and perhaps some under clothes? I'd like to look my best when seeing my parents for the first time since, well, in a long time. At least it'as been a long time since I have seen them with a clear head."

I knew it hadn't been that long a time, or had it? I knew Elizabeth had been in the dungeon for a couple of weeks. How often did one or both parents visit her? If they had been to visit her, what kind of mental shape was Elizabeth in? I had heard stories of people having a hard time getting over addictions to drugs. Elizabeth said she had tried to attack my mother. Did she try to attack her mother, too?

"Come with me. Moss keeps me well stocked with towels and toiletries," I said showing Elizabeth into my bathroom. "I have a nice tan gown that isn't too flashy, and would look great with your skin color." I pulled the dress out. "It has matching shoes, too. Do you like it?"

The dress was really pretty. It was not of the style and quality Elizabeth was used to, but it was a whole lot better than the rag she'd been wearing in the dungeon.

"Yes. That's fine," Elizabeth replied and took the dress and shoes with her into the bathroom. A minute or so later, I heard the water running.

"There is no way she can get out of there, is there?" I asked. "She won't try to run now, will she?"

"Unless she could find a way to go down the drain, I don't think she can get out of the bathroom. If she tries to color shift and sneak out, we'll still see the bathroom door open. So, no, I don't think she can get out of the bathroom. But, just the same, I'll stay here until she comes out," Prince Andrew said as he sat on my couch.

"I need a shower, too. Ben and I need to go and get ready for dinner. Laurel, wait here for me and Ben. I want us all to go down to dinner, together. We can be a united front for Elizabeth. She could use friends right now. It'll be frightening for her to see her father," Mom said as she and Ben headed for my door.

"I'm going to go change for dinner, too. Come on, Forrest, let's go change so that we can get back here," Olivia said as she headed for the door to leave.

In moments, everyone had left except Prince Andrew, Ash, and me. I wondered if the princess would need assistance getting dressed. She was used to people catering to her every need. Should I go help her when the shower turned off? As I was thinking these thoughts, I heard a quick knock at my door and then it opened. Moss stepped into my room.

CHAPTER 15

ELIZABETH FACES HER FEARS AND HER FATHER

G ood afternoon, Miss Laurel. I brought you up a snack. I hope you don't
mind," Moss stated as she set down a tray with a variety of cheeses,
grapes, and small strawberries on it. She also had a pitcher of iced tea.
Then she saw Prince Andrew. "Oh, my!" she gasped and went into a deep curtsy.

"Please stand up. Moss is your name, isn't it?" the prince asked dryly.

Moss stayed in the curtsy with her head down. "Yes! Your highness! How
may I serve you?"

"Stand up. Quit gawking at me and take care of our guest," Prince Andrew
stated impatiently. "You're not here to take care of me."

"Yes, your highness," Moss whispered and then looked to me. "How can I
serve you, Miss Laurel?"

It looked to me like Moss did not have much to do with the royalty. She
seemed extremely nervous.

"Thank you for the snack. Um, Moss, we have a guest in my bathroom. I'd
like you to help her get dressed for dinner, also," I said as Ash, got up to leave. Ash
took some cheese from the tray on his way out. I walked him to the door.

"Stay safe. I love you, and I'll be back soon," Ash said to me as he kissed my
cheek just before he walked out of the door.

After the door closed, the prince sat on my couch in a relaxed manner. "I
don't think he likes me very much," the prince murmured, reaching for cheese.

"You haven't exactly been welcoming," I replied sitting across from him. We
must have looked a sight with our color shifting clothes on. The only thing that
was visible was our hands and our heads.

"Should I be?" the prince asked. "Pour me some iced tea, please," he said.

"Yes, your highness," Moss whispered and poured us each a glass of tea.
"Who is your guest, may I ask?" she asked as she handed me my glass.

"It is Princess Elizabeth," I said and had to quick grab my glass before she
dropped it.

"Princess Elizabeth? Isn't she, ah . . ." Moss said at a loss for words. She
looked over at the prince, but he did not say anything.

"Princess Elizabeth is in my bathroom and will need her hair fixed when she
gets out of the shower. No one knows that she is here. We want to keep it that way.
Right, Moss?" I asked while giving her a pointed look.

"Yes, Miss Laurel. I'll do as you ask, although I've never had the privilege of working with the princess's hair before," Moss said giving me a nervous look.

"I'm sure you'll do just fine," I said taking a sip of my tea. "She needs to be beautiful, tonight."

"Yes, I'm sure she does," Moss said quietly as she straightened things in the room that did not need straightening.

I wondered what Moss meant by that comment. What did she know? Did I dare ask her any questions with the prince sitting on my couch listening to every word? We sat quietly for a few minutes, just listening to the shower run. After I thought Elizabeth probably had used up every gallon of hot water in the palace, I finally heard the shower turn off. Andrew must have noticed too, as he stared at the bathroom door. A couple of minutes later, the door opened, and Elizabeth was standing there with wet hair and my robe on.

"I need some help," she said softly. "I don't usually dress myself, except for stretch pants and hoodies. I don't think I'll be wearing those anymore."

"Your highness, please allow me to help you! While Laurel takes her shower, we can use her bedroom to dress you and get your hair done, if that's all right with you and Miss Laurel?" Moss asked as I handed her the clothes I had picked out for the princess.

"Yes, that'd be great, don't you agree, your highness?" I asked as I walked past them and into the bathroom.

"Yes, that would be fine," Elizabeth said as she started to follow Moss into my bedroom.

"I need to get ready, too. I'll be back in just a few minutes. You'll be fine while I'm gone? You won't go anywhere?" Prince Andrew asked as he stood up.

"Yes, Andrew. I'm not going anywhere, except to that vanity seat so that Laurel's servant can do my hair. Is that acceptable?" Elizabeth asked with a hurt look.

Andrew took a deep breath. "Elizabeth, trust needs to be earned. I'm placing my trust in you now. Please don't let me down," He said as he walked to the door. He turned to face Elizabeth when he got there.

"I won't!" Elizabeth said with conviction. "I'll be here when you get back." She headed into the bedroom behind Moss.

"Okay," Andrew said and then he was gone.

I didn't think that there would be enough hot water for me to take a shower. I kept my shower short. I hoped that Elizabeth wouldn't do something to Moss, or try to take off, but I wasn't sure how in control Elizabeth was. She had admitted she was skilled in manipulation. Did the drugs still have control over her thought processes or were a couple of weeks in the dungeon enough time to rid her body and mind of the immediacy of the addiction?

I opened the closet in my bathroom and took out another robe. I walked into my bedroom a little afraid of what I would or would not find in there. My fears were groundless. Elizabeth was sitting at my vanity and Moss was putting the finishing touches on her hair. While her hair did not have the natural luster of most wood nymphs hair, Moss was able to spray some shine on it to make her hair look healthy. It was going to be awhile before all of the residual side effects from the cocaine were eliminated from her body.

"Do I look acceptable?" she asked me when she saw me in the mirror.

"You look awesome. Moss does an excellent job on my hair, and she did just did a great job on yours," I said as I opened my closet to pick out what I was going to wear. Moss usually did this, but I figured that Elizabeth needed her more than I did at that moment.

Elizabeth looked at her reflection in the mirror and then looked at Moss and said, "I don't think that my hair has ever looked lovelier. I think I'd like you for my personal servant after Laurel leaves, would that be all right with you?"

"Oh, my! It would be my honor to be your personal maid!" Moss said with a huge smile. "I never thought I'd be able to be a servant to any of the royal court, but to be the personal maid to the princess! Oh, my!"

"Well, that's fine, then. You take care of Laurel while she is here, and then you'll transfer your things to the royal staff quarters," Elizabeth said looking at me and smiling.

This was the happiest I had ever seen her. When I thought about it, I hadn't seen her happy at all before this. What did she have to be happy about? She was a drug addicted princess with no friends and a family that was embarrassed by her. Would she think of me as her friend? I wasn't royalty, but I hoped that she would like me as a friend. She was needy now, but would she still like me after she was back in the good graces of her family? Only time would tell.

I smiled back at her and picked out a chocolate-colored dress. I wanted to look good, but I wanted the princess to look better. With her in a tan dress and me in a chocolate one, we would look good together.

Moss gave me a worried look as I pulled out the dress. "Don't worry, Moss. You take care of the princess. I can dress myself. I have done it my whole life," I said as I pulled underwear out of the drawers. Elizabeth really did look to be the same size as me. I handed her a bra and panties. "I hope these fit you, this is the only size I have."

"I'm sure everything will fit just fine," Elizabeth said as she put the underwear on her lap. She still had the robe on.

I wasn't sure if she didn't want to get dressed in front of me, but I knew I didn't want to get dressed in front of the princess. I liked my privacy when I got dressed. It was bad enough to have Moss watch me. "I'll give you your privacy to put on the clothes and get dressed in the bathroom," I said as I carried my things and went into the bathroom and shut the door. I hoped she didn't think I was being rude, but I really did prefer to get dressed alone.

I put on the underclothes and dress. I had taken my time to ensure that Moss had time to get the princess fully dressed. I came out of the bathroom and sat on the side of my bed to put on the shoes. Elizabeth was dressed and standing in front of the floor to ceiling mirror I had behind the closet door.

"This really is a nice dress. It isn't too ostentatious. I don't want to stand out too much, I just want to look good," Elizabeth said as she viewed herself from various angles. Moss bent down by her feet to put on the shoes. "Even the shoes fit perfectly! We could be sisters!" Elizabeth exclaimed happily as she did a whirl in front of the mirror.

I sat in my vanity chair, and within minutes, Moss had my hair up in an elaborate French twist and expertly applied cosmetics to my face. Elizabeth sat on my bed and watched. I didn't see Moss put any cosmetics on Elizabeth. She didn't need any.

"I know you can never be my real sister, but I feel like you could be family. I feel so close to your mom. In a way, I kind of wish she was my mom. I had never had anyone listen to me like your mom listens to me. She makes me feel like I have value. I like you, too. Just you being her daughter helps me feel good about you," Elizabeth said as she came over to me and held both of my hands in hers. "I'm sure we can be friends if I can just get through this evening."

I stood up when Moss nodded that I was finished. "We'll do that. You have friends now. Even Andrew looks like he's coming around. He's your brother. Maybe all he needed was a little mental nudge to realize he loved you all along," I said as I squeezed her hands gently.

I heard a knock. Moss went to go answer it. It was Andrew. He really did change and come back in record time. "Is she still here?" he asked Moss tentatively.

"Is who here?" I asked as Elizabeth and I walked out of my bedroom hand in hand. We looked good and I knew it. I also knew who he was referring to, but wanted to hear him say it.

"Elizabeth . . ." He said as his voice trailed off. "You look beautiful."

"Yes, she does, doesn't she?"

Andrew walked up to his sister.

"Thank you," Elizabeth said and blushed. I had never seen a wood nymph blush before. It was really kind of cute.

"I don't ever recall seeing you look this beautiful before. You look happy. I don't think I've ever seen you look happy before," Prince Andrew said as he stared at his sister.

"I have friends that care about me. That makes a big difference. I know that I have made mistakes, but I can be redeemed. Plus, I want to be happy. I guess I never thought about it before. Does that make sense?" Elizabeth said smiling.

"I guess I don't fully understand. But, you do look happy. Just seeing you smile makes me want to be happy. I never felt this way about you before," Andrew said with a grin.

"I guess it's because I'm not manipulating anyone. I'm being true to myself. Do you think maybe that makes a difference?" Elizabeth said as she gave her brother a hug.

"Yes, I think it does," Andrew replied, hugging her back.

I smiled sadly. While this was really nice to see, I thought of all of the wasted years Elizabeth and Andrew had between them, not knowing or feeling love. I didn't get the feeling their parents demonstrated much love. Mom had shown me love every day of my life. I had no doubt I was loved. I knew Ben loved me, too. I knew I was loved by Forrest and Olivia. Ash loved me. I couldn't imagine what it must have been like for Elizabeth to grow up not feeling loved from the people closest to her.

I heard the knock at my door, and when Moss opened the door I saw it was Ash. He looked better than Andrew in his tuxedo. I walked over to him and put my arms around him and whispered, "It looks as if the royal brother and sister are learning to appreciate each other." Ash looked over my shoulder at Elizabeth and Andrew to see that they were in a deep conversation with each other. I guess that they had a whole lifetime of things to talk about.

Within minutes, everyone was in my room again. It looked like all of the women in my family took extra care with their dresses and makeup. Mom had on a plum-colored gown with a high neck, long sleeves, and pearls. Olivia had on a forest-green flowing dress that shimmered when she walked. Willow had on an off-white gown with a lacy brown overdress. She wore tiger eye jewelry. All of the men were wearing their tuxedos. We were going to be a united front against the king and no one knew how that was going to go over.

"Are we ready to present Elizabeth to her parents?" I asked.

"Let's do it!" Andrew said as he held out his arm for his sister.

I saw Elizabeth give Andrew a big smile as she placed her hand on his arm. "Thank you," she said softly. "This means a lot to me! I'm scared, but if you're with me, I know I can get through this."

"Let's be sure we all stay together!" Forrest called out from his place by the door. We had taken our time about leaving my room. We wanted to be sure that the king and queen were in the reception hall before we got there. They always arrived at exactly the same time, and we were a few minutes after that time when we left my room.

Moss opened the door and we all filed out into the hall. "Good luck," she whispered.

I smiled back at Moss, "Think positively. We'll be fine."

We walked down to the elevator. It was a good thing that these were large elevators, so that we all could fit in as we went down to the main floor. I invited Moss to join us in the elevator. I was sure she didn't know everything that was going on, but she knew where Elizabeth had been for the last few weeks.

When we got off of the elevator, we joined other groups of nymphs heading for the reception room where drinks were to be served before dinner. At first, many of the groups would take a quick look at us, and then turned away. However, a few of them noticed Andrew and Elizabeth walking in the midst of our group and bowed. Andrew walked sedately with his head up proudly. Elizabeth smiled at him and held her head proudly as well. My emotions were running the gambit from feeling like we were going to the guillotine to elation that everything was going to work out fine. I just wished I knew which feeling was going to come true.

Before we got to the door to the reception room, I called Moss over to me. "Moss, have the guards at the door announce the prince and princess." I watched as she ran in front of us to tell the guards to have them announced.

Mom and I went over to the royal siblings. "It's show time. Remember, Elizabeth, this is your destiny. You were born to be here. It does not matter what happened before, what matters is what happens now. Act like you belong in there, and the people will treat you like you belong there as well," My mom said as she gave Elizabeth a hug.

"Yes," Olivia said as she came over to stand by us. "People will treat you in accordance with the way you act. If you act nervous or scared, people will pick up on that and treat you in a manner not befitting a princess. If you act like a princess, people will treat you like one."

"I can do this." That was the last thing that I heard Elizabeth say as she walked into the reception room with her head held high, her hand on her brother's arm.

Was she saying that to us or to herself?

CHAPTER 16
A REUNION

"Presenting Prince Andrew and Princess Elizabeth," I heard the caller at the door exclaim to the assembled group. After the announcement there was a silence so deep I felt like I was listening to a vacuum. If not for the fact that I was looking into the room and could see about forty people in there, I would have thought the room was empty.

I realized that everyone was just standing around. I grabbed Ash's hand and we rushed over to the prince and princess after they had been presented. I saw that a few people had bowed down. Most of the wood nymphs just stared. Did everyone know that Elizabeth had been in the dungeon? I wanted to show support. I had no idea what was going to happen. Mom, Ben, and the rest came over to us, too. We created a semi-circle around them. "We're going to be fine," I said to Elizabeth.

"I sure hope so. Here come my parents. My father doesn't look happy," Elizabeth replied.

I watched as the king and queen walked towards us. The queen look puzzled, but the king looked really angry. He was not even trying to hide it.

When the king and queen came near, the queen came up to Elizabeth and brushed her lips near her cheek and said, "You look lovely, my dear, but what are you doing here?" The king said nothing at all.

Elizabeth gave her mother a gracious smile and replied, "I've come to dinner, Mother. I felt that it was time I was presented to the guests in an appropriate manner. Besides, this is where I belong." Then in a quieter voice, that only those of us right next to her heard, "I promise I won't embarrass you. I have learned my lesson, and with the help I have gotten from Valerie, I know my position in this palace."

"What position would that be?" the king asked just as quietly, but there was a threat in his voice.

I was proud of the way that Elizabeth was handling herself. She stood straight and faced her parents in a direct manner.

"As your loyal and dutiful daughter, I'll take my place as a respectable member of the royal family," Elizabeth whispered to her father and leaned forward to kiss his cheek.

He allowed her to come close to him. "It may be too late for that. You've embarrassed this family enough," the king whispered back. He glared at Elizabeth and then turned to his son. "Andrew, what is the meaning of this?"

Andrew was very calm and put his left hand over Elizabeth's hand that was still on his right arm. I wondered if he thought she was going to try to run away. "I think Elizabeth has changed. I hate to admit it, but I think the counseling she received from the human woman has done her some good. It's possible I've been wrong about the humans, that I have offered bad advice," Andrew replied calmly, patting Elizabeth's hand.

I wondered what that meant. I looked at Ash and he just shrugged.

The moment was getting awkward. I wanted to say something, but what? Would they consider me rude if I said something about Elizabeth? What could I say? There was no way that I could tell the king and queen that I had spent the afternoon in the dungeon with his daughter.

The queen looked at each of us and then said to her daughter, "I'll set a place for you next to me at dinner." Then the queen looked at my mother. "I want you on the other side of me in your usual place. I think we need to talk." The queen had no expression. You'd think she was talking about the weather. But, I could feel her emotions. She was excited, worried, shocked—she was feeling a lot of different emotions.

"Please be sure to have me seated next to my sister. I'd also like the humans grouped near us. You'd do that for me, wouldn't you, Mother?" Andrew asked his mother. His mother gave him a long look.

"Of course, dear. If that's what you would like," the queen replied. She turned to a servant hovering nearby and asked to have Andrew's request honored.

It looked like things were going to turn out all right. The king didn't pull out a sword or a gun and kill me or his daughter in front of everyone. We started walking into the room. Moss came over to me and asked me what I would like to drink, and the other servants took drink orders. I heard a scuffle by the door we had just come in. I turned to see what was going on.

Ten large guards with swords drawn were walking through the doorway. Ben, Forrest, Elm, and Ash tried to surround me and Elizabeth.

"What is the meaning of this?" Andrew asked coldly. I think he knew that there was a death warrant out on someone, but whom? Was it me or Elizabeth and were Aron and his goons going to try to kill me or Elizabeth here and now?

"You need to come with me," Aron stated to Elizabeth in a quiet voice. "Now." I watched her face pale beneath her fair complexion.

"No," Elizabeth whispered. She was terrified. Andrew held her arm.

I looked over at the king. He looked like he was going to say something, when I heard Andrew speak up. "She is going nowhere," Andrew snapped at Aron. "You overstep your boundaries."

Aron grabbed Elizabeth's arm. Even though he moved quickly, I noticed he wasn't being rough with her. "Elizabeth is coming with me."

Something about Aron's emotions. I got it. Concern. He was trying to save the princess! I thought, *You were never going to kill her. You want to save her.*

Forrest and Andrew tried to stand in his way, and I said, "No, let him take her. We'll follow."

Forrest opened his mouth like he was going to say something. I spoke before he could and put my hand on his arm, "This may be a good thing."

Aron was starting to turn away to leave with Elizabeth. Andrew let go of his sister's arm and stepped in front of Aron. "You're not taking my sister anywhere!"

"You dumb selfish twit!" Aron snarled at Andrew. "I'm trying to save her life! Your father wants her dead!" Aron turned and pulled Elizabeth out of the door.

Andrew stepped to the other side of Elizabeth and took her arm again and said to Aron, "I want to know what you are talking about."

Aron and Elizabeth left with Andrew following. Aron had a gentle, but firm grip on Elizabeth's arm.

I looked behind us, and I saw that the king and queen had followed us out of the room. At the door, the king announced to the assembled people, "Please wait here. There's no alarm, we will return shortly."

Aron and his guards led us down to the library where I had seen and heard the king tell Aron to kill someone. Aron and Elizabeth went in first, followed by me, Ash, Forrest, my mom, Ben, the king and queen, and then Ash's parents. Elm was almost dragging Willow into the room. I heard her say, "No, we don't need to be in there with them. He is angry!"

"Yes, that's why we must be there," Elm said firmly and pushed his wife the rest of the way into the room and shut the door behind them.

"What's the meaning of this?" the king roared once the library door was closed. "How dare you interrupt my gathering!"

"I can't allow the murder of your daughter. And it would be murder. It's true I've sworn an oath to you. I swore to protect the royal family. She's part of the royal family. I can't kill her and I can't let you kill her," Aron said to the king.

Aron walked Elizabeth over to a couch. Elizabeth sat down. She was so pale, I thought she was going to faint. She was trembling. Mom and I sat on each side of her. We each took a hand. She gripped my hand tightly. She was terrified. After all that she had gone through, now she had to deal with this!

Aron looked down at Elizabeth on the couch. "I would color shift and enter the room when another guard or your human counselor went through the door. I've watched you suffer in your cell. I've watched you scream in agony. No one knew I was there. I've also watched your rehabilitation. I watched you get better. I saw the spark of light grow in your eyes again. I saw that they were clear of the pain and the drugs.

"I think that because you have experienced human misery, you've become very wise because of it. You're not the spoiled, pampered princess anymore. I believe that you are now a benefit to the wood nymph world."

While I watched Aron talk to the princess, I couldn't believe the emotions I was feeling from him. He was in love with her! I watched the king look over at the other guards. His best guards. How would he handle this situation?

Aron reached down to gently touch the princess's face. There was silence in the room as I watched the tableau. Ash stood next to me, Ben was next to my mom on the other side of the couch. Forrest, Elm, Olivia, and Willow stood behind us. Aron stood in front of Elizabeth. Andrew was on Aron's right side and the king and queen were on Aron's left side.

"I have to think about this. Have you really been watching my daughter transform from a drug-addicted monster to a proper royal princess?" the king asked Aron.

Aron looked at the king and nodded. "I knew that things were bad. I knew you would have to do something about her behavior and could not keep your daughter locked up in a dungeon forever. I don't know what would have happened if the human counselor hadn't come along. I really believe she saved your daughter's life."

"Valerie. My wife's name is Valerie," Ben stated with his hand on Mom's shoulder. "She's not just a human."

Aron looked at Ben and nodded as he said, "No, she is not just any human. She's a counselor. I had no idea what a counselor did until I watched . . ." He paused a moment, "Valerie talk with Elizabeth. That's all she did. Talk. But, she was always calm and everything she said made sense."

Elizabeth put her hands over her eyes and started crying softly. "I'm so sorry for everything I've put everyone through. I've been selfish, but I've also been lonely." She put her hands down and Andrew handed her a handkerchief. She gently dabbed at her eyes and then looked at the king and said softly, "I didn't realize the damage I was doing to myself and everyone around me. Can you please forgive me? I'm truly sorry for everything I put you and everyone else through."

"Oh, my dear child," the queen said as she came over to stand in front of Elizabeth. She reached down for Elizabeth's hands and pulled her to her feet. She gave her a big hug. "I had no idea you were so unhappy before you started using the drugs. I was so busy and I didn't take time with you to know that. I had no idea why you did what you did, and I didn't know how to deal with it after you started running away."

"I too, should have paid more attention. I paid more attention to my son, but neglected my daughter. For that, I'm sorry," King Cornelius said with a sigh. He also hugged his daughter.

I stood up and walked over to Ash and whispered, "Maybe we should let the royal family have some peace and enjoy their family reunion."

The king looked at me. "You. If not for you, we would have never been to Wisconsin. If not for you, we would have never known what a counselor was."

The king then looked over at my mother and said with feeling, "You've brought my family back together. I had no idea how to handle the situation and I was willing to murder my own daughter in my ignorance. But you, you saved her from her demons. You made my family whole again. For that I'll always be grateful. If there's anything I can ever do for you, all you need is ask. If I can do it, I will."

My mother smiled graciously and gave a slight bow. When she stood straight again, she looked at the king and said, "It's almost time for us to go home. You had said that we would be here for a month and a month is almost up. I've taken a leave of absence from my job, and I have to go back. There are others I need to help."

"A week from today you shall all have your flight home. I have learned a lot about humans and they're not the polluting monsters I thought they were," King Cornelius stated and then looked at me. "I see how much you love your young wood nymph and that you have bonded. I agree to the match. However, I must insist on an invitation to the wedding."

I didn't expect that! I was staring at the king at a loss for words when I heard Ash speak.

"Thank you, your highness," Ash replied with a bow. "We are grateful for your permission."

For a moment we all stood there grinning like fools. I wanted to go and hug the king, but I knew that would be inappropriate. I turned and hugged Ash and he fiercely hugged me back. Everything was going to be all right! We all started talking about the wedding and the palace and what we would do when we got home when the king held his hand up for silence. He looked over at Aron.

"Aron, you have disobeyed a direct order. If you had been any other guard or if this had been any other situation, I would levie some kind of punishment. But, you were right. I was going to kill my own daughter. For that I'm deeply ashamed. I can see why you pulled her out of the reception room. However, even though you

131

are a royal prince of the Moors, you promised me fidelity, and I expect you to obey me in my orders from now on. At least until we get your own kingdom reestablished," King Cornelius stated sternly.

All of the happy emotions in the room were so intense that I was getting dizzy.

Aron was royalty? The Moors were royalty? I had to find out more about this! But not right now. As curious as I was, I wasn't feeling very well at that moment.

"Let us go and rejoice in the princess's recovery," the king said with a big smile. He took the queen's hand in his and gave it a quick kiss and a smile as they left the library first.

Aron reached for Elizabeth's hand, and she smiled as she took it. "Tonight, instead of being my father's guard, will you be my prince?"

"It would be my honor," Aron replied with a deep bow.

I looked at Andrew's face. I could sense he was feeling alone. Elizabeth must have noticed because she used her free hand to take Andrew's hand. "You've been the best brother I could have asked for this evening. I look forward to a wonderful friendship with you. I'll always be grateful that you stood up for me tonight," she said as Andrew stood up.

Andrew smiled at his sister as he held one hand and Aron took the other. "I think I like the idea of you being my friend and sister."

Andrew, Elizabeth, and Aron walked out together. Mom and Ben followed, and then Olivia, Forrest, and Ash's parents left the room.

I could feel my face perspiring and took a deep breath. Ash noticed. "Are you okay?" He asked me. He took his handkerchief out of his pocket and dabbed the sweat on my forehead.

"Yeah, I'm fine. It's just a bit much, feeling everyone's jubilant emotions," I said as we followed everyone out of the room.

As we left, I heard the king call to one of the servants to set up the ballroom and band for dancing tonight.

I heard Aron tell Elizabeth, "I'm yours to command."

I heard Elizabeth giggle and Andrew give a fake sarcastic sigh and smile. Even though I didn't feel very good, I still had to smile at the turn of events.

CHAPTER 17
DANCING

Ash and I took our time going back to the reception room. I found a restroom on the way and went in to put a damp cloth to my face. I guess the relief at knowing we were going to live was making me feel faint.

"Do you feel better?" Ash asked. Everyone else was already in the reception room. The happiness in the room was all a bit much. It was a good thing, but too much of even a good thing can be too much.

"Not really. Let's find a quiet place to sit for a minute," I said feeling the blood rush to my head.

We found a bench in the hallway outside of the reception room door. We could hear all of the people inside laughing and talking, but it was a dull roar. Ash and I could talk without raising our voices.

He reached over held his hand out to me and I put my index finger against his. I saw a little flash of light at our touch and I felt a soothing feeling wash over me. I lost a lot of the sick feeling that I had been having.

"Is that a healing touch?" I asked with a smile. I really did feel a lot better.

"I don't know. When I touched your finger with mine, I could feel your nausea. Then the feeling went away. Are you better now?" he asked.

"Yes, a lot better. I didn't know that wood nymphs had a healing touch as ability," I said as I stood up.

"Me, either," Ash replied with a shake of his head. "Is this a link because we are bonded? The other day I wanted to give you my soul. Maybe I created a stronger connection between us."

"Maybe. All of this wood nymph ability stuff is still pretty new to me," I said as we arrived at the reception room.

Moss saw us walk in and brought me a glass of nectar. Ash's servant brought him a beverage. As I sipped my drink, I looked around. I'd never seen everyone look so happy. And I thought I saw a slight glow around Elizabeth. She was smiling and laughing. Aron and Andrew were with her. I looked around and saw the king and queen talking to Mom and Ben. They were smiling and laughing, too. Every now and then, I'd see the king look toward Elizabeth and shake his head as he smiled.

"Let's go talk to Elizabeth," I said to Ash as I started walking towards her. As we got closer, we could hear their conversation.

"Aron, tell me more about where you come from," I heard Elizabeth ask. "I've known you all my life. I knew you were a prince, but not why you served my father."

Aron looked fondly at Elizabeth and replied, "I'm a Moor. We're from Africa. Centuries ago, we were the strongest warriors in the world. Shakespeare's *Othello* is about a Moor general. You've heard of the Spanish Moors? They were my people. We spread out from Africa over one-thousand years ago. But, in some of the Middle Eastern countries, we came across a tribe of evil wood nymphs. Unless you believed what they believed, you couldn't be their friend. They would pretend to be friends to kill us. We couldn't believe that one wood nymph culture would kill another and we trusted them. They insinuated themselves into our society and then slaughtered us in our sleep."

Aron looked across the room at King Cornelius. He sighed and said, "King Cornelius' grandfather sent a contingent of his best guards to the Middle Eastern wood nymphs and slaughtered enough of them to rearrange their thinking about other cultures. We live in peace now."

"How awful! I know humans have had wars on and off forever, but I didn't know wood nymphs did, too!" Elizabeth said in a shocked voice.

"There have been battles and wars with other species, too," Ash said softly. "In North America, at least in Wisconsin, Michigan, and Minnesota, there were the wood nymph/water sprite wars that took place a couple of hundred years ago. While no one really won the war that I know of, we have had a truce for a long time. The Native Americans in the area helped us. They're mostly human."

"I had no idea that war went beyond humans! There really is a lot I have to learn," Elizabeth said thoughtfully as she looked at Ash. Then she looked back at Aron.

"I'll help you, if you like. I can help teach you the wood nymph histories," Aron said as he brushed his hand along Elizabeth's face.

"I'd like that," she replied, looking at him with adoration.

"There are a lot of Moors left, but many are scattered in different parts of the world. They don't realize their powerful history. There are human Moors, too. I'm the last prince of the Moor wood nymphs. I have a father who is a king, and he's trying to gather our people together to regain our rightful place in our home-land of Africa. In the meanwhile, my father thought it would be best for me to learn royal protocol from the king of the wood nymphs and sent me here. Since I am from a powerful warrior society, your father decided to make me part of his royal guard."

"How interesting!" I said. "Does that mean I should call you Prince Aron?"

"Well, that would be my proper title, but no, you can just call me Aron. You are almost family," he said to me with a smile.

"I don't think you should be a guard anymore. I think you should learn more about being a royal and less like a guard," Andrew said thoughtfully.

"I agree! You should be living like a royal prince. We need to talk to my father about moving you to the royal quarters Besides, then I can see you more often," Elizabeth said firmly.

"It would not matter if I was a guard or anything else in this palace. If you want to see me, I will make it happen," Aron replied.

I was looking around at all of the assembled people in the room. Everyone looked happy and I felt a lot of relief in the room. I think everyone was concerned for the princess. I would bet any money that everyone in this room knew that the princess had been living in a cell in the dungeon. I enjoyed reaching out my emotion sense and feeling what other people were feeling, when all of a sudden, I felt hatred. It was so incongruent with the rest of the people in the room. I tried to tune in to who it was. I saw a group of people in a corner talking. I noticed that the nurse was in with that group. Was the emotion I was feeling from her? Did she still hate me that much? I had felt her dislike and hate before, but this seemed intensified. She was looking over at us, but when she saw I was looking at her, she looked away. It was a shame that some people just could not get over their prejudices. I almost felt sorry for her. Here everyone was having a good time but because of her bias against humans, she was not having a good time. I sighed.

"What's with the sigh? Aren't you happy that the princess is back in the good graces of her family?" Ash asked with a smile.

"Of course! You know I am. It is just that I felt hatred coming from Dr. Elder's nurse over in the far corner. Why can't she get over her aversion to humans? If the king can accept us, why can't she?" I asked.

"I don't know. I would have thought that after all of this time that she would have realized that you were a good person," Ash replied as he kissed my cheek.

I was just thinking about the conversation and finishing my drink when we were called to dinner. As we filed in to our places at the table and waited for the king and queen to be seated, I looked around There were forty people at this table tonight. Almost everyone looked happy and relaxed. I had never seen so many wood nymphs smiling. I saw many of the wood nymphs come over and talk to my mother. Most of them had never given any of the humans in our group any notice or attention prior to tonight. I hadn't noticed the wood nymph royal courtiers pay any attention to the Wisconsin wood nymphs either, except for Olivia. Men, wood nymph or human, flocked to Olivia.

As I sat, I thought about all of the changes that had taken place in the last month. A lot had happened just today! It seemed that every day my life was changing in one way or another.

As I sat down, I thought about our situation. Tomorrow I was to go and see Dr. Elder for maybe the last time. The king had said that we could go home next week! The whole time that we had been here, all I could think about was how I didn't want to be here and how I wanted to go home. For the first time, I found that I liked it here. I liked Elizabeth, and Andrew wasn't the idiot I thought he was. I looked down the table at him and thought, well, maybe he was still a little bit of an idiot, but not as bad. The only person I would really not miss was that idiot nurse. I could not understand why Dr. Elder put up with her. Maybe she just had a bad attitude around me. Maybe she was nice around other people—well wood nymphs, anyway.

I had come to England, thinking I was probably coming to my death. Not just my death, but the death of everyone near and dear to me. I had been miserable on and off the last month thinking my new family and my immediate family were going to be put to death simply because I existed.

I looked over at Ben. He was seated next to one of the royal courtiers, and they were having a relaxed conversation. I would never have expected to see anything like that, even a week ago. A week ago, that same wood nymph attendant would not have given Ben the time of day.

I looked over at Olivia. As usual, there was some male wood nymph trying to get her attention, but tonight, she was so relaxed that she actually talked to the guy! Forrest was deep in conversation with Dr. Elder. Every now and then one or the other would look at me. I would just smile at them. I knew they were talking about me, but I didn't care. I knew Forrest would never say anything negative.

My mom and the queen were having a wonderful conversation, as they were both smiling and laughing. This was quite the demonstration. Not that the queen or my mother would laugh loudly, but laughing at a dinner table was new. That was not something I had ever seen before.

"Can you believe it? We no longer have to live our lives as if we're on trial. We no longer have to worry about a death sentence. We're actually going to go home," Ash said to me between the first and second courses.

"It's wonderful news, but it's almost hard to believe. I wondered if this day would ever come. For a while there, I was convinced we would never make it out of here alive," I said as I reached for my water glass.

"I knew we would get out of here. I could not believe anything else. I had just found you. I refused to believe our lives were over before we had really started living out our futures," Ash said confidently.

"A future. What a wonderful concept. Now I know that we'll have a future together, I can look forward to our long and happy life," I replied.

I sat next to Ash and either had my hand on his leg or he had his on mine . I'd smile at him and he'd smile at me. I was contemplating my future and having a wonderful time. The food was excellent. In no time, the dinner was over and we were being escorted to the ballroom.

When we entered the room, it was like being transported to a mythical kingdom. Lights floated in the air above us and looked like stars. The décor looked like a forest glen. The orchestra tuned up in the corner. Just like at the Copper Clan celebrations, I heard instruments I'd never heard before. Chairs and tables had been placed strategically around the ballroom with the center left clear for dancing.

Olivia, Forrest, Ash, me, Mom, and Ben sat at a table. Next to us sat the king, queen, Elizabeth, Andrew, and Aron. Mom sat next to the queen. She seemed to like to have my mom near her, and Mom didn't seem to mind.

After a couple of minutes, the music started. It sounded similar to a waltz. I watched as couples got up to dance. The king and queen were the first to go onto the dance floor. They flowed like liquid across the dance floor. They were so graceful dancing the intricate steps. I felt I was watching the best *Dancing with the Stars* routine, ever.

After watching awhile, I thought, *I can do this*. I had watched carefully. With a good partner, I should be able to do it. I looked at Ash and asked, "Can you do this dance?"

"Yes. I was taught how to dance at a young age. It's considered appropriate to teach the young nymphs the cultural dances early," he replied as he glanced over at the dancers on the floor.

"I think I can do the dance if you lead. Can we try?" I asked tentatively. I stood up.

"Sure, I'd like to dance with you. It's been awhile since I have danced this particular dance, but I think I can remember how to do it," he replied as he stood.

"Where are you going?" Mom asked as Ash and I walked past her.

"To dance," I said, smiling, as Ash took my hand to lead me to the dance floor.

I thought my feet might get caught up in my dress, or I'd trip over my feet, or some other dreadful thing, but it didn't. It seemed that I was a natural. Within moments, Ash was whirling me around the dance floor as if I had been doing this dance my whole life. It was faster than a regular waltz. I could feel my skirt swirl around as I danced. I could feel the rhythm and I felt the beat.

"You dance well, for a human," Andrew said with a smile as he danced close by with a beautiful courtier on his arm.

"Thanks. You dance pretty well for a nymph," I replied laughing. I knew he was just having fun and didn't mean anything mean by his comment. It was amazing how much things had changed in so short a time.

Ash and I danced to a lot of the numbers. However, I did dance with Forrest, and I even danced one dance with Andrew. I had not danced this much in my life. I didn't dance this much at prom.

I had no idea what time it was when I realized I was exhausted. I was happy, but really tired. "I need to sit down," I said as the band started the next song. "I'm getting tired. I guess I just don't have the stamina of a true wood nymph."

Ash escorted me back to the table. "No problem. My feet are tired, too."

I didn't believe that for a moment. He looked just as fresh as he had when he had returned to my room after cleaning up for dinner. He had not one hair out of place and not a bead of moisture on his forehead.

I felt wilted. It had been a good day, but now I was ready for the day to be over. "Do I look as tired as I feel?" I asked as we sat down.

Mom must have heard the question because she answered it, "No, honey, you look great. You also dance great. I had no idea you could dance that well. I know you had some classes as a little girl, but you looked like you've been dancing like that all of your life."

After we had sat down for a few minutes, Mom said to me, "You do look a little tired. The crowd is starting to thin. Why don't you go on to bed?"

I agreed that was a good idea. Ash and I left the ballroom after saying good night to everyone. The king and queen had left already and many of the older nymphs were gone. Andrew and his pretty courtier seemed to be having a good time as they said good night to us. Aron and Elizabeth seemed not to notice anyone but each other. When I said good night to them, they turned away from each other long enough to wish Ash and I a good night as well.

"This has been an eventful day. I doubt we'll ever have this much excitement in one day again," Ash said as we walked to the elevator.

"Yes, it's been quite a day," I replied.

Just as we got to the elevator, I felt light headed. I figured I had danced too much, or had too much excitement. I didn't realize I was weaving, until Ash grabbed me around the waist and said what sounded like from a distance, "Laurel, what's wrong?"

"I . . ." I started to say, and then I felt the floor come up to my face as I fainted.

138

CHAPTER 18
FUTURE LIFE

I was wringing wet with sweat when I woke up on a couch inside Dr. Elder's office. The first thing I saw was Dr. Elder bending over me with a stethoscope and listening to my heart. He saw me looking and said, "Well, young lady, it looks like you overdid it tonight."

I heard Ash behind him say, "Is she going to be all right?"

"Yes," the doctor said as he stood up. "I believe she's going to be fine, but I'd like to run some tests in the morning."

"Oh, Laurel, you scared me so badly!" Ash said as he knelt by my head.

"How long was I unconscious?" I asked. It must have been quite some time to get me here.

"Not long, a couple of minutes. As soon as I realized you'd passed out, I picked you up and jetted up here. I saw the doctor on my way up as he was going to his rooms," Ash replied. He looked frazzled. His hair was messed up and his tuxedo looked a little wrinkled.

"Who else knows that I passed out?" I asked as I sat up. My head and stomach still didn't feel quite right, but at least I didn't feel like I was going to pass out any minute.

"No one. Just us," Ash replied. "Is it too soon for you to stand up?" he asked me the question, but was looking at the doctor.

Dr. Elm replied as he looked at me, "How do you feel?"

"I think I feel okay. I guess I danced too much," I said as I slowly stood up. I was glad my head had stopped spinning.

"Go back to your room and take a bath. That'll make you feel better. However, I want to see you first thing in the morning, back here. Or come back sooner if you have any more difficulties. My rooms are right next door to the clinic," Dr. Elder replied as he escorted us to the door.

I thanked the doctor for his care and apologized for interrupting his evening. He told me it was no problem and to take it easy until he saw me in the morning.

Ash and I walked slowly to the elevator. "Are you sure you're okay?" he asked.

I was getting embarrassed from all of his attention and said, "Ash, I'm fine. I promise. I feel sticky from sweating and would love a warm bath. Let's get me to my suite."

We took our time walking down the hall to my rooms. "Do you want me to stay with you?" Ash asked.

At that moment, as much as I loved Ash, I wanted to be alone and take a long bath. "I think I'll take a bath and go to sleep. But, I appreciate everything that you've done for me. Don't worry, I love you! Why don't you come with me to see the doctor in the morning?"

"If you're sure," he replied hesitantly. I knew he didn't want to leave me alone, but I didn't need any more attention tonight. I was tired, sweaty and felt icky.

"Yes, I'm sure. You need to get some sleep, too. You look tired," I said as I opened the door to my suite. He did look tired. It must have been hard to jet up all of those stairs carrying me to the doctor's office.

We stood in my open doorway for a few minutes just holding each other. I could smell his sweat. I very rarely ever smelled sweat on him. It was different from a human's sweaty smell. It was more of an earthy, musky scent. I wondered briefly if he used underarm deodorant. I did. I could smell myself and it wasn't pleasant.

"I love you. I really don't want to leave you alone right now," Ash stated with a hopeful expression on his face.

"I know, Ash. I love you, too. I smell nasty and sweaty and I don't want you to have to smell that," I replied as I gently pulled myself away from him. "I'll see you in the morning, okay?"

With a sigh, he replied, "Okay, but if you feel even the least bit dizzy, you call Moss and have her call me."

I was in my room holding the door open. I kissed him on the lips and said, "I'll see you in the morning. Please don't worry. Other than feeling tired and sticky, I'm fine."

We said good night and I shut the door. I did feel better, just tired. I didn't feel like I was going to pass out. I leisurely undressed as I filled the bath. I added some bath salts and slowly lowered my body into the warm water. It felt so good to wash the sweat off. I soaked awhile and then got up and drained the tub. I got into my pajamas and went to bed. I think I was asleep before my head hit the pillow.

I woke listening to Moss humming in my outer room. Moss must have heard me yawn. She came in with a breakfast tray. "I was told to bring you your breakfast this morning. I hope you don't mind. I tried to find things you'd like."

When she lifted the lid, I saw an English muffin, some scrambled eggs with cheese, and a cup of diced fresh fruit. There was also a glass of milk and a cup of coffee. The eggs were still steaming.

I ate as Moss pulled out my clothes for the day. "I hear you'll be leaving us next week," she said as she set out my pants suit.

"Yes, that's what I hear, too," I replied as I got out of the bed. News traveled fast. I was saved from answering any more questions when we heard a knock at the door.

"I'll get dressed while you answer the door," I said as I closed the bedroom door. In a moment, I heard Ash's voice outside my door.

"I'll be out in a minute," I called through the door. It didn't take me long to get dressed.

"Good morning," Ash said as he gave me a kiss. "How do you feel today?"

I noticed the scrutinizing look he gave me. I looked at Ash and gave a meaningful look to Moss's back and replied, "I'm fine. Are you ready to go?" I didn't know if she knew I'd fainted last night and I didn't want her to know. I didn't want her worrying about me, too. I didn't wait for a response when I called over to Moss, "I have an appointment this morning. Thank you for bringing my breakfast."

"My pleasure, Miss Laurel. My pleasure," she said as she smiled and then went into the bedroom.

After I shut the door behind me and we were in the hallway outside of my suite, I said to Ash, "She doesn't need to know I fainted last night. She knows that we are leaving next week. She said so. I wonder how she found out so quickly," I said as we walked down the hall. We didn't say much as we took the elevator to the doctor's office. I had barely knocked on the door when the doctor himself answered.

"Good morning, Laurel, Ash," he said as he opened the door. "How are we feeling today?"

I looked around but did not see that nasty nurse. "Fine. I did what you said. I took a warm bath and went to bed. I slept soundly," I replied as I sat in the chair opposite the doctor's desk and Ash took the chair next to me.

"Don't get too comfortable there. I need you in the lab to take some blood tests. I want to know why you fainted last night. I have an idea, but I want to make sure before I say anything," he said as he walked into his lab.

Ash and I got up and followed him. "What do you think's wrong with me?" I asked as I sat in the lab chair.

"Oh, nothing much, my dear, I think something's very right, but I'll let you know shortly," he replied as he drew out some of my blood. "This won't take long. Have a seat by my desk."

Ash and I went and sat by his desk and talked about Wisconsin and wondered out loud about how Chuck, my dog, was doing with Adam.

In a few minutes, Dr. Elder came and sat across from us. He was trying to hold back a smile when he said, "I know why you fainted last night."

"Really? I see that you are smiling. What could be good news that would cause me to faint?" I asked perplexed.

"You are pregnant. Congratulations!" he said with a proud smile. "I'm assuming this is Ash's baby. That makes it three quarters wood nymph and one quarter human."

Ash and I looked at each other in shock. Me, pregnant. Wow! I guess I never really thought of the consequences of our making love. I think I believed that because most of the wood nymphs were having a hard time conceiving a baby, it couldn't happen to me so easily. But, I should have thought about the consequences. My mother got pregnant after one weekend with my biological wood nymph father.

Ash was the first one to process the news. "Laurel, honey! We're going to have a baby! We're going to be parents!" He exclaimed as he reached over to give me a hug. "I love you so much!"

"But we are not even married yet. What will our parents think?" I said with a shudder. I wanted to be happy about having a baby, but having children was such a large responsibility. My mother would have expected us to be married before she received this kind of news. Would she and Ben be angry? I didn't think they'd disown me or anything, but I couldn't stand it if I disappointed them.

"I think everyone will be happy for the both of you. You've bonded, so the wedding itself is more of a human tradition. The king will be interested to hear this news," Dr. Elder said. "He's been very concerned about the rapid decline in the wood nymph birth rate."

The king! He had just said yesterday that we could go home. Was it possible he would think of me and my baby as another science project? "He won't make me stay here, will he?" I asked in concern.

"I don't know. He could, I guess. He'll want to know how the pregnancy progresses, I'm sure," Dr. Elder said thoughtfully. "I'm sorry, but I can't keep this news from him. If he were to find out that I knew and didn't tell him, well, the consequences would be bad for me."

"I want to go home!" I said standing up. I had seen the king angry. I knew that Dr. Elder was right. This was real news for the wood nymph community. There had always been the chance I was sterile. Human and wood nymph scientists had been mixing species for years with mixed results. Almost always, the offspring of two different species were unable to procreate, and here was I, a human-wood nymph hybrid, pregnant with a wood nymph's baby. I didn't expect this. Plus, we were so close to going home. Would the king renege on his promise?

My thoughts kept going back to Mom and Ben! What would they think about my being pregnant before getting married? Would Mom be ashamed of me? What about college? I had always promised my mom that I would go to college!

"I think I should make an appointment with the king and queen to tell them. Do you want to be there?" Dr. Elder said kindly.

"Yes, I want to be there," I said firmly. "It's our life and our baby. I want to see his response to this news." I looked over at Ash and he nodded in agreement.

"We should be there. I don't want anyone talking about this behind our backs. I'm not ashamed about this. I'm proud! We had planned on getting married anyway. Not only are we bonded, I've given my soul. This baby is a blessing," Ash replied.

"But first, we have to tell our families," I said with a little apprehension. I was not sure how our parents were going to deal with this news.

"I'll schedule something with the king and queen tonight before dinner," Dr. Elder said with a smile. "However, I think most all the wood nymphs will find this a blessing. I wouldn't worry too much about how they respond."

"I'm just afraid that the king will make me stay here," I replied as I started walking to the door. "Do you have any idea how far along I am? When's the baby due?"

"Come back tomorrow and I'll do an examination. I had taken blood when you first got here and checked for pregnancy, and it was negative. So, either you were barely pregnant when you got here and it wasn't picked up on by the test or you got pregnant since you have been here. So, you're maybe a month along, but not more. I'm guessing the baby will be due some time in February," Dr. Elder replied as he walked us to the door.

As Ash and I walked to the elevator I said, "We need to tell our families right away. I don't want to have them surprised tonight. I also want my mom there when the doctor tells the king and queen."

We were quiet all of the way down to our hallway. I was excited and thrilled to be having a baby, but what would the consequences be? I kept thinking that I was ready to be a mom. I could handle college and be a parent with help. Ash's family had a lot of money, so paying for college or daycare would be no problem. I looked over at Ash, and he had a big grin on his face. How could he be so happy? I was happy, but . . .

"I'll go to my parent's room and you go to your parent's room and whoever finishes first goes to Olivia and Forrest's rooms, okay? Ask them to come to my room," I said with a sigh.

"Sure. Don't worry! This is awesome news!" Ash said happily.

Maybe for wood nymphs, I thought, but not so much for humans. I knocked on my parent's door and got no answer. I looked over at Ash and he was getting no answer, either. We knocked on all of the doors and got no answer. "Do you think that they're still at breakfast?" I asked.

"Let's go look. We did leave really early for the doctor's office," Ash replied as we headed back to the elevator.

We found everyone finished their breakfast.

"Good morning, Laurel! Ash!" Mom called from her place at the table. "Nice of you to join us. Have some breakfast!"

I sat next to Mom and Ash sat next to me. "I got some news I need to share with you," I said. That got everyone's attention. All eyes were on me. Great.

"Last night, after Ash and I left the ballroom, I fainted . . ." I started and my mom interrupted me.

"Are you okay? You look okay. What happened?" Mom blurted out as she looked me over.

"I'm fine. Ash jetted me to the doctor's office and Dr. Elder checked me out. He said he thought I was fine, but wanted me there for tests this morning. We just left his office," I said as I was scared to death to finish what I had to say.

"What happened in the doctor's office? What did he say?" Mom asked cautiously. "You look nervous."

"I'm nervous. You see, I'm pregnant," I said softly. There it is. It was out there. I kind of wished I could faint right now.

"What? I didn't hear you clearly," Mom said with a shocked voice. She leaned back in her chair. "Oh, my."

"Oh, yes, you did. Ash and I are going to have a baby," I replied. I had to be proud of this news. It was still new to me, but the more I thought about it, I thought about how wonderful this news was. This baby was a blessing and I had to believe it and get everyone else to believe it, too.

The room erupted. Everyone was talking at once. The noise was deafening. I couldn't hear what anyone was saying and I wasn't sure I wanted to.

"Quiet, quiet down!" Ben called from his seat. Then he looked at me with the most loving look. "Laurel, are you okay? I know this is not what you or any of us expected, but the important thing is that you're healthy. What did the doctor say?"

God bless Ben. He saw beyond the negative aspect and just cared about me. I started crying with gratitude for his love.

"Laurel, please don't cry," Ash said with angst in his voice. "I promise you, we'll get through this. This baby is a blessing."

"I know," I sniffled. "I'm just so grateful to have a family that loves me. I'm grateful that our families will help us. I'm fine, dad. Thanks for caring."

Ben came over and hugged me. "I'll always love you, no matter what. Although . . ." He stopped and gave me a smile and a wink to show he was joking, "I'm too young to be a grandfather."

Mom came over and hugged me after Ben released me. "I love you, too. I only want what's best for you. This is just a surprise, that's all. We'll help you any way we can. I always wanted to be a grandmother, just maybe not this soon."

"A baby! We're going to have a baby in our family! It's been way too many years since we have had a baby in the Copper Clan!" Olivia said joyously.

"This baby will be part of our clan too," Elm said loudly, "Ash is the youngest member of our clan. We have had no babies in our clan in a long time, either."

"The important thing is to keep Laurel and the baby comfortable and not too excited," Forrest said sternly. "This child is a blessing, even if it did get conceived before the young couple got married. Everything else is just details."

"Oh, Laurel, I'm so excited for you! A baby! Just think!" Olivia was just beside herself with excitement. "Why didn't I see this coming?"

"Oh, my, how can we help?" Willow asked. She looked happy for us, but nervous.

"There's an awful lot of excitement in this room. I can hear you all down the hall. What's going on? Who's going to help with what?" Prince Andrew asked as he walked into the room and helped himself to some toast and jelly from the sideboard and leaned against the door jam in the doorway.

The room went instantly quiet. He looked around at all of us. We all must have looked like deer in a car's headlights. "Oh, come now, we're friends now, right? What's the good news?" He looked concerned and sad that we weren't telling him our news, feeling hurt by our rejection.

I decided I would trust Andrew. His father was going to know by that evening anyway. For better or for worse, I told him with a smile, "We have big news. Ash and I are going to have a baby," I said nervously. "We just found out this morning."

Andrew pulled up a chair and sat down next to me. "Really?" he said with an almost reverent tone. "You and Ash are going to have a wood nymph baby? That's awesome news! A pregnancy! Now, that is something to be celebrated. I wonder what kind of abilities the baby will be born with!"

I would have never have guessed that Andrew would have been that excited by the news. I expected some form of sarcasm or a snide remark, not meant hurtfully, but sarcastic just the same. I certainly didn't expect this reaction.

"Maybe you are the hope for our future. The future life of the wood nymphs," Andrew said with a big grin. "Awesome. Maybe mixing with the humans would not be a bad thing after all."

With that, everyone started talking excitedly about the baby and the future and names and I couldn't hear all of the voices through the noise and laughter.

"What's going on? Are we having a breakfast party? I want in on it!" I heard Elizabeth exclaim as she came into the room. "What's so exciting?" She sat down next to Andrew.

"Laurel's pregnant!" Andrew blurted and went to hug his sister. "There's a baby coming! When I was young, I never understood the importance of a new life, a new baby, but since there are so few births anymore, well, this is stupendous news!"

"Really? That's wonderful news! Can I be a god-parent?" Elizabeth laughed as she got up and came over to me to give me a hug.

We laughed and talked awhile and then Ben soberly asked Andrew, "What do you think your parents will say about this?"

"I think that they'll be as excited as we are!" Andrew answered happily. "They'll love to see a new life come into the world."

"Will they let us go home to have the baby?" I asked softly. That was the big fear in my mind. I didn't want to be a prisoner so that the king could see what kind of off-spring I would have. He may want to keep me here for my protection. Not like I would actually need protection, but that could be his excuse for keeping us under his roof.

No one answered me. Everyone sat down and pondered the question. There was silence for a while when Andrew spoke, "I don't know. My father can be con-trolling at times. I'd like to think that he'd allow you free will to stay or go home if you want, but he did force you to come here in the first place, but he didn't know you then. Laurel, you're such an interesting person. You're changing life around you no matter where you go!"

"Dr. Elder is scheduling a meeting with your parents tonight to tell them," I said. "I guess we will find out then." I leaned back in my chair and sighed.

"We'll be there with you," Elizabeth said from her seat. "You were there for me, and I really appreciated it. I want to be there for you. I'll back whatever decision you decide on for you and your baby."

I looked over at Elizabeth. Her skin was clear. Her eyes were clear. She looked completely different compared to the filthy and bedraggled woman she had been in the dungeon yesterday. Having her family welcome her back had made a world of difference in her and for her. She looked healthy. "I'd like you there with us when we tell your parents," I said with a smile. "You're my friend."

"Yes, I'm your friend. I'll stand with you, no matter what you decide to do," she replied with a big smile.

We all talked for a while. We debated on what we would do in response to what the king said. I made it perfectly clear I wanted to go home. I also made it perfectly clear that Andrew or Elizabeth were welcome to come and visit us in Wisconsin whenever they wanted, and that I'd come back here to visit. I just didn't want to live here. I wanted to go back to my beloved north woods.

"Do you mind if I bring Aron with me?" Elizabeth asked with a twinkle in her eye. She leaned closer. "I think I'm falling in love with him."

"Of course, you can bring Aron! All of the clan members would love to meet all three of you!" I said as I looked at Elizabeth and then Andrew. They both smiled.

The servants brought lunch as we talked. We sat and discussed all day, all of the aspects and arguments the king could come up with to keep me there. Now we had to get ready for dinner. Soon we would find out how he would react to the news.

Ash and I were the first to leave to get ready. As we stood up, Forrest said, "Wait for us before heading to the reception room. We'll meet in your room and all go down together."

CHAPTER 19
ATTEMPTED MURDER

When I got to my suite to bathe and change for dinner, Moss was in my room waiting for me. "So, is it true, Miss Laurel? Are you really going to have a baby?" She sounded excited as she ran to meet me at the door.

"News does travel fast in this place, doesn't it?" I answered with a smile. "Yes, Moss, the doctor thinks the baby will be born in February."

"Oh, Miss Laurel, that's very exciting news! A baby! Just think!" Moss stared off into space for a moment. Then she looked at me and said, "Oh, Miss Laurel, sit down! I'll get your bath ready for you. We need you to look perfect when the king and queen are told tonight."

"Oh, so you know about that too, huh?" I replied as I sat on the couch. She didn't answer, and I wasn't even sure she heard me as she rushed into the bathroom to run the bath water. In a minute or so, she was back and telling me that the bath was ready for me. When I went into the bathroom, she insisted on undressing me. She held my arm as I lowered myself into the water.

"Really, Moss, I can do this myself," I said with a slightly embarrassed tone to my voice. I was totally not used to someone helping in the bathtub. I found it embarrassing. I could understand someone helping me if I was disabled, but pregnancy was not a disability, and I wasn't even very far along in my pregnancy.

"Oh, Miss Laurel, I want to help you in any way I can. I wouldn't forgive myself if you were to fall in the tub and hurt yourself or the baby," she replied with a worried tone to her voice. "This is the most exciting thing to happen here in a long time. Not only are you a miracle, being what you are—both human and wood nymph—it is so exciting that you're having a baby. If anything bad were to happen to you, well, I'd feel horrible if I could have prevented it."

"I'm fine! Really! Why don't you find me something to wear?" I said as I lathered up my wash cloth. I figured that would give her something to do besides hovering over me. I really hated being hovered over. I watched Moss go into the bedroom. I hoped I wasn't hurting her feelings. I just like to be alone in a bathtub.

A took a leisurely bath and then I came out with a towel on my head and a towel wrapped around my body. Moss had laid out my dress for the evening. It had a princess cut waistline that had a ribbon that wrapped around my body just below my breasts. It was a forest-green and matched the color of my eyes.

148

"That's a perfect choice," I said as I put on my underwear. After I had put on my bra and panties, I looked at myself in the floor length mirror. I didn't look like I had gained any weight. Was it possible that I had? Were my breasts a little larger? Was my waist a little thicker, or were these things just my imagination?

Moss took my mind off of my musings when she said, "If you'll sit on the vanity seat, I'll put your hair up for you."

I sat. In a few minutes, my head was a mass of curls with a couple of tendrils hanging down by my ears. It was an elaborate up-do. Moss then applied some cosmetics, but not a lot. I had a lot of natural color in my cheeks. Was this because I was pregnant, or because I was nervous about how the king and queen would accept my news. "Moss, you've outdone yourself. My hair looks great! How do you manage to get such a wonderful hair style in such a short period of time? The hair dresser at home would have taken hours to achieve this," I said admiringly.

"Thank you, Miss Laurel. Let me help you with the dress," she said as she picked my dress off of the bed.

I raised my arms and she slid the dress on. She zipped up the back. I was afraid it might be tight, but it wasn't. It fit just fine. I put on my pantyhose and slipped on my shoes. I was just looking at myself in the mirror when I heard someone knock on the door.

"I'll get it, Miss Laurel," Moss said heading for the door.

I came out of the bedroom as Moss let Ash in. He was wearing his best suit. "You look great," he said to me.

"You do too," I said as I walked over to kiss him.

"You smell good, too," he said as he hugged me. I wanted to stay that way for the whole evening, with just me and him. But, when I heard the knock at the door behind us, I knew that our evening had begun. Moss opened the door and Mom and Ben were there. "Everyone else is in the hallway. Are you ready to go?" Mom asked as we stepped out into the hallway.

"You know, I forgot to ask where we were supposed to meet up with Dr. Elder," I said. "I don't think we are supposed to go directly to the reception room, but I'm not sure where we're supposed to go."

"I'll take you to the parlor where Dr. Elder will be waiting for you," Moss said as she shut my door and walked past me down the hall.

"Okay," I said. "I'm glad you know where we're going." I looked back at my mom and Ben and shrugged. I saw that Ash's parents, Olivia, and Forrest were right behind us.

"As a servant, it's my responsibility to anticipate your needs and to help you," Moss said proudly.

As we walked toward the elevator, I couldn't help but wonder how the king and queen were going to take the news of my pregnancy. I was still coming to terms with the idea. Ash and I had been together less than a year. We had only been sexually intimate for even less time. I looked at Ash and he smiled at me. He seemed really happy about the idea of having a baby and becoming a family. I wanted a family with Ash, too, but it would have been nice to have had been married, first. I could not help but wonder if the king and queen would accept this news graciously. I thought about the day that we met the king and queen. He had forbid us from being a couple or getting married.

I knew he was happy with my mother. I knew he'd promised we could go home and he wasn't as prejudiced against humans as he had been. But, would he be happy for me and Ash? Would he get angry again? When we got on to the elevator, I turned to face my family. "I'm not sure if it is fair to all of you to have you face the king's wrath if he does get mad."

Olivia came up to me and Ash. "We're family. We will all go in together. For better or for worse, we will stand with you."

"This is my grandchild we're talking about. I wondered if I'd ever have a grandchild. We felt very fortunate to have had Ash. I agree that we'll go in to this meeting together," Elm stated. "There'll be no more discussion."

When the elevator door opened, it was on a floor I had not been on before. "We are on the royal family's personal level," Moss explained as we followed her down the hallway. We came to a door that opened to a very comfortable sitting room. There were overstuffed couches and chairs placed in a way to allow a group of our size to have a relaxing conversation. "I'll be right outside. When I see the door open, I'll go with you to the reception hall," Moss explained and left us in the room.

We were not in the room very long when Dr. Elder joined us. "I chose this room because I expected all of your family to want to be involved in this discussion."

"Thank you, Dr. Elder," my mom said as she found a place to sit next to Ben on a couch. "That was very considerate and thoughtful of you."

Olivia sat next to my mom and agreed, "Yes, very thoughtful. We all care about Laurel and are concerned for her welfare. We wanted to be here to hear what the king would say about the news."

"What news would that be?" King Cornelius said as he entered the room. Everyone stood. Queen Delphine was right behind him.

"I too, wonder why our good doctor has requested we meet here," the queen said as she took a seat. "What's the purpose of this meeting, Dr. Elder?" she asked.

She then turned to her servant and said, "Please wait outside. I'll call for you when I need you. Please close the door on your way out."

Dr. Elder waited until the door closed and then began, "I've chosen this time to give you all of the results of the tests that I've performed on Laurel." He then sat in a chair near me and Ash. Ash and I were on a loveseat holding hands. Ash seemed so relaxed, but I was a nervous wreck.

"I've determined that Laurel does have some wood nymph abilities. She can control sea creatures, can request fish to bite a hook when fishing. We did some experiments with the fish in the pond outside of the palace. At her request, each of the fish in the pond came to her hand when she put it in the water. She told me that the water sprites prefer her not to use this particular ability. However, I have learned from the discussions I've had with Laurel that the water sprites in Wisconsin like her and respect her.

"Laurel can color shift. This ability has only manifested itself since she's been here. She had to be trained to use it. She is sensitive to emotions and can read them well, but Laurel also has a rare gift. She has the call. She told me during one of our sessions of a time last winter when she was caught in a blizzard and called out for help. Both wood nymphs and Native Americans heard the call from miles away." Dr. Elder paused and poured himself a glass of water from a pitcher that had been on the table when we arrived.

I noticed that most of the little tables had pitchers of water with glasses. I poured myself a glass of water, too. My mouth was as dry as the Sahara.

"Last night, Laurel showed a natural ability to do our dance steps. As you know of course, these dances are much too complicated for a human to do without years of instruction with a patient teacher."

"Yes," Queen Delphine said as she smiled at me. "I noticed that. I was very proud of her. I didn't expect her to be able to pick up the complicated steps so easily."

I smiled back at the queen, but she hadn't heard the most important news. Would she still be smiling?

"There is a difference in the blood. It'd definitely show up in a human blood test. The DNA is a blend of human and wood nymph. Laurel is a hybrid of both species. Forrest Oakton, whom you have met and is sitting over there, of the Copper Clan in the small village outside Presque Isle of Northern Wisconsin has ensured that a wood nymph physician has always attended her. When you were visited by the Quince family after they were in Wisconsin you found out that Olivia Oakton had been able to foretell Laurel's birth. Wood nymphs have lived around and worked with humans for years. As per the royal instruction that has been decreed for the past millennium, wood nymphs have not told the humans of their existence. Even Laurel's mother did not know that Laurel's biological father was not a human," Dr. Elder said and took a sip of water.

Just as Dr. Elder took a sip of his water, the door opened and Prince Andrew and Princess Elizabeth walked in. "I'm sorry we're late! We haven't missed anything have we?" Princess Elizabeth said excitedly as she sat in a chair near the doctor. Andrew stood behind her.

"We were just talking about Laurel's abilities. You haven't missed anything," Dr. Elder replied with a smile.

"Yes, yes, I knew about that," King Cornelius said. "I learned that on our trip to the United States. I'm glad to hear that Laurel has wood nymph characteristics. This tells me that the blending of humans and wood nymphs does not negate the wood nymph traits. This has been a concern of mine." King Cornelius looked at Forrest and Olivia. "I'm still not happy that Laurel's birth was kept a secret from me, but I forgive this transgression, especially since I have brought you all here. If I had not brought you all here, I would never have had Valerie here to help with Elizabeth's addiction problem. My daughter is a better person since she has had Valerie help her. I had never heard of counseling before. It is a good thing.

"I'm grateful to have my daughter back. The truth is, in the short time that my daughter has been out of the dungeon, I appreciate my daughter more now than I ever had in the past. I enjoy our conversations and I realize that my daughter has a lot of creative ideas. I think our relationship has never been better," the king said as he smiled at Elizabeth.

Elizabeth glowed with happiness from the praise from her father. Andrew affectionately squeezed Elizabeth's shoulder. She grinned up at him.

"I've never been happier," Elizabeth agreed. "I have a better relationship with both my parents and my brother."

The king smiled for a moment and then became serious. "However, it appears that there's more to this conversation than just discussing the wood nymph part of Laurel. I can see Laurel is nervous. As I look around, I notice that most of the people were nervous, but not Andrew and Elizabeth. They seem to know a secret that they are happy about, but this secret was making the other humans and wood nymphs nervous. There would be no reason for anyone to be nervous, unless there is something to be afraid of. What is it?" King Cornelius asked impatiently.

For a long moment, no one said a word. The king scrutinized the different faces in the room, including mine. I looked around the room and saw that the king was right. No one looked comfortable except for Elizabeth and Andrew. They were still smiling broadly.

The doctor opened his mouth to speak, but my mother held up her hand to stop him. "I'll tell him. I'm her mother." My mother took a deep breath and continued. "When I met Laurel's father, we had a wonderful weekend together. During that weekend, we were intimate. I'm not the type of person to sleep with a man that quickly, but the truth is, within a day of knowing him, I knew I loved him. After that weekend, I never saw him again, but I was pregnant.

"I had no idea that Leif wasn't human. I was devastated when we had agreed to meet the next weekend and he did not show up. I did not know that he had died," my mom said sadly. "However, I was able to eventually find another love." She reached for Ben's hand and he smiled at her.

"Touching, but I already know that part. I heard it before. I want to know what's making you all nervous today. I already said that you could return to the United States next week. There's obviously a problem. What is it?" The king asked impatiently.

"Last night after the dancing, on the way to their rooms, Laurel fainted. Ash jetted her up to my clinic and after a quick examination, I could find nothing wrong. I had Laurel come back to my office this morning. After another test we found out that Laurel is pregnant," Dr. Elder said with a gentle smile.

"This is great news! With the severe decrease of the wood nymph birth rate, anyone having a pregnancy is exciting news!" Elizabeth gushed. The king and queen stared at her.

"Laurel has some wood nymph characteristics and this baby will be three quarters wood nymph! I'll bet the baby will be able to jet, even though Laurel can't. That is one of the things she's been unable to do."

The room was as still as a tomb for a couple of minutes. "Laurel and her family have been afraid of how you'll react to the news," Elizabeth said to her father in a quiet voice. "The doctor confirmed it this morning and told Laurel that you had to be told immediately. Andrew and I just happened to walk in at the moment Laurel was telling her family the news. Please be happy for them."

The king and queen looked at each other and the king said, "We have to think about this. In the meanwhile, we'll go to the reception room and then to dinner. We'll discuss this again tomorrow at breakfast. I wouldn't worry. I'm not angry. I just have to think about the consequences of this event."

The king and queen got up and left the room. Elizabeth said, "Don't worry! He's concerned, but he's not angry! This will turn out fine, you will see!"

"Elizabeth is right. I've seen my father angry, and he's certainly not angry. In fact, I think he's as excited as we are, but doesn't know how to show it," Andrew said. "Let's go down to the reception room."

"I hope you're right," my mom said. "We don't need problems so close to going home."

When we got out into the hallway, Moss and the rest of our servants were there to greet us. Moss led the way to the reception room. When we got there, Elizabeth's servant brought her a beverage. Elizabeth looked at me and said smiling, "This is my favorite mixture of fruit juices. Try it and see if you like it!"

I took the glass and sniffed it. It didn't smell bad, but I didn't think I'd ever smelled anything quite like it before. I took a sip and it tasted okay, but there was a funny aftertaste. I had just noticed the after taste when I violently vomited on the floor.

"Laurel, what's wrong?" I heard Ash call out to me.

I felt hands holding me up. I was on my knees and violently threw up until I had the dry heaves. I had never thrown up so hard in my life. It only took a minute or so, but it exhausted me. I was having a hard time catching my breath, the vomiting was so intense. Dr. Elder rushed over and personally jetted me to his office. Before we left the reception room with me in his arms, I heard him tell someone, "I want all of that vomit in a sterilized container and brought to my office immediately."

I must have passed out on the way to the clinic. The next thing I remembered was that I was lying on an examination table with my dress off and in a hospital gown. Ash and my mother were on each side hovering over me. "Laurel, can you hear me?" I heard my mother ask in a weird voice.

I opened my eyes and looked at her. She had been crying. I looked over at Ash, and he was stone white. He looked terrified. "What happened?" I asked.

"You were poisoned," I heard Dr. Elder explain from across the room. "There was a toxic substance in the juice you drank similar to what humans use for rat poison."

"Is my baby okay?" I asked in a weak voice. I felt exhausted.

"I believe so. Your body ejected the substance as soon as you drank it, so I doubt that it had time to reach your blood stream. Wood nymphs do not vomit like humans do. There are times when they can vomit, but they don't do so easily. If a wood nymph had drunk that juice, it very well could have killed him or her. I will do preliminary tests to make sure that the fetus isn't damaged." The doctor explained.

The fetus. The doctor did not even call my baby a baby. It was just a fetus. Did this mean that there was reason to be concerned? The doctor came and drew blood from my arm. Ben and Forrest came into the room. "Now I said that only a couple of people could be in here at a time," The doctor said with a sigh. "I need to get to my patient."

"We'll move when you need to get to her," Forrest said grudgingly. Then he looked at me. "How do you feel?"

"I feel like I vomited my stomach as well as its contents out on the floor. My stomach hurts, and my throat burns," I replied with a scratchy voice.

"Excuse me," Dr. Elder said as Ben moved out of the way. The doctor held out a glass to me. "Drink this. It'll make your throat feel better and help settle your stomach."

The stuff tasted like chalk. It was thick but it did make my throat and stomach feel a lot better after a couple of minutes.

"Who could have done this to Laurel?" Mom asked angrily. "Why would someone want to kill her?"

"I don't think that the juice was meant for Laurel," Dr. Elder said thoughtfully. "I think it was meant for the princess. Think about it. The juice was given to Elizabeth. She just wanted Laurel to try it."

Willow asked from the back of the room, "Is it possible that Elizabeth knew the drink was poisoned? Do you think that she intended to poison Laurel?"

"No," I said with conviction. "We're friends. She wouldn't try to poison me. I'm certain someone else was trying to poison Elizabeth."

Ben came over to stand next to me. "If you are right, then there's a potential murderer in the palace," he said thoughtfully.

Dr. Elder came and stood at the foot of the examination table. "You're right. That is a horrifying thought, but someone put that poison in the juice. I think Elizabeth is in danger. I need to contact the king."

"I'll go get him," Forrest said. "I think he needs to know about our theory. The princess needs to be protected."

I watched Forrest disappear as he jetted to find the king. "Ash, would you go find the princess? I am worried about her. What if someone really is trying to kill her?" I asked as the full implication of what we were talking about really sunk into my mind. I truly believed that someone was trying to kill the princess.

"Okay. I'll be right back," Ash said as he jetted out of the room.

"Who would want to kill the princess?" Mom asked. "Does she have any enemies? I know that her brother and parents were not real happy with her and that her father had considered having her killed, but I don't think he wants to kill her anymore. Just today he said that he was happier with her now than he had ever been before. I can't believe it would be her father. But, I definitely believe that the target was Elizabeth and not you."

We were quiet for a while as we digested this information. "I hope Ash finds Elizabeth quickly."

CHAPTER 20
FINDING A MURDERER

Forrest was back with the king before Ash returned with Elizabeth. "What's going on?" King Cornelius demanded. "Is the rumor true that someone is attempting to commit murder in my palace?"

"Yes, your highness, that's what the evidence tells us. Laurel drank a juice drink with a toxin in it. Her human digestive system was be able to vomit out the poison. A wood nymph's system would not have been able to reject the toxin and probably would have died. The drink was the princess's, and she'd drunk it she'd probably be dead now," Dr. Elder stated somberly. "I feel horrible that Laurel suffered, but she'll be fine."

"Did the poison harm Laurel's baby?" King Cornelius asked with concern in his voice. "I've thought about this baby and I've been thinking about wood nymphs and humans. There may come a time in the not-too-distant future that we may have to tell the world of our existence. I'm not ready for that yet. However, if another wood nymph should become bonded with another human, I believe that we should maintain our secret, at least for the time being. The human will have to be able to maintain the secret. But, I won't forbid such a bonding. Laurel and Ash are the first wood nymph-hybrid wood nymph couple to have a baby. I'm very curious to see how this baby turns out. It appears there are a lot of life changes going on around here."

"Does that mean we'll still be able to go home in a week?" I asked from my examination table.

The king turned to look at me and smiled. "Yes, you can go home. But, you have to promise to keep in touch with us and let us know how you're doing. Elizabeth was telling me about a thing called the Internet that humans have. She thinks we could wire the palace with this Internet thing and be able to communicate immediately. She told me we could send photos and be able to look at each other to talk with this technology. I'm very curious about human technology and how we can combine this with wood nymph natural abilities. We used a combination of human and wood nymph technology to build the lifts and lighting in the palace."

I sat up and thought, wow! That is the most I've ever heard him say at one time. "Yes, your highness," I said happily. "I'd be happy to keep in contact with your family and keep you apprised of how my pregnancy progresses."

It had been an hour or so since I'd gotten sick. My throat was still a little sore, but I was feeling a lot better. The medicine that the doctor gave me made me did wonders. I was even getting a little hungry.

I was wondering where Ash and Elizabeth were. Just as I was getting really concerned, I saw them come in through the door. "Where have you been?" I asked with concern. "Someone's trying to kill you!"

"Oh, Laurel, I'm sorry you had to go through that experience. How is the baby? Are you okay?" Elizabeth said as she sat on a chair next to me. "It is hard for me to believe that someone would want to kill me. As far as I know I have no enemies in the palace." Then she took my hand with a concerned look and said, "How are you?"

"I'm fine, now. As sorry as I am to have experienced that horrible vomiting, as I understand it, the poison would have killed you. I saw it was your normal servant that handed you your juice. Did she mix the juice or did someone else mix it? How long have you had her for a servant?" I asked as I put my legs over the side of the table.

"Laurel, are you sure you are ready to sit up?" Ash asked with concern. He sat next to me on the table.

"I feel fine. Between the vomiting and the medicine, I feel a lot better. In fact, the vomiting happened so fast, my body eliminated the toxin before I realized that I was even sick," I replied. "I'm even getting hungry now. However, I'm really worried about a potential murderer in the palace."

"Yes, that's something that needs to be addressed immediately," the king stated as he headed for the door. "Bring me Elizabeth's servant immediately!" he thundered as he walked out of the clinic.

"Can I get up now?" I asked the doctor.

"Yes, I should think so. I think you expelled all of the toxin before any of it had a chance to do any damage to you or the baby," Dr. Elder replied. "However, if you feel even the least bit sick, come to me immediately. Where's nurse Thornbush? She should have been here. Lately that woman is never here when I need her."

I watched as Dr. Elder went into the office part of the clinic as I stood up. "Elizabeth, do you have a food taster?" I asked.

She laughed when she replied, "Food tasters have not been used since the dark ages. No one uses food tasters anymore."

I looked at her somberly when I replied, "Elizabeth, until the murderer's found, you need to have someone taste your food and drink."

She sobered up when she replied, "How awful. I just hate knowing someone in our palace wants me dead."

Andrew put his hand on his sister's shoulder and looked her in the face. "I am really proud of the way that you have been handling yourself since you left the

157

dungeon. I no longer feel like I have to put you under lock and key. I also enjoy our conversations. I had no idea that we felt the same way about so many things. No, I am certainly not the one who wants you dead." Andrew then looked at me and glanced at everyone else still in the room. "I don't believe anyone here would want my sister dead. However, there is someone in this palace who does. I agree she needs a food taster from now on, at least until we find the person responsible for what happened today."

"I know I missed the cocktail hour, but did I miss dinner?" I asked as I heard my stomach grumble.

Andrew laughed and said, "I guess you are hungry. No, I think the cooks have been holding dinner. We should go down as soon as you get dressed. It's a good thing that you didn't vomit on your gown. We'll wait in the hall for you."

Mom helped me get dressed. I looked in a mirror and noticed that some of the curls had come loose, but other than that, my hair looked presentable. My face was a little pale, but that could have been due to being sick or the shock of knowing a potential murderer lurked in the palace.

After I got my shoes on, Mom and I headed for the hallway. I saw the doctor in his office. "Are you coming to dinner, Dr. Elder?" I asked.

"Yes, I'll be down shortly. I just have to check something," he said distractedly. He seemed to be looking through some cabinets of medicines above his desk.

"Okay, we'll see you there!" I said as we opened the door to the hallway. He mumbled a reply. He seemed really involved in whatever it was that he was doing. I wondered if he had an experiment going bad. I was hoping it had nothing to do with me.

Ben, Ash, Elm, Willow, Forrest, and Olivia were waiting in the hall for us. "We didn't take too long, did we?" I asked as I walked up to Ash.

"No, honey, you're fine. I'm just really grateful that you're able to get up and get around. I'm extremely grateful that you and the baby are fine," he replied as he kissed my hand.

"I'm still trying to get used to the idea of my daughter having a baby!" Mom exclaimed.

"Oh, calm down, Grandma," Ben said affectionately as he gave Mom a hug.

My mom playfully pushed him away and said, "Just remember, that makes you a Grandpa!"

"Oh, I hadn't thought of that. Grandpa Redmond. It has a nice ring, don't you think?" Ben asked Mom.

Olivia answered for her, "I think it does. I can't wait to meet my new little cousin."

"I'll have a great niece. Just think. I already have a great niece," he said as he gave me a hug from behind. Ash and I were walking in front of everyone except Andrew and Elizabeth. They were in front of us.

It was nice to have some humor in a scary situation. I really liked it that everyone was trying to lighten up the mood, but the truth was, someone in the palace was trying to kill the princess. The more I thought about it, the more I was sure that Elizabeth should have a food taster. "Maybe I should be Elizabeth's food taster," I mused out loud.

Elizabeth stopped and turned to look at me. She was furious. "No way! You got lucky this time. What if the next poison got into your system and killed you and the baby! I won't have that on my conscience."

Andrew put his arm around Elizabeth, "Elizabeth's right. You did get lucky this time. The next time could be tragic. You will not be the food taster."

"I'm human. I could do it," Ben suggested.

Everyone rejected that idea at once. Everyone in our group protested loudly at the very thought of another human being a test subject for a possible poison. "Okay, okay, I give up. I won't do it. But, someone has to. Who?" Ben asked.

We had been standing in the hall long enough for Dr. Elder to come up to us as we waited for the elevator to take us down. "I think I have an idea," he said. "I'll explain later. For now, let us go down to dinner."

The majority of the guests were already standing behind their chairs, waiting for the king and queen. The king and queen were waiting for us. Once we were all one big group, the king and queen led the way into the dining room. The queen beckoned me to come and walk with her. "How do you feel, my dear? I feel dreadful that something like this happened to you."

"Right now, I feel pretty good. The baby is fine, too," I replied.

"That is good news," the queen said with a large smile. She was really pretty when she smiled. I could see where Elizabeth got her good looks.

Dr. Elder went up to the king and whispered in his ear. The king gave him a long look for a moment and then nodded. I wondered what that was all about.

At that moment, Aron, the Moor prince came up to Elizabeth and gave her a big hug. "I've been worried about you. I heard Laurel drank some juice meant for you and it was poisoned. I also heard it would have killed you if you'd drunk it."

"That's all true," Elizabeth whispered. "Sit next to me at dinner. I'll tell you all about it." Elizabeth had a server move the place settings around to ensure that Elizabeth and Aron could sit together. Once the king and queen sat in their chairs, everyone else sat down.

After everyone had been seated, the king raised his hand and said, "We have an announcement to make that should be heard by the entire palace staff. Would all available servants and staff members please locate all of the palace personnel and bring them to the dining room so they can hear this announcement. It won't take long."

The servers served the first course and then jetted off to find other palace staff not involved with the dinner. I noticed that Dr. Elder was seated next to the king. I saw Elizabeth next to Dr. Elder and Aron next to her. Ash and I were together on the other side of the table across from Andrew and a pretty young female wood nymph I had not noticed before. Andrew looked at Aron and said with a smile, but in a serious voice, "Please take care of my sister."

"No harm will come to the princess while I'm here," Aron said with a scowl. The look on his face scared me. I sure wouldn't want to be a person Aron was mad at.

The king had a pretty young scullery maid taste the princess's soup. The poor girl was terrified to do it. But no one disobeyed the king, absolutely no one. While I could see by Elizabeth's face that she wanted to argue with her father, she did not want to make a scene he would have won anyway. No one knew what could be poisoned. We all watched the horrified girl dip the spoon into the soup and stare into the princess's eyes. We could all see the compassion in the princess's eyes. She glanced at the king and saw no compassion. He wanted this over and done with. She took a deep breath and sipped the soup. She closed her eyes as she stood there. I wondered if she was thinking that she was going to keel over at any moment. After a minute she opened her eyes and looked surprised, and then happy. The soup was not poisoned.

"Stand here for a couple of minutes, please," the king said to the young woman. The woman nodded, fear coming back into her eyes. Everyone knew that my reaction to the poison was instantaneous. It was clear that the king did not believe the threat was over. After five minutes, the young woman said, "Sire, the soup tastes really good."

"Very good. You're dismissed. You'll receive a bonus with your next check. I will also talk to your supervisor about a better position for you," the king replied.

The young woman had a huge smile as she left the dining room. She survived the taste test and was given a better position with greater pay. Her relief was palpable.

After that, we all enjoyed the wonderful creamed asparagus soup. There were no incidents at the table and everyone relaxed and talked. As the second course was being served, the king said to the doctor, "Let's have Nurse Thornbush taste the salmon."

"A splendid idea," the doctor replied. The second course was more of an appetizer—little slices of smoked salmon with caviar and a cracker. "Nurse Thornbush, I would like you to taste the princess's salmon, please."

160

Nurse Thornbush had been standing along the wall with the rest of the palace staff brought in to hear the announcement the king was going to give. No one knew if the king was going to give the announcement during the dinner, between courses or after dinner. All of the walls of the entire dining room had people waiting to hear the news.

"Why me?" she asked. She looked really nervous. I could see the sweat bead up on her face from across the room.

The doctor cocked his head to one side and said, "Come now, Nurse Thornbush. Why not you? It is only fair that a different member of the staff take a risk with tasting the princess's food. I believe it's your turn."

"Please, Dr. Elder. Can't someone from the cleaning crew do the tasting? I have an important position as the palace nurse," Nurse Thornbush was really getting nervous and starting to wring her hands in agitation.

"It's true. You do have an important position, although lately it seems that whenever I've needed you, you've been nowhere to be found. This will make up for your absences. Plus, it'll ensure that you get the higher education you've been asking for," Dr. Elder stated calmly.

"But, but, the food could be poisoned!" Nurse Thornbush stammered. She tried to back away from the table.

"Yes, my dear Nurse Thornbush. All of the princess's food needs to be tasted before she can eat it. We can't let the princess be murdered," replied the doctor calmly.

Nurse Thornbush looked around the room as if looking for a way out. I and probably everyone else at the table were watching her. Then a strange thing happened. She stopped being frightened and got angry. She shook her head in apparent disgust and said, "Someone should be sacrificed for the princess? Her own father was going to kill her. She's a drug-addicted embarrassment to her family!" she shouted at the doctor.

The king looked really angry and opened his mouth to say something but the doctor whispered in his ear and he didn't say anything.

"See? The doctor knows what I'm talking about. She doesn't deserve to live," Thornbush whined.

"I have no idea what you think I know. But, I've asked you to taste the princess's salmon and caviar and I expect you to do it now," the doctor said firmly.

"You know, don't you?" Thornbush asked in horror to the doctor. "How could you know I was the one trying to poison the princess? I didn't mean for the human-mixed girl to get poisoned, but it would not have bothered me one bit if she and her mutant baby were killed instead," the nurse snarled at the doctor and then looked at me.

I had never seen anyone look so evil. While I knew she had never liked me, I had never expected her to hate me so savagely. I leaned into Ash. Her look was so venomous that she frightened me from across the table.

Very calmly the doctor asked his nurse, "Why do you hate the princess so much that you want to see her dead? It couldn't have been because she was an addict. At any time while she was in the dungeon, it would have been easy for you to tamper with her food. Why now?"

The nurse looked back at the doctor and then looked with absolute hatred at the princess. "Because the man I love wants her. I've always wanted Aron for myself, but he never gave me a second look. He's always been in love with Elizabeth. She didn't know it, but I did. I saw the way he looked at her. She was so lost in her own world, she didn't notice anything."

"I heard that her own father was going to kill her. That was when I really started having hope that I could have Aron for myself. I had originally hoped that once everyone knew she was an addict of human drugs that Aron would realize what a loser she was and lose his interest in her." She stopped to take a breath and looked around the room. She looked back at Elizabeth and then the king and said, "I was overjoyed when I heard that our king wanted to kill his own daughter. That would simplify matters. The princess would be gone and I could have been there to comfort the broken hearted Aron. He would have fallen in love with me, then."

She gave a loving look to Aron, but if looks could kill, the nurse would be dead on the floor. Elizabeth had her hand on his arm. I thought in any moment that Aron was going to jump out of his chair and kill the nurse with his own hands.

Then Nurse Thornbush glared at my mother. "But, no, a human counselor was brought here and she actually helped the stupid princess. I would've poisoned your food, next. You're too smart for your own good. You might have figured out that it was me."

The nurse looked back at the doctor. "I never would've guessed you'd figure it out. You've always been more interested in ailments and the differences and similarities between humans and wood nymphs to be concerned with what I was doing. Ever since the human girl came, that was all you talked about or worried about. I didn't think you'd even miss me. You never let me in the room while she was there." She glared at me and then the princess. She looked at Aron and sighed. She then said to the doctor, "How did you figure it out?"

The doctor leaned back in his chair and sighed. Then he looked at her and said, "It was the poison you used. The only place in the palace that has that toxin is in the cabinet above my desk. I saw it was missing. The only person who could have taken it was you. The door pad to the clinic was set for the touch of your hand or mine, and I knew I didn't take the toxin. Plus, you've been acting strange lately. The final piece of evidence was when the king questioned the princess's servant and she said you checked to make sure the juice was just right for the her. This was the juice that Laurel drank. So, now eat the salmon and the caviar."

"No, I won't eat it," the nurse said firmly. She tried to back away from the table, but two of Aron's guards grabbed her arms and held her in place.

"It's a quick death for wood nymphs. You won't suffer long. It's a death sentence for anyone to try to kill a member of the royal family. You know that," the doctor said. "It may be the easiest death for you."

"If you don't eat the caviar and salmon, I'll let Aron and his guards have you," the king said in a voice low with anger. "No one decides the punishment for anyone in my family but me. I also decide the fate of any wood nymph of the palace and throughout the world. You have tried to murder my daughter and you're acting more evil than I have personally seen any human act. I never would've believed that a member of my staff could attempt murder. If the salmon and caviar do not kill you, then you'll go to the dungeon until Aron decides on a way to execute you. It's your choice."

The nurse shrugged and glared at everyone around the table. She walked up to the princess's plate and took the princess's fork and stabbed the salmon and caviar. She was glaring at the princess. I looked at the princess. She was nervous and leaning into Aron, but would not back down from the hateful gaze she was receiving from the nurse. The nurse then looked at Aron and said, "I would've been good to you. I would've made a good Moorish Princess."

Aron leaned across the princess to spit at Thornbush. "You're a disgrace to the wood nymphs. You're a disgrace to the medical field. Death from this poison is too good for you. You disgust me."

I knew at that moment that Nurse Thornbush was going to eat the salmon and caviar and that this was the food that she had poisoned. I looked at Ash and said, "I can't watch this. I can't watch anyone die, even someone who wanted to murder someone else and almost murdered me." I buried my face in Ash's shirt. I heard a gasp from many of the wood nymphs around the room and I heard the thud as her body hit the floor. "Let me know when her body is gone, okay?" I said as I cried into Ash's shirt. "I just can't look."

I heard some shuffling and believed I was hearing the nurse's body being removed from the room. "I'm sorry for this disturbance," I heard the king announce in a somber voice. "I, myself, have no appetite for salmon and caviar and request the servants to please remove all of the plates."

"You can look now. The body's gone," I heard Ash whisper in my ear. I looked up and I watched the king sigh.

"This has been a terrible event. It appears that wood nymphs have other mental health issues. I never would've thought jealousy would cause a wood nymph to want to hurt another. It's not as if the nurse and Aron had bonded. I won't tolerate anyone hurting my friends and family.

"However, I did bring everyone here for a happy reason, not an execution. We have a pregnancy to announce. There'll be a baby born within the next year," the king said proudly.

Everyone started talking at once. The king had to hold up both hands to get the people at the table to quiet down. "Quiet, quiet. I haven't told you who the mother-to-be is."

From a loud uproar to silence as everyone wanted to know who was pregnant. "Is it the queen?" I heard someone from across the table ask.

"No, we've been blessed with two children. There will be no additional royal children, although I do wish that the proud parents will allow one or both of us to be godparents to the child. Our guests Laurel and Ash are going to be parents. While they're not conjoined yet, we can put together a quick conjoinment before they go back to Wisconsin in the United States."

I whispered to Ash, "Should we get married now? I guess if it'll make the king happy, we could have another ceremony in Wisconsin, right?"

"Whatever will make you and the king happy will make me happy. I would marry you right now, if I could. How many real wood nymphs get to get married at the wood nymph palace?" Ash whispered back.

"I heard that!" the king shouted. "We'll have the conjoinment tomorrow!"

"Oh, my," I heard Mom say. "This is all so sudden." I saw her look at Ben.

Ben smiled at my mom. "It'll be fine. Who would have guessed that our little girl would be married in a palace proceeded over by some elder wood nymph?" Ben asked with a shrug.

"This is all so sudden. Excuse me, but who does the officiating at the wedding?" my mother asked the king.

He smiled grandly and said, "One of our older wood nymphs. He is the one that handles our essence ceremony and all of the fairies like him. The fairies will come to the conjoinment and give their blessing. There are fairies in this room right now that'll go out into the world to bring back additional fairies for what you call a wedding and we call a conjoinment. After the ceremony, we'll have a small essence ceremony that celebrates the young couple. This will be a happy occasion. We've had too many negative experiences lately."

I believed he was talking about the death of the nurse. Since she ate the poisoned food, did that make what she did a form of suicide, even if it was coerced? The whole thing creeped me out. I wondered if he was bringing up the news of my pregnancy and holding this conjoinment to take everyone's minds off of the death of the nurse.

When we came here, we weren't sure if we'd leave alive. Now, not only were we allowed to leave alive, the king wanted me and Ash to get married here. I thought, *I don't even have a dress appropriate for this.*

"We'll eat in celebration of the upcoming conjoinment that we'll have tomorrow," King Cornelius stated with joy in his voice. "Bring the next course."

CHAPTER 21
A DEATH AND A WEDDING

Even though I did not actually watch, I knew the nurse had died. I was positive that I'd have no appetite. But, when the next course was served, my stomach growled and I tasted it. It was duck in an orange sauce. This was one of my favorite dishes. I surprised myself by eating it. No one seemed concerned that the nurse may have poisoned any of the other dishes. However, I did see the king and queen talk to members of the kitchen staff. I guessed that the kitchen staff must have stated that the nurse was only near the salmon plate.

After dinner, the queen and her closest attendants whisked me, my mom, Olivia, and Willow away to what appeared to be a seamstress's room. The princess was already there and had half of a dozen seamstresses lined up to take my measurements.

"This is your wedding, Laurel. I know it is rushed, but you should have the dress of your dreams. Every young woman wants to have her gown made exactly like she wants it to be made. Here is a book with a variety of gowns. You can pick and choose different aspects of any dress and have it put on your dress. Our seamstresses will have your dress ready for you tomorrow," The princess said as she sat me at a table with a lot of different designer gown books on it.

Elizabeth sat on one side of me and Olivia sat on my other side. "Who do you want to stand up with you tomorrow?" Olivia asked me quietly.

I looked at her. She was smiling, but seemed hesitant. "You, of course! Can I have you as the Maid of Honor and Elizabeth stand up with me, too?" I said as I reached over to give her a hug.

"I wanted to be in your conjoinment!" Princess Elizabeth said happily and opened the nearest book. I read the designer name and thought that never in my life would I have ever have been able to afford a knock off of any of these designs.

"How is this different from a human wedding?" I asked. I'd never been married before, so I wasn't entirely sure what I needed to do for a human wedding, either.

"You pick out the dress and the fabrics and we will take care of the rest," the queen stated to me. I saw her look over at my mother, who appeared a little lost and she sat my mom down with her at another table. "The mother of the bride should look fabulous, too. This book has my favorite designer's gowns for this year. Take a look and pick out a style and color. Your dress will also be finished before the conjoinment. I'll ensure that all of our seamstresses will have everything perfect by tomorrow afternoon."

We talked for hours about fabrics and styles and what colors would go with the dress style I ultimately picked out. It would be made of satin and lace. The sleeves had little caps with lace sleeves. The bottom of the dress and the bodice had lace over the satin. It had pearl buttons going up the back. The veil was ankle length in the back, made of the same lace on the dress. The seamstresses found satin shoes that would match the dress perfectly.

Mom, Olivia, Willow, Elizabeth, and the queen all coordinated their colors to compliment each other. I was exhausted by the time all of the measurements were taken. I was ready for bed when the seamstresses started putting it all together.

"Miss Laurel, your dress will be delivered one hour before the ceremony," One of the seamstresses said shyly. "You will be so beautiful."

"After the conjoinment part of the ceremony, we will go outside of the palace in the valley for the essence part of the ceremony. After that, we celebrate!" The princess shouted happily.

I saw her mother give her a worried look and the princess went over to her mother and gave her a hug. "I know, mother, no alcohol for me. I can celebrate and have a good time without drugs or alcohol." I saw the relieved smile that the queen had on her face behind her daughter's back.

I did not see Ash before I went to my suite. I looked around for him, but my mother told me it was bad luck to see the groom the night before the ceremony. I was asleep before my head hit the pillow.

When I woke up in the morning, my mother, Olivia, and Willow were already in my room with Moss. "Here, eat your breakfast. It's time to get up!" My mother exclaimed from the foot of my bed.

"Didn't you sleep last night?" I asked with a yawn. "What time is it?"

"It is time to get you ready for the wedding. First we go to the spa, then we get your hair done, and then it'll be lunch time, and then the dress will be delivered," Elizabeth said as she entered my bedroom. She was grinning so big, you'd have thought she was the one getting married. "There's a lot to do today, so eat your breakfast and get up!"

That's exactly how we spent the day. Mom and Willow were telling wedding stories and comparing human weddings to wood nymph conjoinment ceremonies. I was glad to see Mom and Willow getting along. I had Olivia on one side of me and Elizabeth on the other the whole day. Everyone was very excited. I was excited too, I just wished I had more of an idea of what was expected of me. I didn't want to make a fool of myself. Before I knew it, we were back in my room and Moss was putting the final touches on my hair.

"How will I know what to do?" I asked, suddenly quite nervous. "I don't want to make a mistake."

"Oh, honey, it'll be fine. I'll be with you, guiding you along. There's a form of a chapel in the palace. While it's not exactly Christian, it's close enough that you'll know what to do. Your dad will walk you down the aisle. When you get to Ash, your dad will place your hand in Ash's hand and sit down. Someone's explaining this to your dad, as we're explaining this to you. The cleric will guide you once you're with Ash. Just don't trip on your gown walking up the aisle!" Elizabeth giggled.

Olivia laughed and said to Elizabeth, "Don't tease her. She'll get even more nervous." Olivia then reached down to give me a hug. "This should be the happiest day of your life." Olivia stood up and pulled a chair next to me and sat down. "I just wish I got conjoined with Hawthorn years ago. I wish he was here, now," she said with a sad sigh.

"Oh, don't you get gloomy! We'll plan your conjoinment or wedding when we get back to Wisconsin. It'll be your turn. Then you can get pregnant and our babies can grow up together!" I said happily.

"You make it sound so easy. Wood nymphs are not getting pregnant. Our birth rate is really low, which is one of the reasons that the king is so excited about this baby," Olivia said worriedly.

"I believe that you'll get pregnant, soon. I just know it. My baby needs a play-mate!" I said as I heard a knock at my door. "Is that the dresses?" I asked.

"The dresses are here! Each of you take your dress and meet back here in half an hour," Elizabeth said as she pulled her gown off of the rack. Her maid took it from her and followed her out of my room. In a moment, it was just my mom, me, and Moss in my room.

"Are you okay?" Mom asked kindly as she sat on the stool Olivia had vacated. I was getting white rose buds put in my up-do.

"Yeah, I think I am. This is happening really fast, but I couldn't have asked for a better dress. Just look at it! I could never have afforded a dress like that, and I wouldn't let you pay that kind of money. But, since the king and queen insisted, I guess I shouldn't feel funny about wearing the dress. Everyone's been so kind. The spa was fun. I'd never been to a spa before. I really liked the body massage. I would've thought I'd feel funny having a strange woman running her hands over my body, but it really was relaxing. It was also fun having us all together. Do you think all of the men are pampering Ash as much?" I asked just as Moss stood up.

"What do you think?" she asked as I looked in the mirror.

"You look like a goddess," Mom said with a smile. "I wish I had a camera. I hope someone had the forethought to bring one."

Mom went to get her dress on while Moss helped me on with mine. She was just finishing up with the tiny buttons on the back when we heard a knock at the door. It was Elizabeth. She also had her hair in an up-do with yellow roses that matched her yellow dress. Right behind her, was Olivia. Olivia had on a pale-pink dress with pale-pink roses in her hair. They were absolutely gorgeous.

"Laurel, you look perfect!" Olivia gushed as she came over to me to check me over.

"Yes, you really do," Elizabeth agreed. "Oh, I found a photographer to take pictures. I hope you don't mind. That'll be my gift to you."

Another knock on the door was the florist. My bouquet held white, pink and yellow roses with baby's breath and other flowers that I could not identify, but smelled heavenly. Olivia's bouquet was similar to mine, but slightly smaller and mostly pink roses with a couple of white roses and a couple of the other flowers, and Elizabeth's was like Olivia's bouquet, only with yellow roses with the white roses and other flowers.

My mom and Willow had corsages. It seemed bare minutes had gone by when all of the women were back in my room. Most of them were drinking some kind of champagne. "I'm sorry you can't have any," Mom said with a sad smile. "This time it is not because you're underage, but because it wouldn't be good for the baby."

"I don't mind. I've never been a drinker. I don't plan to start now," I replied with a happy smile.

"That's good," Elizabeth said handing me a glass of juice. She clinked her glass to mine. "We can be the teetotalers. I have better things to do with my life than pollute it with alcohol or drugs."

"Are you okay with other people drinking around you?" Mom asked with concern. She put her wine glass down and came over to Elizabeth.

Elizabeth sighed. "Yes, I am. I made a fool of myself because I couldn't control my behavior while under the influence of alcohol and drugs. I like me better sober." She looked at my mom and laughed. "You should know that. You taught me! Go ahead. Have your wine. You know how to handle it. You don't abuse it."

I was just finishing up my drink, and checking my reflection in the mirror when I heard another knock at the door. Since all of the women I knew were here, who was at the door? I was curious when Moss went to the door. It was Spruce, my mom's servant. "It's time."

I walked in the middle of my crowd of women. The only one missing was the queen. I looked over at Olivia on my right and Elizabeth on my left. My mom and Willow were behind me. Moss was in front leading the way.

I heard the music before we got to the chapel. I never thought to ask what the wood nymphs called the place, but it did look like a Christian chapel without the cross. There was no podium looking thing, either. But, the benches looked like what I would expect to see in a chapel.

Where the podium would be, I saw what appeared to be an Essence Bowl. It looked a lot like the one used by the Copper Clan in Presque Isle. This one was more elaborate and set with large precious gems. I could see the rubies, diamonds, sapphires and emeralds from across the room. There was what appeared to be a mist coming from the bowl. It reminded me of the fog used in concerts.

Moss held me up at the entryway. Mom and Willow were guided to their seats by Aron and another large guard in ceremonial uniforms. They were very handsome. I could see Ash, Andrew, and Forrest at the end of the aisle by what must be the cleric. The cleric had on formal attire that reminded me of the pope's robes.

Ben came up to me and put his arm out. "Are you ready for this?" he asked kindly. I wondered what he'd do if I said no and wanted to make a run for it. The thought made me smile. I'd never run from Ash. The music changed. It wasn't the wedding march I was familiar with, but it had a kind of pomp and circumstance sound to it, but in a soothing way. I thought if New Age music and the wedding march were combined, it might sound like this.

"Here I go!" whispered Elizabeth. She walked sedately down the aisle. When she was about halfway down, Olivia reached over and gave me a kiss on the cheek.

"My turn!" she whispered and started walking. I pulled my veil over my face. When she was all of the way to the end of the aisle, all of the attendants and Ash turned to watch me and Ben walk down the aisle. "Let's do it!" I whispered with a smile.

"I love you. You'll always be my little girl," Ben whispered as we started walking down the aisle. I had my hand on his arm. He patted my hand with his other hand. There were a lot of people in the small chapel. It didn't seem to matter if there was a bride's side or a groom's side. The place was packed with wood nymphs. Mom and Ben were the only true humans in the place.

When we got up to Ash, Ben placed my hand in his. I wondered if he could see the love in my eyes through the veil. I heard the cleric speak, but didn't understand all of the words. I only had eyes for Ash. As long as he was with me, I could handle anything. I was told what to say and I said it. Then Ash did the same. At what would have been the end of the ceremony, the fog billowed into the air and settled onto me and Ash as if it had a mind of its own. A peaceful feeling came over me. Ash lifted my veil from my face and kissed me. We were now conjoined in the wood nymph tradition.

I'd insisted on a cake. It was a beautiful multi-tiered cake. Moss's mother brought the cake out. Moss told me that her mother had made it. I knew it would be the best cake I had ever had, and it was. The wood nymphs ate cake, but did not use it in their conjoinment ceremony. Most of the wood nymphs I heard talking about the cake thought that it was a fun tradition and would use it in their ceremonies from now on. I had incorporated a human tradition into a wood nymph tradition. I also explained the tradition of tossing the bridal bouquet to the single women. I was not surprised when Olivia caught my bouquet.

Before going to the banquet, we went to the valley for the Essence Ceremony to celebrate the conjoinment. Someone had placed wooden bleachers in the stadium-shaped area similar to what I had seen at the Copper Clan ceremony. The same cleric came out with the dancers. I listened to the music and squeezed Ash's hand. I was overjoyed that the king and queen were allowing us to combine human traditions with the wood nymph ones. Mom and Ben were allowed to sit in the stands, but were told that because they were human, they would not be touched by the essence. They understood and were just glad to be there.

When the lightening bolts of light came out of the bowl, the first shot of light was not as bright as what I usually saw at the Copper Clan. But what happened next, amazed me. The light went into my mother. I saw her look of surprise, then she looked at me and then she closed her eyes in rapture. The next shot of light went into Ben. He was too busy looking at my mother and did not see it coming. He too looked surprised and looked over at me before he closed his eyes in rapture. I watched as wood nymphs all around me were getting struck by the light and leaning back in rapture. I looked at Ash and neither he nor I had had the light touch us. Just as I was wondering about that, I saw a brilliant light come out of the bowl. Much larger and brighter than any light I had seen before.

It was large enough to hit Ash and me at the same time. We were holding hands at the time it hit us and I felt this almost electrical charge shoot through my hand to his and back again. I felt a wonderful feeling of warmth in my belly and I knew my baby was getting his or her share of the essence. While in the rapture I kissed Ash and the light got brighter for just a moment. The wonderful feeling was so intense that I thought I would pass out from the joy of it.

When I opened my eyes, I saw that everyone was looking at us. "I have never seen that happen before," The king said solemnly. "I have never heard of humans being touched by the essence or having the essence coming out and striking two persons at the same time. There is magic happening here, but of a kind I have never seen before."

I just stared at Ash and relished the moment. I didn't think about magic or what it meant. It was good and it was right. That was enough for me.

"Let's dance!" Andrew called from the palace doorway. We all filed back into the palace to the ballroom. When we first got there, I just sat and stared at Ash. I didn't feel too bad about staring at him, as he was staring just as intently back at me. We were both smiling. "Hello, Mrs. Woodson," Ash said with a grin.

"Yes, I am Mrs. Woodson now, aren't I?" I laughed and kissed him.

"Hey, you two! Come and dance with your fellow revelers. You'll be alone to-gether soon enough!" Elizabeth took Ash by the hand. "Come dance with me."

Andrew came and took my hand and we danced a waltz. After the waltz, I danced with Forrest, and a slow dance with Ben. I think I danced with every man I knew there. Finally Dr. Elder came over to me and stated, "Enough for tonight. We don't want you to faint again."

"Your place or mine?" I asked as we said our goodbyes and thanked everyone that had come to our celebration.

"Yours," he said. "I like your bed better." We walked to my room and I opened the door. Ash picked me up and carried me over the threshold.

"Is that a wood nymph tradition also?" I asked as he set me down and shut the door.

He turned to look at me. "No, it is a human tradition, but I thought you would like it."

"I did," I replied. "Thank you."

We were married now. We no longer had to sneak around to be together alone. I hugged him. "You are all mine now," I said with a laugh.

He pushed away and gave me a mockingly serious look and said, "Oh, no, you have it all wrong. It is that you are all mine now!"

"Well, if I'm yours, what would you like me to do?" I asked trying to sound sexy.

"I'd like to undress and then ravish you," he said trying to sound threatening.

"Yeah, yeah, promises, promises," I teased as I turned my back to him. He immediately started undoing all of the little buttons on the back of my dress.

"I'd rip this dress off you, but it's so beautiful. I hope our daughter gets mar-ried in it," he replied when he was about halfway down my back.

I twisted to look at him. "Is that what you think? You think we'll have a daughter?"

"I truly hope so, and I hope she's as lovely as you are," he replied finishing with the last button and pulling my gown over my head. He continued to slowly undress me.

"Your breasts are larger," he murmured as he put his face between them.

"Pregnancy will do that," I replied as I pulled away to undress him. I took my time, watching his face watch my breasts as they moved. I could smell his musk scent quite strongly by the time I got him naked.

He was very ready for me by the time we got to my bed. In moments, he had me just as ready for him. We spent the night in marital bliss, over and over again. I had no idea what time we actually got to sleep. I just knew it was very late. I hoped Moss was not coming to bring breakfast.

When I woke up, I noticed Ash was not in bed with me. Just as I sat up and wondered where he had gone, he came in with a tray of food. "I rang for Moss to bring us some breakfast. It just arrived. I would have woken you up," he said as he gave me a kiss and put the tray on my lap.

We spent the entire day alone. A couple of times during the day Moss brought food and probably gave everyone else updates on us. At one time, she gave us an update. King Cornelius had arranged our transportation back to Wisconsin. We were going home.

The next morning I woke up and saw Ash lying next to me. I watched his breathing as he slept. I still could not wrap my head around the idea that we were conjoined. It was still a miracle to me that I would be able to wake up every morning, every day for the rest of my life with Ash. This was our last day in England. King Cornelius was true to his word. He said we could go home.

"Wake up, wake up, wake up!" I whispered in his ear. I could tell when he woke up because before he opened his eyes, he smiled. I wanted to spend our last day with Elizabeth and Andrew. This was it. We were scheduled to leave the following day.

Ash gave me a big grin as he stretched and said, "What time is it?"

"We have a little time together before meeting everyone for breakfast. I wanted a little extra alone time before we got in with the group," I replied as I climbed onto him and kissed him.

"I like that idea!" He said as he wrapped his arms around me and then we lost track of time. We were rushing to meet everyone for breakfast.

My hair was still damp from my shower when we got to the breakfast room. "It looks like the newlyweds are doing well," Olivia said with a smile.

I blushed. I couldn't help it. Everyone at the table must have noticed it because they all laughed. I decided to change the subject when I noticed that Elizabeth, Andrew and Aron were all sitting with our families.

173

Elizabeth waved a piece of baguette at me. "Good morning! Come sit by me. I'd ask you what you did all day yesterday, but I think everyone can guess!" She laughed.

"I can't believe that you're leaving us tomorrow morning. I'll miss you! I never thought I'd really like humans, other than to use them, but, well that was another life," Elizabeth stammered.

Andrew looked at his sister and realized that she was embarrassed. He stood up and shook Ash's hand. "It is true, mate. We will miss you around here. It seems that you just got here and now it is time to go."

"It only seems a short time because really, we have only been friends for a short time. You had your ideas about humans and I'm really glad that you like us, now. It is easy to pass judgment on a population of people when a few people do bad things. I believe that's how stereotypes get started," I said to Andrew. "I'm really glad you like us, now."

"We all are glad that you like us, because we like you. We never had any pre-conceived notions about wood nymphs because to us, wood nymphs were myth and legend. I really hope you'll come to Wisconsin. Maybe we could take a tour around the United States. There are many interesting things that humans and wood nymphs have created in the United States. It would be fun to try to determine if it was human technology or wood nymph gifts that have created some of the things to be seen," my mom said as she handed her cup to a server for a refill.

"I plan to be there for the birth of this baby," Elizabeth said opening up a soft-boiled egg in an egg cup.

"I will be there with you," Aron said giving Elizabeth a kiss on her cheek.

"Me, too. I won't be left behind," Andrew said as he sat down next to Ben. Then he said to Ben, "I'd like to learn more about the American Army. As the next king of the wood nymphs, I would like to know about technology to protect my people."

Ben sighed and said, "I'll tell you what I can. However, there are many books and articles that can give you much more information than you can get from me. You'd only get limited information from me."

We spent the rest of the day together, as a group. It seemed no one wanted to be away from our new friends and our new friends liked spending time with us. In no time at all, it was time to dress for dinner. The king said that he had something special for our last night in England.

After we were dressed, my family and Ash's parents met us in the hallway out-side of our suites. This would be the last time I wore a formal gown for dinner. I was thinking I'd miss this when we went back to our normal lives in Wisconsin.

We were the last group to get to the reception area and had time for one beverage before we were called to dinner. Once we were seated, the king clapped his hands and we were given a dinner show. It was a program that went back to the early history of the wood nymphs when the druids worshipped the wood nymphs at Stonehenge. Stage sets showed what Stonehenge had looked like in the early years. Each stage set showed how the druids began to depend upon the wood nymphs too much and how slowly the wood nymphs disappeared from their world into the underground palace where they lived today.

It was interesting to see how at one time wood nymphs and humans associated, but the humans treated the wood nymphs like gods. I learned a lot of history during that dinner show. It took about three hours. After the dinner and show, the king and queen came over to us. "When I brought you all here, I had no idea of what would happen or how I would deal with humans knowing that we exist. In all truth, I was very angry that humans were made to understand that wood nymphs live in the world. But, I was happily surprised when I found that human training in mental health can be better than any wood nymph gift. Valerie saved my daughter. I hate to think of what I may have done in my ignorance if not for Valerie's help," King Cornelius stated solemnly. "I hope you don't mind if we come to visit from time to time. There may be a time in the not-too-distant future when I'll allow all humans to know that wood nymphs exist. However, I'm not quite ready for that yet."

"We fully understand, sir," Ben said to the king. "We respect your right to determine when, if ever, you choose to enlighten the rest of humanity to your existence."

"Thank you," King Cornelius replied.

We spent the next hour discussing plans, baby things, and just about everything except leaving. When it was time to retire for the evening, the queen said, "I am sorry to see you leave, but we will keep in touch. My daughter has told me about some human technology called Skype that will allow us to see and talk to each other. I promised her that we would buy the equipment. She says that you already have the equipment."

"I do," I said. I was feeling sad. While I wanted to go home, I was going to miss my new friends.

The next morning we got up, had breakfast with the royal family and then we were escorted to the door of the palace with servants carrying our luggage.

"We'll see each other soon. I promise," Elizabeth said with tears in her eyes. "Don't forget me, because I'll never forget you." This last part she said to my mother.

While counselors don't usually give hugs, when Elizabeth put her arms around my mother, my mother hugged her back.

Whitey Pine was waiting for us at the door. The servants came with us to the train. In no time at all we were at the airport and on our flight home.

The End